They were too close again. Zak was in her personal space.

And Caitlin liked it.

Of course, all that previous talk about keeping the lines drawn flew right out of her head and all she could breathlessly hope for was that he'd grab her and kiss her stupid. Maybe kiss her so hard that she'd forget that it was a terrible idea and probably ranked in the top three most reckless things she'd ever done in her life.

Okay, it was *the* most reckless thing, but she didn't want to pull away or remind him that they'd agreed it was a bad idea.

But how often did opportunities like this drop into a woman's lap? She wasn't dead below the waist. Zak was very handsome and he smelled like citrus and male skin, something that had never really made her quiver, but it certainly did now.

Oh, God, he was moving in. His lips were tantalizingly close to hers.

This was happening.

Zak was going to kiss her.

She lifted her lips, ready to feel his mouth on hers.

* * *

Dear Reader,

There's nothing sexier than an emotionally wounded hero with a stoic outside and a wicked sense of humor, right? Pretty much my opinion, too. I always knew Zak Ramsey's story would be fun to write because even though he was the calm voice in the chaos that was at the heart of Red Wolf, the elite ex-military team he worked for, deep inside, he had his own storm brewing.

I also knew it would take a special someone to tame his wild heart, so when Dr. Caitlin Willows appeared in my head, the wheels started turning.

I hope you enjoy the latest wild ride with the Red Wolf team as they work to save the world and as Zak and Caitlin fall madly, deeply in love while doing it!

I love hearing from readers. Connect with me on Facebook, Twitter, or drop me an email at alexandria2772@hotmail.com.

Happy reading!

Kimberly

SOLDIER PROTECTOR

Kimberly Van Meter

Recycling programs for this product may not exist in your area.

ISBN-13: 978-1-335-66200-2

Soldier Protector

This edition published by arrangement with Harlequin Books S.A.

For questions and comments about the quality of this book, please contact us at CustomerService@Harlequin.com.

Printed in U.S.A.

Kimberly Van Meter wrote her first book at sixteen and finally achieved publication in December 2006. She has written for the Harlequin Superromance, Blaze and Romantic Suspense lines. She and her husband of seventeen years have three children, three cats, and always a houseful of friends, family and fun.

Books by Kimberly Van Meter

Harlequin Romantic Suspense

Military Precision Heroes

Soldier for Hire
Soldier Protector

The Sniper
The Agent's Surrender
Moving Target
Deep Cover
The Killer You Know

Harlequin Superromance

Family in Paradise

Like One of the Family
Playing the Part
Something to Believe In

The Sinclairs of Alaska

That Reckless Night
A Real Live Hero
A Sinclair Homecoming

Visit the Author Profile page at Harlequin.com for more titles.

Chapter 1

"If people could just stop being egomaniacal assholes, that would be great," drawled CJ Lawry, echoing Zak Ramsey's private thought as their team leader, Scarlett Rhodes, went over their next assignment in the conference room at Red Wolf Elite headquarters.

The pounding in Zak's skull made grinning in solidarity an effort but he had to point out the obvious. "Without assholes who want to rule the world, we'd be out of a job."

"Solid point," CJ agreed with a grumble, kicking out his feet to use the chair next to him as an ottoman. "Okay, so what's the deal this time around?"

"This time it's pretty serious," Scarlett said, her expression puckering into a sour frown. "I'm talking end-of-days kind of shit."

"You've got my attention," Zak said, perking up, curious because Scarlett wasn't prone to dramatics. "What's going on?"

"Look, we all know the next war isn't going to be some politician pushing a button and sending a missile this way. We've got plenty of fail-safes against that kind of threat. No, the next threat to America is far more insidious—it's going to creep up on us while we're too busy on social media perfecting the ultimate selfie, too self-absorbed to notice that we're in deep shit. By the time we realize there's a problem we're all going to go out puking and crapping our brains out as our insides melt like rancid butter left in the hot sun."

"Well, ain't that a lovely picture," CJ said with a grim shudder. "If things don't work out for you with Red Wolf, you ought to write Christmas jingles, TL. Very uplifting."

"I'm serious, jackass. The threat is real and it's here."

Zak waited for Scarlett to continue, knowing that whatever was going down had to be big, because nothing scared their team leader—and she looked freaked out.

"All right, shut your trap, CJ. This sounds worth listening to," Zak said, looking to Scarlett, whose expression was hard as nails but colored with worry.

"At 0300 hours there was a breach in a top-level, heavily classified lab in Vermont, where the sample of a highly dangerous biological agent was stolen. I'm not going to sugarcoat anything when I say this is Armageddon-level shit and it landing into the wrong hands spells trouble for everyone."

"Of course it does," CJ quipped with a dark glower. "For crying out loud, what I want to know is why scientists have to mess around with that scary shit anyway? I mean, it always lands in the wrong hands, every single time. No one plays nice or fair, so the best thing for everyone would be if they'd just stop messing with that scary shit, because no one deserves to die like that."

"Yeah, tell me about it," Zak agreed. "So what are

we talking? Bubonic plague? Swine flu? Or some Outbreak Monkey-don't-have-a-name-hell-fire-level-up kind of disaster?"

"My guess is the monkey one," CJ retorted.

Scarlett nodded. "Apparently, the researchers were trying to reverse engineer a cure but the sample was stolen before they could perfect the formula. We have to find that sample and protect the lead scientist."

"A twofer." CJ chuckled, rubbing his hands together with pretend glee. "My favorite."

"What about the FBI?" Zak asked. "Why weren't they called in?"

"Because this sample recovery wasn't sanctioned in any way. It was stolen from a country without official authorization, so technically, it shouldn't even be here in the States. We're being hired to handle this quietly and beneath the radar."

"So if we screw up, Uncle Sam has his friggin' hands clean," CJ said, to which Scarlett nodded. They all knew why they were being tasked with this project but hey, the risks came with the job, and they had all signed on the dotted line understanding that simple fact.

"Here's how this is going to shake out. CJ and I will run point on the investigation while you, Zak, will be in charge of protecting the asset."

Babysitting? Not his favorite detail but CJ was too hot-tempered to deal with people on a regular basis. He was much better out in the field doing reconnaissance or blowing shit up. For that reason, Zak didn't begrudge their TL her choice but he wasn't looking forward to babysitting some nerd in a lab when the fate of the world rested on his team.

"All right, tell me about this scientist I'm supposed to be babysitting."

Scarlett slid the file across the desk and Zak caught it with his fingertips before flipping it open. Straight, shoulder-length Nordic-blond hair and blue eyes, glasses that obscured her face, and a list of academic achievements a mile long—should be easy enough to keep her safe. "Are you sure I shouldn't come with you and CJ? We are a man down with Xander being a big shot with the FBI now. You might need the backup. We can always send a new recruit to babysit the scientist."

"We can't risk someone getting their hands on Dr. Willows. She's the only one who can reverse engineer a cure, which puts her in a dangerous position. I need you to take point on this, Zak."

Zak nodded, accepting Scarlett's reasoning. Now wasn't the time to sulk and pout about being handed the less-than-exciting assignment.

Scarlett continued, "You're to be with her 24/7. If she goes to work, you're right behind her. If she goes home, you're stationed outside her bedroom door. It's imperative that her safety is assured. You worry about the doc and we'll worry about the recovery. Got it?"

"Loud and clear."

Scarlett nodded, satisfied. "Your flight leaves in two hours for Vermont. Details are in the packet."

Zak scooped up the file with no time to waste. He needed to pack and then hit the airport.

Scarlett stopped him before he left the conference room. "You know I'm not an alarmist but the intel on this biological is scary as shit. If this doc can reverse engineer a cure…that means she's a target. You're going to need to keep your head on a swivel."

"Always do."

"I know. That's why I need you on this job. Don't let us down."

"Never will."

Zak left the building, made quick work of packing and then hit the airport.

The flight wasn't long, only about an hour and a half, but it gave him the chance to really study the doc.

Caitlin Willows, thirty-three, originally from Wisconsin, had moved to Vermont to work for Tessara Pharmaceuticals five years ago. She'd worked up to lead research scientist relatively quickly, which meant she was either a workaholic or crazy smart.

Probably both.

Thankfully, workaholics tended to keep to themselves, so accommodating a bunch of extraneous people within her circle wouldn't likely be necessary.

The intel in his hands would be considered intrusive—or borderline illegal—by most standards but he'd long since stopped caring or questioning how the intel crossed his desk. All that mattered was the job. He'd let the politicians sort out the details.

And if Red Wolf failed this mission…there'd be no details to sort.

Everyone would just end.

Caitlin Willows couldn't believe what her superior was saying to her—honestly, it all seemed something out of a movie. She kept waiting for the nightmare to end, to open her eyes and discover it'd all been a terrible dream.

One minute her orderly life was filled with comforting routine, and the next, nothing made sense—the equivalent of Bill Murray's iconic speech in *Ghostbusters*, "Dogs and cats living together—mass hysteria!" Because the scariest thing imaginable had just happened and now her life was in danger.

"Red Wolf Elite will be sending a highly trained soldier to watch over your safety while you recreate the sample. He should be like a shadow, always there but never in your way. You don't have to worry about anything but your work."

Still unable to wrap her head around the last twenty-four hours, Caitlin rubbed at her fingers, a nervous habit she'd had since she was young. "I don't understand. How did someone break into the lab with all of our security protocols? It practically takes Harry Potter magic to get through all the fail-safes."

Her immediate superior, Stan Obberon, wasn't amused by her comment, but then, Stan was allergic to humor most days.

"Now is not the time to make jokes," he said, frowning with what appeared to be distaste. "If you can't understand the gravity of the situation I don't know how you can possibly fulfill the task you've been given."

Caitlin nodded, immediately chastised. No one would ever think to call her the office jokester—she was quite the opposite, actually—so the fact that Stan was calling her mild comment inappropriate was unsettling.

But then, everyone was on edge, too. Tessara was a huge pharmaceutical company with multiple locations, but the largest facility was in California. The Vermont location was smaller in scale but the work they did was just as important.

The fact that Caitlin had been tapped to head up the ultrasecret project had been both exhilarating and intimidating.

To reverse engineer a cure for a new biological agent capable of decimating an entire population within weeks...well, it was simply mind-boggling, and of course a matter of national security. But she'd only gotten halfway through the formula before the sample had been stolen, and now she could practically hear the clock ticking on humanity.

Was it her fault somehow? How else had someone gained access to her lab? Her head hurt from the questions that hammered at her and her stomach felt permanently clenched from anxiety.

And now she was being assigned a supersoldier for protection? Never in her life had she ever been so out of her element. She lived a quiet life of research and study—she was not adventure prone.

She didn't even like to go hiking. Her idea of living on the edge involved enjoying a glass of milk with her cookies when she was mildly lactose intolerant and knew she'd suffer a bellyache later.

Caitlin smothered a shiver at the potential ramifications of everything that'd happened. "So when is this soldier supposed to be showing up?" she asked, drawing a deep breath. The world had been tipped on its head and she couldn't seem to get her bearing.

When she got to the lab this morning, there'd been mass chaos and it'd taken a minute to fully process what she'd been seeing—her lab destroyed and her research stolen.

It was enough to make a scientist's heart stop.

On the surface, having a highly trained soldier to protect her was a good thing, but Caitlin wasn't much of a people person and the knowledge that she'd have someone in her bubble 24/7 was upsetting to say the least.

"He should be here any minute," Stan answered, checking his watch with a short, agitated motion. "He's supposed to be the best."

She wasn't worried about his qualifications—no doubt this soldier was a proficient killing machine—but she hated the idea of having him as her shadow. Caitlin enjoyed working alone and was accustomed to solitude. Having someone in her bubble for longer than a socially acceptable conversation length promised to be excruciating.

And the prospect filled her with anxiety.

As if on cue, the door to Stan's office opened and the biggest man she'd ever seen came striding into the room, sucking up all the oxygen and filling the space with all of his male energy.

Oh, good gravy. This wouldn't work. The protests were immediate and shrill in her mind, but her mouth wasn't quite working.

He had to be at least six feet four inches, 275 pounds of pure muscle capable of pounding a person into a hole with one hand.

"Dr. Willows," he said, extending a hand with polite courtesy, which she accepted on autopilot. She stared in shock as his hand dwarfed hers. He released her hand and moved on to Dr. Obberon with the same attention, but Caitlin could still feel the warmth of his calloused hand against her palm. Thrusting her hands in her lab coat, she tried not to fidget too much but her entire body felt as if she were vibrating with nervous energy.

"My name is Zak Ramsey, Red Wolf Elite. You can rest assured I will do everything in my power to keep you safe while my team works to bring in whoever breached the lab."

His assurances sent an odd bubble bouncing down her vertebrae. Why did he have to be so tall? Standing next to him made her feel like a child. No doubt he could tuck her under his arm and cart her off like a Viking with his spoils if he chose to.

And that name? Zak? Sounded like a rock star's name.

Her mind was rambling, but thankfully, her mouth hadn't started flapping yet—one saving grace, she supposed.

"I'm not used to having a bodyguard," she blurted, her hold slipping. "I don't know the etiquette. Am I supposed to bring you hot tea or something? Coffee? Because I don't drink coffee and I don't fetch coffee, either, just so we're clear."

"I can get my own coffee."

"Caitlin, honestly," Stan said, his mouth pinching at her odd question. "Just do what you normally do and he'll take care of the rest."

"What I normally do, I do by myself," Caitlin couldn't help pointing out. "I'm just saying… I don't know how to act around a bodyguard."

"I'll do my best to fade into the background."

She wanted to bark a short laugh. Him? Fade? Impossible. He was practically a beacon of male energy pulsing for every single—and unhappily attached—female in the building. She may not be interested but there would be plenty of women who found the idea of a virile soldier traipsing through the halls too tempting to resist.

And given their present situation, a disruption of that magnitude…well, it just seemed like a bad idea.

She drew herself up with a faint scowl, saying, "Well, I happen to think this is overkill but it's not my dime, so as long as you stay out of my way, we'll get along just fine."

"Ma'am, your safety is tied to the safety of the world. I can promise you nothing will stand in *my* way of doing my job and keeping you safe."

Their gazes met—they were both determined to do things their way—but the question was…whose way was going to win?

Caitlin pulled her gaze first, her fingers curling inside the privacy of her lab coat. To Stan, she said, "I'll be in the lab, cleaning up the mess. We have a lot of ground to make up and we have no idea of knowing how unstable the sample is wherever it's being held."

"I'll need to vet each of your team from this point forward," Zak said, his tone firm. "There's a chance this was an inside job."

"Not possible. I handpicked my team," Caitlin said, affronted by the suggestion. "I'd know if I had a traitor on my team."

"Not likely, but it's not your fault. You're not trained to search out evidence of deception."

"I can appreciate that, but I know my team. Your efforts are better spent looking on the outside."

Stan interjected with a gruff approval to Zak, "You do what you feel is necessary." To Caitlin, he said, "And I trust you'll do whatever is necessary to ensure he has what he needs to accomplish his goal in keeping this lab secure."

"Of course," she replied stiffly, hating being told what to do in her own lab. "But I feel it prudent to point out that Mr. Ramsey's energy can be spent pursuing more fruitful endeavors than areas that I already know are dead ends."

She expected pushback but Zak simply said, "We'll see," and left it at that, which gave her little to argue further. Stan nodded, accepting the end of that particular discussion, even though Caitlin wanted to squash the theory that anyone on her team had been responsible.

Stan turned to Zak. "I'll leave you to your work," he said, before exiting the conference room.

She was alone with Zak now. Within seconds the silence between them blossomed to excruciating levels and Caitlin was almost relieved when Zak gestured for her to lead the way to the lab with an ultrapolite "After you."

Caitlin spun on her heel and tried to pretend she didn't

have a sanctioned stalker. But her body seemed hyper-aware—an ordinary activity such as walking was suddenly outside of her wheelhouse and she stumbled on imaginary obstacles.

"Are you all right?" Zak asked, reaching out to steady her but she shook off his help with embarrassment.

"I'm fine," she insisted, her cheeks heating. "I was distracted." *You distract me.*

This was her new reality, she realized. A tall, handsome, movie-star-looking bodyguard trailing her every move, breathing down her neck, probably thinking to himself that he'd definitely pulled the short straw for this gig.

Lord help me.

High school hadn't felt this awkward and high school had been hell.

Chapter 2

Caitlin walked briskly to her lab, trying to somehow forget that she had a giant shadow on her tail that smelled faintly of mint aftershave and machismo, but that was like trying to forget that lions had teeth or that the IRS never lost an opportunity to collect their due.

Her assistant, Rebecca, looked up from her computer as they entered, her jaw dropping in an uncharacteristically girlie manner, and Caitlin resisted the urge to frown as this was exactly the kind of behavior that she'd wanted to avoid.

Rebecca, a few years younger than Caitlin, but sharp as a tack and one of the most brilliant research scientists in her field, quickly grabbed her cane and rose to greet them. With a smile as bright as the gleam in her eyes, she stretched her hand out. "My goodness, you must be our newest team member," she said, openly and unabashedly flirting. "My name's Rebecca Childress. Pleasure to meet you."

"Ma'am," Zak said, his handshake quick and perfunctory, which Caitlin approved even if she hated him being there. "Zak Ramsey, Red Wolf Elite."

"Red Wolf… So official," Rebecca practically cooed and Caitlin had had her fill of the nonsense.

Caitlin cleared her throat and addressed her team. "We all know the lab security was breached and a highly classified sample was stolen, so I'm not going to waste time dancing around the issue. The elephant in the room is plainly visible, so let's also not pretend we don't see it. Mr. Ramsey is here on official business, and as such, I would expect each of my team to act professionally." Caitlin cast Rebecca a meaningful glance before continuing. "Mr. Ramsey will be here until such time as Tessara believes his services are no longer necessary, but we are to go about our business as if he weren't here."

Jonathan, one of her junior assistants, spoke up first. "Is our safety at risk?" he asked.

"Of course not," Caitlin answered, refusing to let fear cloud anyone's work performance. "But I won't sugarcoat the situation—we don't know who has the sample or to what end. So it's imperative that we continue our work on the reverse engineering for the cure. That's our top priority."

"But why would Tessara hire a supersoldier unless there was a threat?" Jonathan persisted. "I'm not going to put my personal safety at risk without some kind of compensation, like hazard pay or something."

Caitlin nodded. It was her job as the lead supervisor to take the concerns of her team seriously and Jonathan had raised a solid point. "I'll talk to Stan and see if we can't offer some kind of hazard pay during this time," she said, trying to appease her team. "But until then, I suggest we just do what we normally do and everything will be fine."

"I feel safe with Mr. Ramsey around," Rebecca said, directing another smile his way. "Would you mind sharing with the team your qualifications aside from being super handsome and built like a Roman god?"

Caitlin suppressed an embarrassed gasp at Rebecca's silly comment. How was Zak supposed to take them seriously if Rebecca kept acting like a lovestruck teen? Her mouth firmed in a tight line but Rebecca ignored her silent cue to stop.

"I assure you, I'm more than qualified to see to your team's safety," he answered with a brief but professional smile. Caitlin had to give him credit—he wasn't moved or swayed by Rebecca's attempt at flirtation or flattery. Rebecca was more than cute, not that Caitlin paid attention to those things, but if she were forced to answer, she'd admit that Rebecca probably didn't have any trouble finding dates for a Saturday night.

The last date Caitlin went on had been abysmal for both parties and definitely hadn't sweetened her opinion about online dating. In fact, afterward, she'd immediately deleted her ill-fated profile and tried to forget she'd ever stooped so low as to make one.

As far as she was concerned, Science_Lover17 need never see the light of day again. Scrubbing the memory, Caitlin pushed forward. "See? Everything is going to be fine, but we have a job to do. So if everyone could just go back to doing that, that would be great."

Rebecca must've seen that Caitlin's patience was wearing thin. "You're the boss," she acquiesced with a subtle pout, returning to her research with a sullen gesture that Caitlin was willing to forgive for the moment.

Trying to cling to some semblance of professionalism

when everything felt as if it were crumbling all around her, Caitlin turned to Zak. "I'm sorry. We're not accustomed to having visitors back here and the circumstances aren't exactly normal."

"Of course, totally understandable. I'm going to take a look around. I'll be back in a few minutes. Do not leave the lab until I return."

Caitlin bristled a little. "Am I on lab arrest or something?"

"Your safety is my concern. Do not leave the lab," he repeated.

His firm tone invited no argument. Suppressing the shiver that danced on her spine, Caitlin managed a stiff nod. "I have work to do anyway, so I have no need to leave," she said, spinning on her heel and going to her office. She plopped into her seat and flicked on her computer, determined to ignore Zak and the fact that her stomach was trembling.

It wasn't until Zak was out of the lab that she managed to release her pent-up breath. But her relief was short-lived, as Rebecca scuttled into her office, her eyes sparkling. "Are you kidding me? That guy is your bodyguard? He's, like, Hollywood-hot. I'm talking movie-star quality. How are you not drooling all over him?"

As smart as Rebecca was, she talked like a bubble-gum-chewing, hormone-riddled teen, and the incongruity was beyond Caitlin's comprehension. Irritated, Caitlin looked at Rebecca, reminding her sharply, "You need to focus. Our lab was breached and the safety of the world might be at stake. I'm less interested in the beefcake bodyguard than I am in finding the cure for that bloody biological agent. I suggest you redirect your attention, as well."

Chastised, Rebecca said, "Of course. It's just not every

day someone like him shows up like a Christmas present on our front doorstep."

Caitlin found Rebecca's fascination an additional irritant to her already raw nerves. "His facial symmetry aside, you need to concentrate on the task at hand."

"I will," Rebecca said, but she couldn't let the topic drop. "Is he going to live with you?" she asked, cocking her head to the side, curious. "Imagine waking up every morning to that mug. Yikes, there are worse punishments in the world, am I right? I wouldn't mind knowing he was watching over me."

Caitlin wasn't going to respond. She didn't know how to process the fact that Tessara was forcing Zak to shadow her every move, which meant that wherever she went, Zak followed. She worried her bottom lip, her anxiety climbing a notch. Someone else in her private bubble? She didn't even have a cat. She was accustomed to silence and solitude. All she needed was a good book, some takeout and her classical music playing softly in the background, and she was a happy girl.

But now a ten-foot-tall, armed-and-dangerous muscleman was going to be tramping around her cozy house, sucking up all the oxygen and contaminating her bubble with all that testosterone.

She couldn't think about that right now. She stared pointedly at her assistant until she got the idea that it was work time, not story time, and Rebecca let herself out and hobbled back to her desk. God bless America, Zak had been there for only thirty minutes and he was already causing epic levels of disruption in her life. How was she supposed to pretend that everything was fine and business as usual when, in fact, it was the exact opposite?

No, this couldn't continue, she decided. She'd just have

to convince Stan that having Zak around the lab wasn't conducive to a productive working environment.

Yes, that was exactly what needed to happen. She just needed to put her foot down. This was her lab, her work. Zak Ramsey was simply too much of a distraction and the work, too important.

Rising with purpose, she left her office and headed for the door. But before she could slide her key-card, it opened on its own and there was Zak, a frown forming on his face as he stated, "I thought I told you to stay put."

"I—I needed to speak with my ultvisor," Caitlin said, feeling as if she were actually shrinking beneath the shadow of his building scowl.

"About what?"

You. Caitlin swallowed, hating that her voice sounded so small and meek when inside she wanted to roar like a lion. "It's classified," she finally answered.

"I have top clearance, but if you need to leave the lab, I'll accompany you."

"This is ridiculous," she said, shoving her hands in her lab coat to hide the fact that she was shaking. "I'm perfectly safe within the building."

"My orders are to have eyes on you at all times. So that's exactly what I'm going to do."

"That's very intrusive and unnecessary," she said, wrinkling her nose at the very idea. "What about when I go to the bathroom? Am I to have no privacy?"

He didn't necessarily refute her sarcastic question, which was worrisome. But he said, "I will do my utmost best to protect your privacy as long as it doesn't compromise your safety." He stepped aside with a polite gesture. "Now, if you'd like to speak with your supervisor, I'm happy to escort you."

"Oh, good gravy," she muttered, knowing she couldn't

storm into Stan's office with the intent to assure him she didn't need the bodyguard when the bodyguard was right behind her. She wasn't fond of confrontation—her introverted nature cringed at the thought—which left her little choice but to spin on her heel with a quick "Never mind" thrown over her shoulder as she returned to her desk.

Zak shrugged and took his spot, standing like a sentinel at the door, ever at the ready, while she sat glued to her chair, feeling trapped.

In the space of twenty-four hours her entire life had been tipped upside down, and there was little she could do about it.

The best she could hope for was a quick resolution to the theft issue so that her bodyguard could return to wherever elite soldiers came from and she could return to her quiet and orderly life.

In the meantime, she supposed she'd better figure out a way to deal with the fact that at the end of the day, Zak was, indeed, going home with her.

Heaven help me, she muttered, resisting the urge to sink lower in her chair and completely disappear.

For a small thing, she was surprisingly fierce. Oh, don't get him wrong, she may appear meek and mild but Zak could sense a warrior spirit beneath that nerdy act. One thing was for sure, she wasn't happy with the current arrangement and she was spitting mad. He was willing to bet his savings account that she'd been heading for her supervisor's office to have him sent home, which would've been an exercise in futility.

If Caitlin was less than happy with his presence, her coworker Rebecca was throwing him looks that clearly said, "I'm available and willing," but he never messed around on the job. There was a time and a place and this wasn't it.

Besides, Rebecca, although not hard on the eyes, didn't do a thing for him. If anything, Caitlin was more the kind of girl who might turn his head if they were at a bar together. She had that cute, nerdy-girl thing going for her that he found interesting. Not that he could imagine Caitlin being in any place where he would be.

Something told him they didn't run in the same circles. For one, let's get real, standing next to her, he must seem dumber than a post. Caitlin was wicked smart, the kind of brilliant that left most people scratching their heads with no way to relate. He'd been okay in school, nothing special, but he'd been more interested in sports and messing around than hitting the books.

The military had been an easy choice for a guy like him. He had excellent hand-eye coordination, decent memory skills and a knack for knowing when shit was about to go down—a sixth sense that you couldn't teach.

He sneaked a look at Caitlin through his lashes. She was no-nonsense, quite obviously flustered by the turn of events, and trying unsuccessfully to find her footing in this new environment. He respected her stoicism even if her quills were a bit sharp.

Rhodes had been very clear about Zak's responsibility—keep the scientist safe while they chased down the thief—and even though he'd rather be on the chasing side, he wasn't one to question orders.

And to be honest, the last job had been a bit of a doozy, so babysitting a nerdy scientist was almost like taking a vacation.

Except the scientist didn't seem to like him very much and found his presence distasteful.

Aside from that, yeah, walk in the park, bring on the margaritas.

He'd done a quick perimeter check, marked all the exits and determined where the worst defensible spaces were, and then he'd returned to the lab to survey the people in their environment. He would start interviewing lab assistants tomorrow but he wanted to observe first.

If his gaze kept straying to the doc, it was only because he wanted to keep her in his sights at all times, not because there was something about her that he found frustratingly interesting.

Caitlin worked with her hair tucked behind one ear, her expression intent, a slight frown furrowing her brow as if she were ready to argue with her computer at a moment's notice. A half-eaten, forgotten bagel sat to her left. It was anyone's guess how long the bagel had been there, hardening and turning stale, a fact she seemed to remember when she took an exploratory bite and then dropped it into the trash with a grimace.

He smothered a smile and returned to his observations.

It was a small lab—only a few were cleared to work at this level, which made his job easier because it meant fewer people had access and every entry was logged through a key-card and recorded with a time stamp.

Whoever had broken into the lab had bypassed the key-card, going for a brutal smash and grab, obliterating the electronics and gaining access through simple blown circuitry.

They'd known exactly what they were going for—which suggested whoever had taken the sample had had knowledge of the lab layout—because they'd bypassed everything but the biological agent Caitlin and her team were working on.

According to the intel Rhodes had given him, the players in the room were Rebecca Childress, Jonathan Petranski and Robert Vepp, all of whom answered to Caitlin Willows.

Rebecca and Jonathan he'd met, but Robert Vepp had called in sick today, so he'd have to meet Vepp tomorrow. In his line of work, everyone was a suspect until they weren't. He didn't have the luxury of believing everyone was innocent until proven guilty. He figured that if a person was innocent, it would become apparent soon enough.

Unless you were being framed by the government, like what'd happened to his buddy and former teammate Xander Scott, but that wasn't your ordinary everyday, run-of-the-mill circumstance. Not that trying to save the world from extinction wasn't extraordinary, but when you were fighting your own government, it just made everything that much more difficult.

Good God, Zak was so glad that situation had worked out. It could've been a real shit-show if Xander hadn't been a stubborn son of a bitch and his TL, even more so.

A smile threatened but he squashed the impulse. Time to focus. His gaze roamed the room, picking up on the not-so-subtle looks Rebecca kept throwing his way. He made a point not to react and returned his focus to Caitlin, who was still absorbed in her work. A bomb could go off and she'd hardly notice. He envied that kind of concentration. Rhodes often lamented that wrangling the Red Wolf team was often like corralling a bunch of preschoolers, except the preschoolers had semiautomatic weapons, unhealthy coping mechanisms and inappropriate senses of humor.

God, he missed his buddy Xander. He was always down for a good, really inappropriate joke at the worst possible moment. Like a fart joke at a funeral. But he didn't begrudge Xander's good fortune. Hell, if anyone deserved a fresh start, it was Xander. It wasn't every day that a man uncovered a massive conspiracy deep within the nation's capital, saved himself from a well-executed frame job and kicked a raging opioid addiction. So, yeah, "Good on ya, mate," as the Aussies would say.

Caitlin stretched for a brief moment, breaking her intense concentration, and he wondered what it was like to be in her head, to be scary smart like that. What'd high school been like for Caitlin?

She was probably bullied, made fun of, picked on because she was different.

He'd known someone else like that.

Someone who might've grown up to do great things just like Caitlin.

That familiar tightness squeezed his chest and he shifted against the feeling, hating that he'd let the door open a crack when usually he kept it slammed shut.

Now was not the time.

But then, as far as he was concerned, there was never a good time to think about Zoey. Not when every damn time it always seemed to hurt like a son of a bitch, no matter how much time had passed. Zoey was his hot stove.

And he'd learned a long time ago to avoid things that scorched.

Chapter 3

Caitlin's eyes burned as she fought against the yawn that forced her jaw open. It was late—everyone had long since left—but she was dreading having to face the real situation of her bodyguard accompanying her home.

She never had male visitors.

To be honest, she rarely had *any* visitors. She wasn't exactly what anyone would call terribly social. She liked people—sort of—but she preferred the quiet of an empty house.

But now, her empty house would have to accommodate a plus-one.

There was something about interacting with people that always left her feeling more awkward than usual. And now she was supposed to play hostess to a man who not only made her uncomfortable but made her social deficits feel that much more pronounced?

"How much longer are you going to be burning the midnight oil, Doc?" he called out from his sentinel post.

Maybe she'd hoped that he would tire of waiting and decide to check into a hotel without her, but as the hour ticked on and he hadn't budged, she'd ditched that hope for the realization that no matter what, Zak was stuck to her like glue. She didn't know Zak at all, but what she did know was that he took his job very seriously. True to his word, he had trailed her every step the entire day. Not only was it unnerving, it was annoying, as well. She felt like a prisoner when she hadn't done anything to deserve any punishment.

"I'll be ready to leave in a few minutes," she answered, ignoring the strange flutter in her chest. Her stomach grumbled. She hadn't eaten all day, and as far she could tell, he hadn't, either. She mentally checked her refrigerator at home and realized she had nothing to offer in the way of hospitality.

Was she supposed to provide him with a beverage? What was the etiquette of this arrangement? She hadn't a clue. "I should warn you that I am not much of a hostess and if you want food you will need to get your own."

Caitlin cringed at how prickly she sounded to her own ears. She knew how people talked about her behind her back. She pretended not to notice that no one asked her to participate in the office pools—not that she would anyway—but it was the principle that mattered. Rebecca seemed the only person who didn't mind her less-than-social personality, but Caitlin didn't feel right engaging on a personal level when she was Rebecca's superior. So most days Caitlin ate her lunch at her desk, alone.

And now, she was sniping at the man charged with keeping her safe. "I'm sorry," she said, frowning around her own awkwardness. "I'm just trying to say I don't know how to feed you."

He smiled as if he understood, but he couldn't possibly. Caitlin was painfully aware of how she was often off-center when it came to social interactions. Most times, people just made little sense to her. They said things that were silly, did things that were equally so and engaged in activities that were perplexing in their uselessness. Yet, Caitlin had always secretly yearned to understand what she was missing. Sometimes her intellect was a cumbersome burden.

Such as right now. "I make poor food choices," she admitted forlornly, unsure of how to proceed, gesturing to his well-defined musculature. "Something tells me you eat things like vegetables and lots of lean protein. I don't have anything like that in my house. Unless you consider squeeze cheese a protein."

To his credit, Zak made a solid effort to hold back his grimace but it was written all over his face that he did not, in fact, consider squeeze cheese a protein, or even food at all. "How about we stop by the store on the way to your place?" he suggested.

Caitlin was not excited about making a stop at the grocery store. Her routine was already woefully unrecognizable but she couldn't very well expect the man to starve, could she? "I suppose that's reasonable," she said with a heavy sigh that bordered on sullen but couldn't stop herself from adding, "I didn't really plan on traipsing up and down the aisles after work. I'm tired and just want to get home."

He nodded, understanding. "I can make what you have work for tonight," he said, conceding to her discomfort, and somehow that made her feel worse.

"I do my shopping on designated days," she justified, as if that would make her sound any less churlish at this point. "I prefer to stick to a schedule."

"Duly noted."

She cast him a gaze filled with suspicion. "Are you being condescending?"

"Not at all."

Maybe she was being difficult—she supposed there was no sense in denying it—but why should she disrupt her entire life unnecessarily? Honestly, this whole situation was ridiculous. They had no actual proof that whoever the thief was had any interest in her. As far as Caitlin was concerned, likely they could give two figs about her. They had the sample. Why would they come after her? But no matter how she tried to phrase her rationale to her superiors, they kept flatly turning her down.

In fact, her last conversation with Stan via email had been quite terse. Well, of course it was difficult to ascertain tone from an email but his response had seemed clipped.

Which meant she was stuck with Zak for now. Perhaps the hardest part to deal with was the fact that there was no endgame in sight. If Stan had come to her and said, "We need you under surveillance for the next twenty-four hours," she could've handled that because there was a definitive finish. People could handle anything as long as they knew there would be an end. Open-ended details had a tendency to squelch morale.

Unable to put off the inevitable, she finally shut down her computer and closed the office, moving past Zak with a frown. "I'm sorry but you'll find that I am not the most entertaining hostess."

"I'm not here to be entertained."

Of course he wasn't. Not that she would know anything about entertaining a man like him. He was so far afield from anyone she would ever have cause to date or even socialize with that she was at a complete loss as to how to interact with him at all.

"I do have some frozen potpies," she said, trying to sound less inhospitable. But he would discover soon enough that she was no Martha Stewart. "I'm a terrible cook. I'm sorry if you were expecting someone more accommodating."

"It'll be fine," he assured her, still waiting patiently for her to finish up.

She bit back a sound of frustration. Was this how their interactions were going to go for the foreseeable future? Good grief, this was like talking to someone in customer service. She'd almost rather he showed a bit of personality and told her to stop being such a pill, but that would be unprofessional and he'd never do that.

"Okay, fine. I'm glad we have that sorted," she grumbled, hanging her lab coat and shouldering her purse as she locked up and exited the lab. Her short stride was nothing compared to his long, looping gait. Every three steps she took equaled one of his. By genetic standards, his DNA was superior to hers in that by comparison she seemed a stunted version of humanity.

"You know, a hotel would probably be more comfortable," she suggested as they approached her car. "My house is very small. I'm not even sure you'll clear the doorframe."

"I go where you go." He slid her a mildly sardonic glance. "But your concern is touching."

As they reached the car, he gestured for her to hand over the keys and she balked. "You're not driving my car," she said, shocked that he would even think that she wouldn't drive her own car.

Again, his patience was maddening. "I know this seems strange but I need to be in control of the situation. Tomorrow I will drive you to work, but for now, in order to get your car back to your place, I will drive your car."

Now she was losing her ability to drive herself? She wanted to stamp her foot. "This is getting ridiculous. Why can't I drive my own car? I'm a very good driver, I'll have you know. I obey all safety laws and I've never had a speeding ticket."

"You sound like a model driver," he agreed, which told her that was not a point in her favor. "You don't have defensive driving skills. If in the event someone tries to chase us I need to be able to get us out of the situation quickly and safely and that usually means driving in ways that you aren't capable of."

Was she living in a James Bond movie? "Who would try to chase us? Who in the heck do you think is after me? I can't believe this nonsense. Look, I know that Tessara is playing it safe but there is honestly *no* threat to my safety. All of this is a huge waste of your time. I tried to talk Stan into letting you go but he seems to believe that you need to be here. I disagree."

"The validity of your employer's opinions is not my concern. My job is to keep you safe and I will do that through any means possible. Now, if you wouldn't mind taking a seat on the passenger side."

He wasn't going to budge. It was surreal. And she could tell by his expression that he would not change his mind. She wasn't about to stand in the snow freezing her tail off, arguing the fact. She wanted to get home. She was tired and hungry, and the whole day had been one she'd like to forget.

With each passing moment her discomfort grew, but she was out of options. She handed over her keys with little grace and stomped over to the passenger side, saying, "You'd better not put a single scratch on my car. It's a lease!"

* * *

Zak had never met a more irascible woman. "I'm going to take a wild guess and say that you're a little OCD?" he said, making conversation as they pulled out of the parking lot.

She stiffened. "I've never had an official diagnosis but if you're asking if I like things done a certain way, yes. Why do you ask?"

"Because people with control issues usually are."

"I don't have control issues," she denied, her scowl deepening. "Just because I don't want to be squired around like Jessica Tandy in *Driving Miss Daisy* doesn't mean I have control issues."

"It's not an insult," he tried to smooth her ruffled feathers but it was a little entertaining to see how easily she was riled. "The world needs obsessive people. Keeps the rest of us organized."

"Well, there is something to be said for being organized," she said with a small sniff. "Okay, so I'm going to take a guess that you're disorganized and chaotic in your everyday life? You probably wash your colors and whites together."

He didn't deny it. "I like to live dangerously."

A derisive snort followed as she said, "And you probably have more than a few pairs of pink socks in your dresser drawers."

"It happens. Good thing socks are cheap."

"If you separated your whites from your colors you wouldn't have that problem."

"Yeah, but who has that kind of time?"

He was baiting her, not sure why. Normally, he wouldn't chat up someone he was guarding but she was so damn stiff that he couldn't help testing just how rigid she was willing to remain. He wanted to see if he could coax a smile out of her. Maybe it was because, on the surface, the job was seemingly easy that the challenge of breaking through Caitlin's shell was enough to keep his mind engaged, or maybe he just liked the idea of seeing her smile. Either way, he should've just kept his mouth shut but he didn't.

"So you've never accidentally thrown in a black sock with a load of whites?" he asked. Her horrified expression was answer enough. He chuckled. "Been there, done that. I don't recommend it. I had to buy a bunch of new T-shirts. Hazards of bachelor life, I guess."

She didn't respond, not that he expected her to, exactly, but he thought she might've shared some of her own laundry mishaps, maybe to break the ice. He should've known better. Instead, Caitlin did the opposite of inviting more conversation by turning her gaze out the window, effectively shutting him out for the duration of the car ride.

They arrived at her house and after he did a quick perimeter search—which Caitlin handled with more sourpuss expressions—they walked into the small cottage. "You weren't joking, your place is small," he said. "But at least I can clear the doorframe, so that's not an issue."

He'd hoped for a smile but she was ten times more nervous now than in the car, which he hadn't thought possible. She was practically vibrating with anxiety and he knew he had to find a way to get her to trust him or else this detail was going to be a nightmare for them both.

"Very cute, though," he said, trying to appeal to her pride of ownership. "It has a very warm vibe, comforting. I bet this is your sanctuary."

"It was," she grumbled beneath her breath but then realized she was being rude and amended her comment, admitting, "I'm not exactly a social person. Being around a bunch of people is very uncomfortable for me. My home is where I know I can be myself and just relax."

"Except now I'm in your space and it's freaking you out," he finished for her and she simply nodded. At least she was honest. "Look, I get it. I'm a stranger. I wouldn't enjoy it, either, if someone came into my private space and hung out, unless they were expressly invited. But believe me when I say the threat to your safety is real enough that I can't blame your employers for taking precautions."

"You really think the threat is real?" she asked.

"I think that no employer would be willing to pay the kind of money they are paying Red Wolf to keep you safe if they didn't believe the threat was credible," he answered.

He didn't want to freak her out more than she already was, but he needed her to understand that the danger was real and if putting up with a little discomfort was the cost of her safety, it was something she'd have to accept.

Caitlin's unhappy frown spoke volumes as she admitted with frustration, "I don't know how to act with you here. As I said, I'm not a social person and I don't entertain. So having you here…it's just awkward. It feels like the world's worst blind date."

"Ouch," he said. "Been on many blind dates?"

Caitlin paused before she confessed, "No, but the ones I have been on were excruciating. The concept has always baffled me."

"I'm not one for blind dates, either. I prefer to know what I'm getting myself into before I get to the restaurant. Surprises of that nature have a tendency to end badly."

Curiosity must've gotten the best of her because she asked, "You date much? I mean, in your line of work, isn't dating difficult?"

Damn near impossible. He shrugged. “I’m married to the job and she’s a jealous mistress.”

“Right, of course.” Caitlin must’ve realized they’d somehow wandered into territory that was outside of her comfort zone, for she abruptly disappeared into the kitchen. He started to follow, when she reappeared with a bag of pretzels and an orange juice. “So, um, it’s late. I’m going to, uh, decompress in my bedroom. I need my alone time.”

He’d already determined her bedroom was secure. “That’s fine,” he allowed, ignoring the faint scowl on her part because he understand it was probably involuntary. “I’ll just poke around the kitchen, if you don’t mind. See what I can scrounge up.”

“I won’t lie. There won’t be much. I wasn’t kidding when I said I wasn’t much of a hostess.”

“I believed you when you told me the first time,” he said.

“Since you’re going to be here for however long, there’s no point in trying to hide the fact that I have terrible eating habits. But I’m not accustomed to having to defend my dinner choices, so I’m sorry for the poor selection. You’re welcome to whatever you can find.”

“I like pretzels,” he said with a disarming smile, which seemed to work in his favor a least a little bit. “Don’t mind me. You do what you normally do. I’ll try to stay in the shadows.”

“Having a man skulking in the shadows of my house is weird,” she said flatly. “It doesn’t matter how well you try to fade into the background. I’ll know you’re there.” She tossed a handful of pretzels back and said, midmunch, “I have to shower.” And then took her “dinner” and disappeared into her bedroom, closing the door behind her.

Zak sighed, realizing this detail was going to be more

difficult than it had appeared at surface value, not because he couldn't handle the potential of bullets flying but because there was something about Caitlin that tugged at him in a way that felt different than anything else.

And he wasn't sure what to make of that.

If anything.

Just keep her alive, finish the job, go home.

Easy enough.

Yeah...sure.

Chapter 4

Showered and in her pajamas, she was effectively hiding in her bedroom with her bag of pretzels and orange juice. She couldn't bring herself to hang out with Zak as if they were college roommates.

Not that she'd had a roommate in college.

Her cell phone rang; it was her mother. Even though it was late and she didn't want to answer, she was the dutiful daughter and clicked over in case it was an emergency.

"Hello, Mother," she said. "Is everything all right? How is Dad?"

"Your father is fine. We are concerned about you," her mother said, bypassing any chitchat. "We heard about the break-in at Tessara. What happened?"

"Mom, why are you even awake? It's late," she said, hoping her mother would go to bed soon.

"You know I have insomnia," her mother chided and Caitlin instantly felt guilty for not remembering. Of course she'd forgotten that her mother in particular rarely slept regularly, not uncommon in elite academic circles. Supposedly, the higher the intellect, the harder it was to find sleep.

Except in her case. In spite of her high IQ, she often fell asleep like a baby. Her father called her a unicorn. "I'm sorry, Mother," she said, wishing she'd let the call go to voice mail. "But I don't really want to talk about the break-in. It's all very new and the investigation is ongoing."

Caitlin shifted with discomfort. It was true the research community was small and word traveled quickly, but it was worrisome that her parents had already caught wind of the break-in when Tessara was doing its best to keep it hush-hush.

Her parents, both retired research analysts, were as introverted as their daughter, but they'd also been tops in their respective fields, even courted by Tessara, which they'd turned down.

The fact that Caitlin had followed where her parents had refused had always been a bone of contention between them but secretly Caitlin had enjoyed the notoriety. There was something darkly thrilling about working for a company with such a checkered yet brilliant past. However, she didn't dare admit that to her mother. She was also loath to concede that this recent turn of events was a little too real for comfort.

"How'd you find out about the break-in at Tessara?" she asked.

"Does it matter?"

"Of course it matters. You know how strict the security is at Tessara. My lab is already under scrutiny—I don't need more attention."

"I've told you before that Tessara was a bad move.

They're dangerous. This recent incident only further validates our position."

Even if her parents' argument held a modicum of merit, Caitlin resented having to defend her choices when she was a grown adult. If she wanted to work for the pharmaceutical equivalent of the "evil empire," she was well within her rights to do so. She fought to keep the anger from her tone, remembering that to win any debate was to keep emotion out of it. "Mother, Tessara is on the cutting edge of pharmaceutical research. It's very good for my career to have Tessara on my résumé, not to mention that the work I'm doing is important. I would rather have your support for my career than your shrill criticism. You've made your feelings perfectly clear about Tessara—feelings I don't share—so if you don't have anything else to say, I'm very tired and would like to relax before bed."

Caitlin could hear the frown in her mother's voice as she said, "You're a brilliant scientist but sometimes your decision-making skills border on reckless. Your father and I worry that your decision to work for Tessara is less about their pharmaceutical gains and more about the thrill of working for a company that has a reputation for skating the edge of safe and sane with their work."

"You have to stop judging Tessara from incidents that happened in the past," Caitlin said, irritated. "The company was exonerated and the people responsible for a few isolated incidents were removed. You can't blame an entire corporation for a few bad eggs."

"A few bad eggs?" her mother repeated in an incredulous tone. "People who have worked for Tessara have disappeared, or become ill with afflictions no one in the medical community has ever heard of—and those are only the incidents we're aware of. I worry your stubborn refusal to admit that Tessara might be a dangerous place to work is more about your relationship with me than anything else, and that proves my point about your innate recklessness."

"In your exhaustive research into my employer did you miss the fact that Tessara is leading the world in cancer research as well as neurological diseases?" Caitlin said. "They do important work and I'm proud to be a part of it."

"I never said they weren't doing positive things but it doesn't cancel the negative," her mother returned.

A flash of anger rippled through Caitlin. She hated these conversations with her mother because they were unfruitful. Her mother never budged and Caitlin was left feeling unheard and marginalized. "Was there anything else, Mother?" Caitlin asked, every muscle in her body tense, her jaw already aching from clenching it too hard.

"That work is going to get you killed," her mother said quietly and Caitlin swallowed some of her anger. For all of her issues with her mother, she was aware that her mom really did care. Then her mom dropped a bomb Caitlin wasn't expecting. "I know that you were reverse engineering a cure for a deadly biological, man-made virus. Caitlin, do you understand what you're getting yourself into?"

She wanted to say with confidence, yes, she knew how dangerous the situation was, but maybe she'd walked into the situation with a little bit more blind naivete coupled with ego than she wanted to admit. Instead of answering, she rebounded with "How'd you find out about that?"

A real frisson of alarm replaced her pique. "No one is supposed to have that information."

"It doesn't matter how. What matters is that it's true. We're very concerned," her mother said. "We want you to come home until this blows over."

"Come home to Wisconsin?" Caitlin couldn't imagine. No way. Especially not now. Thankfully, she had a great excuse. "I can't. I'm under 24/7 guard. Not to mention I'm needed for when the sample is recovered. I can't just up and leave. It's not like cashing in vacation time. You know that, Mother."

Her mother's heavy sigh said as much but Caitlin heard the worry and forgave her. Her mother could make nagging an Olympic sport but the underlying fear in her tone was the marked difference.

"Pharmaceutical espionage is nothing new," Caitlin said, trying to ease her mother's fears. "And you should see the bodyguard they've hired to watch my back. He's like ten feet tall and built like a rock wall. Nothing is going to get past him. I feel very safe with him around." That much was sort of true. She definitely felt no one was going to get past Zak to hurt her, but she might hurt herself by tripping on her own feet because her awkwardness had kicked into overdrive. At this point, walking into a closed door and breaking her nose was a distinct possibility.

Her mother made a small, distressed sound. "Caitlin Grace, this only reiterates my point. If Tessara has hired a personal bodyguard for you, they believe there is a threat to your safety. This makes me very nervous."

"I'll be fine," she promised, though it occurred to Caitlin for the first time that she was making assurances to the one person who would actually care if she were removed from this earth. She swallowed the sudden lump in her throat. "Zak is very thorough. Honestly, I think it's just a precaution. Probably an overkill, even. I'm sure they'll discover his services aren't needed, but for now, they're just covering all the bases."

"That's your final answer?"

The disappointment in her mother's voice was hard to miss but Caitlin couldn't leave.

"I can't."

"No, you won't. There is a difference," her mother said quietly but left it at that. After a beat of silence, she said, "Your father and I stumbled upon a lovely organic skin care company in northern Virginia that I think you would do very well with. I'm going to email you the particulars so you can check out the company yourself. Not only are they doing good things for skin care but they aren't harming the earth while they do it. Very responsible. I was so impressed with their operation that if I was ten years younger, I'd come out of retirement. They wanted to hire me on the spot. Of course, I mentioned your name and they wanted to know more about you. I took the liberty to send them your LinkedIn profile. If you were to change your mind about Tessara, I think you could make a very good career choice with this company. They are very progressive, forward-thinking."

Caitlin sensed this was her mother's attempt at processing her fear by focusing on something else, and forwarding job opportunities elsewhere seemed to fit the bill. Even though Caitlin had zero interest in chasing after the fountain of youth when she was actually doing work that mattered at Tessara. "Thanks," she said. "I'll take a look."

"Thank you, Caitlin," her mother said, even if they both knew she was just saying it to end the conversation. "It's a start, at least."

"It's been a long day. I'm exhausted and I want to go to bed."

"All right," her mother conceded, but Caitlin knew this wouldn't be the last of the conversation. "Let me know what you think of Patricia Adele Cosmetics."

"Right. As soon as I get a chance."

"Soon."

"Mmm-hmm. Good night, Mother."

"Caitlin…be careful."

That lump returned and she nodded, even though her mother couldn't see her. "I will." She clicked off and tossed her phone, emotionally exhausted by the events of the day and her conversation with her mother. Her parents were brilliant, had flourished within their own careers, but had given her no small amount of grief from the moment she'd taken the job with Tessara. Sometimes being an only child was a burden that only single children could understand. She wanted to live her own life, not the life her parents wanted her to live.

Maybe she was being stubborn—she wasn't ignorant of Tessara's shady past—but she truly was doing important work at Tessara and that was something she had to cling to.

Even if there was a shred of truth to her parent's concern.

Caitlin wasn't about to abandon her work.

While Caitlin seemed content to lock herself away in her room, Zak took the opportunity to check in with his TL.

The late hour didn't matter; Scarlett picked up on the first ring.

"How's things with the scientist?"

"Boring." He didn't pull punches. No sense in lying. "She's not winning any personality awards but I've secured the lab and her personal home. I feel confident I should be able to keep her safe until you guys can determine who stole the sample. Speaking of, any word?"

"Pretty quiet on the dark web but it's just a matter of

time before someone starts posting queries for sale, and when they do, we'll be there to catch them."

"And what if money isn't the motivator for the theft?"

"Money is always a motivator at some point."

If the past was any indication, Rhodes wasn't wrong. In all the missions, assignments and details he'd been involved in, money was never far from the jumping point. "Tessara has a history of trouble," he said. "So far, Dr. Willows's team seems clean but that's just surface looks. I will interview everyone more extensively tomorrow."

"Tessara has a checkered past but it's amazing how a shit-ton of money can make people look the other way."

"Wasn't Tessara involved with that soldier's death a few years ago, something about an amnesia drug that went bad?"

"Yeah, but you won't find their name on any official report. Anything with their involvement was redacted. Tessara is in bed with all the right people."

"And we're doing business with them, why?"

He could hear Scarlett's amusement. "Because at the end of the day, saving the human race is more important than standing on a moral high ground—and Tessara pays extremely well."

"Deep pockets hold a lot of coin."

"That they do. In the meantime, we're looking into the usual suspects, those with terrorist ties, to see if they've been causing trouble."

"I can't imagine anyone better at chasing down dirtbags than you, TL."

"It's my favorite pastime," she quipped and they both chuckled. A dark sense of humor was necessary in their line of work. Scarlett sobered to add, "Look, I know this assignment seems tame but you know that's when shit usually goes bad. Keep your head on a swivel."

"Always."

They clicked off just in time for Caitlin to reemerge from the bedroom with an awkward expression as she held some blankets and a pillow. "I'm sorry, this is all I have to offer. The couch is pretty comfortable, though. I've fallen asleep there more than once doing research."

He accepted the blankets. "Thanks. I'm sure it'll be fine."

She nodded and then, with an equally awkward good-night tossed over her shoulder, Caitlin returned to her bedroom, shutting the door quickly.

That woman had the soul of a Victorian nun. It was no wonder she lived alone.

After another perimeter search during which he double-checked locks and windows, he settled onto the couch with the surprisingly warm and cozy blankets tucked around him.

The faint scent of laundry detergent clung to the fabric, reminding him of his sweet granny before she died. In spite of his shitty parents, his granny had been the brightest spot in his short childhood. She'd always had something delicious to put in his hungry belly but she'd been old when he was born, passing before he'd turned eight.

But he remembered her kindness, even if he couldn't exactly remember the sound of her voice or the color of her eyes.

Sleep never found him easily. He wasn't surprised when he found himself staring at the ceiling, listening to the night sounds.

What kind of childhood had Caitlin had? Had she always been so reserved? Had something happened to make her mistrust people? Hell, why was he digging at something he had no real need to know? Probably because his brain was an unruly beast and he usually had no choice but to follow where it led.

And Caitlin was interesting.

There was something to be said about deep wells and still water.

Caitlin was exhausted and yet sleep eluded her. Maybe her mother's insomnia was finally catching up to her. Each time she closed her eyes, she saw Zak in all his muscled glory and her eyes popped open, but being awake only reminded her that Zak was in the other room.

Sleeping on her sofa.

A man was sleeping on her sofa.

A handsome, well-built man.

Of all the things that should've kept her awake and taken center stage—such as the current crisis facing the world at large—it was Zak who loomed large in her mental theater. She didn't know if she should be worried about her character or her mental health.

Okay, so break it down, her analytical brain suggested. She wasn't interested, of course, but she wasn't blind. Caitlin could admit that Zak was an excellent specimen of the male species. He probably had women chasing after him all the time. Did he ghost women when he was no longer interested? Why was she thinking of Zak's dating MO? Strictly speaking, from a scientific point of view, Zak was the kind of man that would be very popular in the sperm bank catalog. He seemed to check all the boxes.

Athletic: check.

Good-looking: check.

Smart: Not sure yet but he didn't seem dumb and that was another point in his favor.

Courteous: check.

Manners: check. He sort of had a Southern-charm thing going on, though she didn't detect an accent.

Sexy: okay, yes, check.

That last part made her cheeks burn. Thank God it was dark and she was alone. When was the last time she'd gone out on a date? Let's just say it was before Trump became president.

And it'd been horrific—a blind date set up by her friend Jeanice. She'd only agreed to meet the guy because Jeanice wouldn't stop asking and Caitlin figured one date couldn't be all that bad.

Oh, God, how she'd been wrong.

At first glance, they should've been a decent match. Their careers were compatible—he was also in the scientific field—but whereas she was quiet and reserved, he was a know-it-all blowhard who loved the sound of his own voice.

Anything that might've been remotely interesting about him had drowned in the wash of self-congratulatory nonsense flowing from his mouth like a flash flood.

She'd barely managed to choke down her dinner before quietly ending the evening with the excuse that her stomach wasn't feeling well.

Not exactly a lie.

After that she'd blocked his number and tried to forget the awkward almost-kiss that he'd tried to pull as he walked her to her car.

She'd never moved so fast in her life than when she'd ducked that pucker.

A shudder followed the memory. How could he not see from her body language that he made her skin crawl? Oh, well, that was a long time ago but it'd been a sufficient reminder that she wasn't cut out for social entanglements.

Caitlin preferred the solitude of research to the confusing dance of modern dating rituals.

Huffing a short breath, she adjusted her pillows and pulled her blankets more tightly around her, but a comfortable spot continued to elude her. She never suffered sleep issues. Ever.

But then again, she'd never had a complete stranger sleeping in the next room.

Was this to be her reality until Tessara determined her bodyguard was unnecessary? Lord in heaven, she hoped not. She needed a solid eight hours of sleep or else her brain suffered.

As it was, she was past her own bedtime.

Thanks, Mother.

Forcing her eyes to close, she practiced a tried-and-true meditation that never failed to calm and relax her.

A blank clockface. Numbers appearing one by one, followed by the hands. As the hands marked the hour, the number disappeared, cutting into the clockface until nothing but a black sheet of nothingness remained.

Ah, almost there.

She slowly drifted into that familiar place where sleep was found.

Until Zak's face returned to her mental theater and ruined her calm.

Again! A blank clockface…

It was going to be a long night.

Chapter 5

Caitlin growled beneath her breath as she took the passenger side of Zak's black Tahoe, which had been delivered early that morning. It smelled new and everything gleamed with the freshness of a vehicle untouched by humans or Taco Bell.

Clicking her seat belt as he maneuvered the beast down her driveway, she prepared to ride in silence, but Zak had other plans.

"Tell me about your team," he said, getting onto the highway.

Even though she was tired and grumpy, she tried to remain professional. "What would you like to know?"

"Let's start with the easy questions. Did you personally vet every member on your team? How did they come to you? Do you trust them?"

"Those are the easy questions? I'd hate to find out what you consider difficult questions." Drawing herself up, she said, "Of course I trust them. I personally vetted every single person working for me. I take my job very seriously."

"Of that I have no doubt," he said. "I'm not trying to imply that you've fallen down on the job or been careless, but whoever stole the sample knew exactly where to look, which suggests that whoever came into that lab had inside information."

"That's a plausible theory, but I'm sure there are many theories that could apply," she said, refusing to believe that anyone on her team had anything to do with the theft. "I'd advise you against marrying yourself to one particular agenda without first acquiring facts to back up your belief."

If she sounded defensive, she couldn't help it. To imply that one of her team had violated her trust was too much to consider, and she simply wouldn't allow a stranger to throw around accusations without letting him know exactly how she felt.

And Zak got the message, loud and clear. "Look, I understand you want to protect your team but we've got bigger issues than loyalty. The safety of the world may rest on your ability to separate your feelings about your team from this investigation. I need to know everything you know about every single person who has access to your lab."

"It's not only loyalty that you're questioning," Caitlin said. "It's integrity. And I can assure you, everyone on my team is solid."

"I hope you're right," he said. "But we have to look under every rock just to be sure."

Shrugging with annoyance, she said, "Well, clearly, Rebecca isn't a suspect."

"And why is that?"

"She has a disability," Caitlin answered, frowning. "Do you really think that Rebecca broke into the lab, smashed the controls and made off with the sample with her one good leg?"

"On the surface, I agree that Rebecca is seemingly easy to discount, but appearances can be deceiving. I take nothing for granted even if that means placing a woman with a disability under a hot bulb."

"That's ridiculous. It's not Rebecca. Although, she'd probably be happy that you consider her a potential suspect simply for the fact that she always feels people treat her differently because of her leg," Caitlin said, shaking her head at the odd logic. "I can tell you that Rebecca may act like a hormone-riddled teenager but she's brilliant."

"Exactly why we can't discount her."

"She would definitely find that flattering," Caitlin mused with private amusement. "But I can say with confidence, she's not a suitable candidate for your list of suspects."

But Zak wasn't entirely convinced. "What else can you tell me about her?"

Caitlin found his persistence annoying, especially since she knew Rebecca better than anyone else did in that lab. "What would you like to know? Would you like to know if she's single? Because she's very single. But dating is a challenge, which is probably why she's so damn thirsty all the time." Wow, that had come out all wrong and from a weird place. She hadn't meant to sound so judgmental. Caitlin bit her lip with embarrassment. "That was unprofessional. I'm sorry. What I meant to say is, she's incredibly smart but she's boy crazy, as my mother would say, so don't be surprised if she tries to get you to take her to dinner. She's harmless, though."

He chuckled and asked, "How long have you been friends?"

Zak's casual question threw her. Friends? She and Rebecca weren't friends. Friendships within a working environment, particularly between a supervisor and an employee, created problems. "She's not my friend," she corrected, shifting in her seat against the wave of loneliness that the simple statement created. "We're colleagues and she just happens to talk a lot."

And Rebecca was a sharer. Something Caitlin definitely was not. However, Rebecca didn't seem to notice and kept right on sharing, which was why Caitlin knew everything that was happening in Rebecca's life and why Caitlin knew Rebecca couldn't possibly be the one who broke into the lab. Quite simply, between her penchant for karaoke and volunteering down at the local animal shelter, the woman didn't have the time.

"But you like her," he concluded and she could only shrug in answer. She liked Rebecca well enough but it wasn't as if they went out on Saturday nights and whooped it up at the local bar. Oh, goodness, the very thought made Caitlin anxious. Zak pressed a little more. "What else do you know about her? Where does she come from? What is her background?"

Caitlin stiffened, crossing her arms. "If you prefer I can just have HR send you all of the team's personnel files. When I hired my staff, I looked at their professional qualifications, not their personal lives. I have no idea what they do on their off time. Nor do I care."

"And yet you seem to know that Rebecca was very single and apparently ready to mingle."

Her cheeks heated. "Like I said, Rebecca likes to share and I don't like to be rude."

At that he chuckled again. "Well, what else has Rebecca shared? Did she have money problems?"

"How should I know? I have no idea what her personal finances look like. That's...well, personal. I don't ask those sorts of questions. And why would you ask?"

"Money is a great motivator. Whoever stole that sample is likely going to try and sell it to the highest bidder. That means millions—possibly billions—of dollars. So someone with money troubles might jump at the chance of selling the world's most deadly and toxic biological agent to whoever is willing to pay the price."

"I can't imagine that Rebecca would steal something that we were all working on. Money might be a great motivator for some people but for us it's about the science."

He corrected her, "No, for you it's about the science. Everyone else is suspect."

"I work with these people every single day for long hours—morning, noon and night, and some weekends," Caitlin protested. She refused to believe they had anything to do with the break-in. "There's no way anyone on my team was involved."

He realized she wasn't going to budge on Rebecca and suggested, "All right, let's move away from Rebecca for now. What about Robert?"

She huffed a short breath in irritation. This car ride was beginning to feel like an inquisition. "What about him?"

"He wasn't at the lab yesterday."

"He called in sick."

"Seems a little suspect."

"People get colds. Do they forbid sick leave at Red Wolf Elite?"

He smirked, amused by her small jab. "Does he have a habit of calling in sick?"

"Not really, but there was a virus going around the lab a few weeks ago. So it's not far-fetched to believe that he caught the bug that had bounced around. And it's our strict policy that if you're sick in any way, you call in, because we can't risk contamination."

Zak accepted her answer. "What's he like?"

"Not single."

He laughed. "Good to know. What else can you tell me?"

"His research is exquisite."

Zak's brows shot up. "Exquisite? I've never heard anyone describe cold, hard facts as exquisite. Isn't that something you reserve for, like, key lime pie?"

A smile found her even though annoyance was still riding her hard. "Well, it's true. The first time I read his work I was stunned by its beauty. His work is clean, no mistakes. Unlike some people who lead with their egos, when he doesn't have an answer, he doesn't pretend to know what he doesn't know. I wish I had an entire team just like Robert."

"Seems very efficient."

"He is," she agreed.

"And would probably make an excellent assassin."

Caitlin chuckled. "I guess it's a good thing he chose science."

A moment of silence followed. Just as Caitlin began to relax, thinking that perhaps Zak was finished with his line of questions, he started in again. "Are you aware that Tessara has a shady past?"

Her shoulders tensed. "Everyone has a chapter in their story they don't like to talk about."

"Does that sentiment apply to corporations?" he mused.

"Of course."

"So you're okay with Tessara's past?"

She sighed. "You sound like my parents."

"Elaborate."

She didn't know what possible use sharing how her parents felt about Tessara was to the investigation. But at least he wasn't grilling her about her team anymore, so she indulged him. "My parents were top research analysts in their fields and Tessara courted them back in the day but they turned the lab down."

"Why?"

"Because they had serious reservations about what they felt was a conflict in ethics at the time."

"But you don't have the same concerns?"

"Nope."

"Interesting."

Was that judgment in his tone? "That's a pretty heavy rock you're holding while you stand in a very delicate glass house, wouldn't you say?"

He barked a short laugh. "Touché."

"My parents have a difference in opinion about where I should work but I'm not living their life, I'm living mine. They don't understand how important the work is that we're doing." She loved her work and wasn't ashamed of it, either. "I love what I do and that's enough for me." *And it was exciting.* That part pinched a little with guilt because her mother's worry was real and not just her typical nagging, but Caitlin had to ride this out. "Anyway, nothing in life is ever black-and-white, right? You're always the villain in someone's story. Just depends on whose story you're telling."

"True enough," he agreed. He seemed to understand her point. Maybe his own parents had given him grief about his life choices and he understood how it felt to be alone in his conviction that he'd made the right choice for himself. Still, it was weird to be talking about such personal things with a virtual stranger. She wasn't cut out for small talk but then she didn't enjoy sharing deep topics, either, which was probably why she was a loner at heart.

Even so, she was staunchly loyal and she'd defend her team to death. "I can promise you everyone on my team is devastated over this break-in. Every single one of us feels violated. We want to find out who did this, but honestly, we really just want to get back to work."

Zak blew out a heavy breath, as if knowing he was about to become really unpopular with his next statement but was going to say it anyway, "Look, I admire your loyalty to your team. I get it, I really do. I'm alive today because I put my life in the hands of my team. In certain situations, you have to believe that your team has your back and take that belief to the bank. But you also can't ignore facts to your own detriment." He ignored her gathering scowl, putting the facts as he saw them on display. "Caitlin, someone knew exactly where to go to get that sample. The theft was an inside job," he concluded with a firm shake of his head. "That means someone on your team is guilty and dangerous."

She dug her heels in. "I refuse to believe that."

"You're being stubborn."

She flashed a hot look his way at his admonishment. Just when she thought they were reaching some kind of accord, he went and ruined it. "Well, there you go. I guess there's nothing more to say about the subject. If you don't mind, I'd like to finish the ride in silence."

Zak accepted her request and she unhappily turned her gaze out the window. There was a simple comfort in clinging to the assertion that no one on her team was guilty of the break-in. She didn't want to think about the possibility that a traitor was working right beneath her nose. It made her question everything she thought she knew about her team and, worse, about her own skills as an administrator.

She struggled against the helplessness that the situation put her in, but there was also something about Zak that poked at her in a way that was worrisome. She just wanted him to leave so she could stop feeling this way. But if Tessara was right and her life was truly in danger, she couldn't imagine anyone else who could do a better job than Zak at keeping her safe.

And that caused a riot of feelings she didn't want to feel, either.

Honestly, the whole situation made her want to climb into bed and pull the blankets over her head.

She felt bad for being short with Zak, but her lips remained seamed shut, and she couldn't manage a simple apology. Blame it on the lack of good sleep, the need for strong coffee or the fear that somehow she'd inadvertently been to blame for this disaster. Inside, she felt like a miserable little bitch. No wonder no one invited her to anything.

Chapter 6

He'd hit a nerve but he couldn't spend too much time worrying about hurt or bruised feelings when he had a clear objective. Even though his TL was running down leads from her end, he knew the theft had been an inside job. His intuition told him he was on the right track, which meant he had to keep pushing forward.

Even if it meant pissing off his prickly scientist.

After securing Caitlin in her office—ignoring her sour, withdrawn looks—he started his individual interviews, starting with the previously absent Robert Vepp.

The man was lanky, wore glasses and had knobby knuckles. Zak had never seen a man play a stereotype to a tee like Robert Vepp. Sometimes people with ridiculously high IQs suffered from a low social EQ, which could present like a guilty conscience because they didn't like to make eye contact, seemed shifty and avoided conversation.

He was prepared for awkward.

But Robert Vepp wasn't awkward at all.

He thrust his hand forward for an aggressively manly handshake as he and Zak found a quiet corner to talk. "So sorry I missed the introductions yesterday. I heard it was quite the hubbub having someone such as yourself roaming our halls."

Zak smiled, faintly amused. Was Robert flirting with him? *Well, that's certainly a different track to travel.* Not that it mattered, but he wondered if Caitlin knew Robert was gay. "Who'd you hear about me from?" he asked, curious as to who was talking after hours. He knew it wasn't Caitlin, because the woman had only spoken to her parents and then had gone to bed with a bag of pretzels.

"Am I on the record?" Robert teased with an amiable smile. Robert was easy to like, which Zak filed away for future reference. Sociopaths were often likable. Zak returned the smile and waited. "Ah, so we are," Robert said, shifting in his seat. "As you might've heard, I was home with a stomach virus. But I'm friends with Jonathan Petranski, and when he called to check up on me, he let me know about our new visitor—you."

Were Petranski and Vepp a couple? "I'm sorry if this question seems inappropriate, but do you and Jonathan have a romantic relationship?"

"No," Robert assured Zak with a laugh. "Just friends. Jonathan is very straight, but we like to bowl together and sometimes after work we grab a beer at the local pub. He's a decent guy but a terrible bowler. How's your bowling game?"

"Haven't bowled in years, so I'd wager a guess—probably worse than Petranski."

Robert chuckled. "It's like riding a bike. I'd be happy to be your partner if you're looking to brush up on old skills."

Zak just smiled and kept moving forward. "So Petranski told you about the break-in?"

"Yes."

When Robert didn't automatically elaborate, he prompted, "Do you know of anyone who might've wanted to get their hands on that sample?"

"Just wagering a guess, every criminal mastermind on the planet with money to burn and a general hatred for the human race. Let's get real, that biological agent was Armageddon in a vial. Anyone in possession of that virus would be the most powerful force in the world."

"And how do you feel about your part on the team?"

"I feel pretty good. We're the good guys. Why wouldn't I want to be on the right side of that equation?"

"And you feel Tessara is on the right side?"

"Don't you?"

He shrugged. "I don't have an opinion."

"Sure you do."

Zak smiled. "I've heard things about Tessara but it's not my place to judge. I'm just here to find who took the sample and protect Dr. Willows."

Robert accepted his answer but said, "I don't envy your job. Caitlin isn't an easy person to get to know."

"She speaks highly of you, of her entire team, actually."

"Yeah? She's not big on praise. Hard to tell."

"Do you need praise?"

"No, of course not, but I'm not like everyone else. I'm confident in my work quality but others, such as Rebecca, could use a little pat on the back now and then."

"Dr. Willows is very defensive of her team. I'd say that says a lot about her faith in who works for her."

Robert smiled. "Indeed."

Zak considered the man before him, a contradiction in

every way. If he'd gone off first impressions, he would've been wrong. "You're an interesting guy," he shared, cataloging every reaction. "What made you go into science?"

"It's what I'm good at," Robert answered. "And, in the right labs, it pays well."

Zak slid his gaze to Robert, curious. "Tessara pays well, I assume?"

"Considering you can just look in my personnel file and find out what I make a year, I'll just go ahead and answer...yes, I'm happy with what I bring home. Tessara takes care of its employees. No complaints there."

"What complaints do you have?"

"None worth sharing."

"Indulge me."

Robert laughed. "Okay, the cereal bar is never stocked with my favorite cereal, in spite of several complaints, and it seems the office manager has some kind of bias against poppy-seed muffins because they're never available in the cafeteria."

"So, food complaints? That's it?"

"Pretty much. Like I said, Tessara takes care of its employees."

Zak smiled and leaned back. "Kinda rare these days, huh? Finding an employer that actually cares about its employees."

"The rarest."

A beat passed before Zak said, "So there's no one you can think of that might have a beef with Tessara?"

"Nothing big enough to risk their lives over."

"Interesting choice of words."

"How so?" Robert asked.

"It implies that Tessara's bite has teeth. Most people who work for a giant corporation have a more relaxed view of theft. I mean, who hasn't taken home a few pens from the office supply closet, right?"

Robert chuckled. "Tessara pays well enough that we don't feel the need to steal pens. Or anything, for that matter. That's all I was saying."

"Got it. So you can't think of anyone who might be willing to risk everything for a potentially big payout. I mean, let's get real for a minute, no matter how well Tessara pays, it's not a billion-dollar payday."

"Some things aren't for sale."

"If the number of zeroes is right…you'd be surprised how quickly people flip on their values."

"Speaking from experience?"

Zak smiled, making a mental note to keep watch on Robert. "Let's just say I've seen a lot."

"I bet you have. You've got the look of an all-American hero, with a SEAL-Team-Six vibe. You must be pretty popular with the ladies."

Interesting how Robert kept circling the conversation back to Zak. It could be classic deflection or it could be that Robert was passive-aggressively mocking him. Either way, Zak wasn't playing. He closed his notebook, signaling the end of their conversation. "I appreciate you taking the time to chat with me."

Robert nodded and rose from his seat. "I'm here any time. Like most of Caitlin's team, I pretty much live here at the lab. Who needs a social life when you're saving the world, right?"

Zak responded with a short smile that he immediately dropped as soon as Robert left the room.

Time to do some research on Robert Vepp. His instincts told him that the man with the "exquisite" research might be worth watching.

* * *

Caitlin managed to block out the knowledge that Zak was hovering around her lab, but each time he took someone into the adjoining room for a private interview, her breath caught in her chest.

She hated to admit that she had control issues. But there was no denying that fact, now that she was faced with situations she had absolutely no control over.

The anxiety was crowding her brain, making concentrating difficult.

Not to mention she was exhausted. She suddenly had a newfound appreciation for her mother's ability to function at such a high level with so little sleep.

Rubbing at her eyes, she tried to focus but it didn't help that Rebecca couldn't seem to stay on track for two seconds before she was rambling on about Zak and his physique.

"What was it like having him stay the night? Where did he sleep? On the couch? Or in your bed? I mean, if he's supposed to keep you safe at all times, he'd probably need to keep you within close proximity, right?"

Caitlin didn't want to dignify that silly question with an answer but she knew Rebecca would keep asking, so she answered with a curt "On the couch." She then pointedly returned to her notes in the hopes that Rebecca would get the hint but, of course, Rebecca was too enthralled with the unorthodox situation to notice.

"I'd probably insist that he sleep with me," Rebecca said, dropping down into the lone chair across from Caitlin's desk. "I mean, for safety purposes, it only makes sense to have him within arm's length. What if someone sneaked into your bedroom and was hiding in your closet, just waiting for the right moment to slit your throat?"

That was decidedly macabre imagery. She flicked her eyes to Rebecca. "That's not going to happen."

"Which part? The person hiding in your closet or Zak sleeping in your bed?"

Her cheeks flushed with heat as she replied, "Neither. Was there something work-related you needed to discuss?" Caitlin asked, bringing the conversation back to more appropriate topics.

"No. Not really. I just can't understand how you can be totally unaffected by the fact that a certifiable hunk is your personal bodyguard. Are you blind?"

"Not blind, but certainly irritated," she muttered, meeting Rebecca's gaze. "However, I'm equally puzzled as to how you can be so nonchalant about the fact that we were burgled and the single most important sample in the known world was stolen. You do realize we are still on a ticking clock, right?"

"Of course," Rebecca said, apparently shifting with guilt. "Maybe it's my coping mechanism. If I focus too hard on the fact that someone gained access to our lab, it sends me down a spiral that I somehow must've been responsible. I've gone over the protocols a million times since that night and even though I know I've followed every rule, I still worry that it's somehow my fault."

"How could it possibly be your fault?" Caitlin asked, frowning. "Whoever broke in smashed the control panel to gain access, which is not something we were prepared to handle."

"Yes, but how'd they know which lab to target? Tessara had literally hundreds of ongoing experiments and minilabs throughout the building but somehow they knew the sample was here, in our lab. What if… I don't know, someone hacked my emails or bugged my house and overheard me talking in my sleep about the project?" She threw her hands up, frustrated and riddled with anxiety. "I mean, there are too many variables to consider and the sheer scope of it paralyzes my brain! So, yeah, I tend to focus on things that are far less intimidating, such as your sexy bodyguard, who, if I'm totally honest, I would've been climbing like a tree if he were protecting me. You have the restraint of the Queen's Guard."

For the first time ever Caitlin saw Rebecca in a new light. "Wow, I never thought I'd meet someone with more anxiety issues than me," Caitlin said in a rare moment of commiseration. She understood Rebecca's fears—even though they sounded totally irrational when spoken out loud, they were plausible. Her own apprehensions with the thinnest thread of plausibility kept her awake at night. "Look, it wasn't you. It wasn't anyone in our lab," she assured Rebecca. "Zak and his team will find the thief and then life will go back to normal. Until then, we just have to fake it until we make it."

"What do you mean?"

"I mean, we have to keep moving forward, even if we're not sure of what we're doing. Eventually, everything will slip into place."

Rebecca remained dubious. "That's not very scientific."

"No, not at all, but it does work. Mind over matter. Tessara is counting on us. The world is counting on us. Do we have much choice? Failing isn't an option."

Rebecca nodded, rubbing at her nose. "Yeah, I guess you're right. It's still really weird to have Zak around, though. He's super hot. Not exactly the type we're used to seeing running around the halls."

That much was true. He was a terrible distraction. "The sooner Tessara releases him, the better. I, for one, am ready for some normalcy."

"Just because something is what you're used to, it doesn't mean it's good," Rebecca said glumly. "Just because we're into science doesn't mean we have to settle for pale-faced lab rats."

Caitlin laughed at the absurd idea. "My parents were both lab rats as you call them and they aren't particularly pale or unattractive. Be careful for stereotypes—they'll bite you in the butt every time."

But Rebecca wasn't ready to concede, not yet. "C'mon, be real for a minute, Caitlin. That guy is hotter than Georgia asphalt and you'd have to be blind to miss that. You can't tell me that having him in your house isn't a little distracting."

"Oh, it's a lot distracting and I don't like it," she said, finally finding something she could agree with. "But it's temporary and I can handle a little discomfort for the time being. However, I need you to focus on your work, not on the temporary distractions, okay? What we're doing is super important and we can't let anything stand in our way of success. Tessara is counting on us."

"Why are you so damn loyal to Tessara?" Rebecca groused. "Did they pay off your student loans or something? You sound like the poster child for employee gratitude."

Rebecca's attitude shocked Caitlin. She'd never seen her act so churlish. It was a side to her assistant she didn't know how to process. "I think we do good work and the work is important," she answered. "Don't you?"

"Yeah, I guess. I mean, if you overlook the fact that the sample we were working on was stolen from someplace else and the rumor is that it was stolen from a Tessara lab in South America, then, yeah, I guess we're doing good work."

She hadn't heard this rumor but it made her intensely

uncomfortable. "Well, we can't put much stock in rumors."

"There's a grain of truth to every rumor," Rebecca reminded her with a small smile before rising and leaving Caitlin's office.

Caitlin tried to focus on work but her mind kept returning to Rebecca's comment. What if it was true? What if the sample they'd been working on had been created in a Tessara lab and if that was true, why were two Tessara labs working against one another? It didn't make any sense.

Which was precisely why listening to rumors was counterproductive.

Doubling down, she refocused and pushed all thoughts of conspiracy from her head.

Chapter 7

Caitlin hadn't lied when she said she wasn't a cook. The woman lived off Cheez-Its and apple juice with the occasional pretzel surprise thrown in.

Her body might thrive off junk but his did not. The first order of business was stocking her house with actual food—vegetables, fruits and dairy—so he could cook something that wasn't processed to death and had some actual nutrition.

He wasn't a health nut but he relied upon his body remaining strong and healthy for his job.

Let's face it, he couldn't kick some ass if he was draggin' ass.

Caitlin surveyed the food he'd purchased with an overwhelmed expression. "Do you know what to do with all this stuff?" she asked, grabbing the spaghetti squash in total confusion. "What the heck is this?"

"That is squash and it's a good substitute for pasta. You can make spaghetti out of it."

"What's wrong with actual pasta?"

"Nothing, but too many carbs make you sluggish. When I'm on assignment, I need to stay light on my feet, keep my reflexes sharp."

"So you go low-carb when you're on the job?"

"Depends on the job."

"I would die without carbs."

"Carbs are delicious," he agreed with a wink, adding, "but after you try my squash marinara, you'll forget all about traditional pasta."

"Doubtful, but I appreciate your enthusiasm."

He chuckled. "How you operate that giant brain of yours on the crap you eat I'll never know, but while I'm here, you're going to try a few things different from your usual fare of convenience-store food."

Her cheeks flushed and she muttered, "Don't knock convenience-store pizza until you've had it."

Zak laughed, amused at how prickly Caitlin got over the smallest things. She was wound so tightly she fairly squeaked. Zoey had been like that, too. Often he'd been the only one who could make her laugh.

He ignored the immediate cloud that never failed to gather when he thought of his sister. There was a reason he kept that crap private. Turning so Caitlin didn't catch his slip, he started preparing the squash, grateful to have something to focus on until he got a handle on his feelings.

Since meeting Caitlin, he'd spent more time pushing away thoughts of Zoey than he had in years. There was just something about Caitlin that reminded him so much of his sister that the memories of Zoey kept resurfacing.

"Do you need any help?"

He turned to find Caitlin standing awkwardly, arms crossed, yet with an odd earnestness that seemed out of character. Not wanting to dishonor the fragile moment, he gestured toward the waiting vegetables. "You could make the salad," he suggested, picking something easy.

"Salad…like lettuce and tomato, right?" she clarified.

He nodded. "Maybe throw in a cucumber or two, if you want to get fancy."

"Don't push your luck," she grumbled but grabbed the lettuce and started preparing, albeit a little awkwardly. But Zak couldn't care less about presentation. He just liked to eat good food; it didn't matter to him if the dish looked like a train wreck. After a few minutes, she said, "So you're a health nut…what else should I know about you?"

"Is this where we bond?" he teased, trying to get her to smile at least a little bit. If he didn't have to spend so much time fighting her on every step, maybe he'd make more progress. When she didn't respond to his subtle teasing, he returned to his pot of shredded hamburger. "Well, what would you like to know?" he said.

"I don't know. I've never known someone like you. How did you get into the bodyguard business?" she asked. "What is Red Wolf Elite anyway?"

Zak was relieved to talk about something other than the case. "Red Wolf is a paramilitary outfit that specializes in operations that are difficult to categorize. Shadow ops, high-profile client protection, even some jobs overseas. Basically we do anything that the government wants to be able to claim no part of." He understood Caitlin's pride in her job, even if others found it shady, because he was proud of his job, too.

"Sounds very dangerous," she murmured. He turned to find her regarding him warily. "You've probably killed people before, right?"

"Yes," he answered without equivocating. "But I can

promise you, if they ate a bullet from my gun, they had it coming."

That broke a tiny smile. *That, of all things, broke a smile?* "Methinks the quiet scientist is a little savage."

She chuckled, admitting with the tiniest of shrugs, "Maybe a little."

He liked this hidden side of Caitlin. Private people were the most interesting. He preferred deep wells to shallow pools any day. "Tell me what it was like growing up in the Willows household."

"It was quiet. I read a lot. My parents were gone a lot." As if to prevent any pity coming her way, not that he was about to offer any, she quickly added, "But I liked my alone time. Actually, it suited my personality very well, not having my parents hover around me all the time. Gave me the chance to develop my own set of skills and coping mechanisms without their influence. I think I'm very lucky to have grown up the way I did. Although my mother did enjoy her share of nagging."

He sensed loneliness beneath the brave words but he had the sense to keep his observation to himself. "School wasn't my thing. I joined the army as soon as I was able."

"Makes sense, given your current field."

He laughed. "Yeah, not a lot of jobs out there for former army rangers. My skill set isn't exactly directly transferrable to the civilian sector."

"I suppose not. But then I'm not sure I'd feel as safe with an insurance salesman guarding me, either."

He chuckled, conceding her point. "Probably not." Finishing his sauce before grabbing the spaghetti squash from the oven to pull out the fleshy strands, he said, "You're an interesting woman."

Caitlin blushed but she still agreed with him. "Yes, I am."

"Has anyone ever told you that you're a contradiction?"

Her expression melted into wary confusion. "No. In what way?"

"Well, you're clearly an introvert but you work for a company known for their dangerous associations, which tells me that on some level you crave adventure. You're private but not afraid to assert yourself when the situation calls for it. I don't know, you're just hard to categorize."

"Should I be flattered or worried?"

He shrugged. "My observation isn't meant to flatter or worry. I make my living by being observant and, to some extent, figuring people out."

"And you're saying that I'm hard to figure out?"

"Definitely."

His breath hitched slightly as her tongue darted to tease her bottom lip. The unintentionally arousing gesture punched him in the gut.

The smell of gently simmering sauce filled the small kitchen but there was more than savory marinara in the air. His heart rate quickened as their eyes met and his gaze dipped to that sweet, petulant pucker. He knew it wasn't right and that he should pull back but they were both being pulled and it was almost mesmerizing.

"I think your sauce is burning," she whispered, her pupils dilated as he instinctively leaned forward, his eyes on the prize. *Sauce. Saucy. Yeah, she was saucy all right.*

But suddenly, what she'd said actually penetrated the fog in his brain and he whipped his head around to see that, in fact, his sauce was burning and he hurried to turn down the burner. The quick motion helped evaporate the haze, leaving him to question what the hell was wrong with him.

He needed to apologize. Drawing a chagrined breath,

he turned to find Caitlin had split the kitchen, leaving him, the scorched sauce and his unfortunate lapse in judgment behind.

Had he been about to kiss her? Caitlin couldn't quite process what had almost happened.

Did an almost-kiss count?

Was it inappropriate to feel disappointed that his damn sauce had ruined what might've been the most exciting kiss of her life?

She touched her lips from behind the safety of her bedroom door. He had exquisite lips. Who was she kidding, the man was crafted from perfection. It'd probably been on his résumé when he'd applied to Red Wolf.

Adonis-like face: check.

Greek-god physique: check.

Lethal in every way: check.

Well, she didn't actually know much about Red Wolf but it sounded exotic, and exotic employers had extraordinary requirements.

Her stomach yowled. God, she was hungry. Whatever he'd been cooking had smelled incredible. Way better than convenience-store pizza. How was she even alive? Zak was right—she treated her body like a garbage can.

But she really hated vegetables.

She much preferred food that was fast, greasy and probably loaded with carcinogens.

Caitlin smothered a giggle. Perhaps Zak's casual observation was on point—she was a contradiction. She knew better, she understood the mechanics of biology and the necessity of good nutrition, and yet, she rarely ate anything that could remotely qualify as good for her.

Snack cakes were her weakness.

It was a wonder she wasn't four hundred pounds. Her

metabolism was holding strong for now but she knew it was just a matter of time before the dam broke and her metabolism slowed to nothing.

She startled at a sound outside her window. Probably an owl or something. Or a raccoon. Still, after quickly composing herself, she returned to the kitchen to find Zak had set a nice table and the food was ready and waiting.

"You returned. I was afraid I was going to have to leave your dinner outside your door."

"I just left to use the bathroom," she lied. If he knew that she'd fled like the devil was on her tail, he politely didn't mention it. She sniffed at the aroma in the air. "Smells good."

"Embarrassing sauce moment aside, it turned out pretty great."

"You didn't have to do this," she said but her mouth was watering. "I don't expect you to cook for me."

"We both gotta eat," he said by way of simple logic. "Have a seat."

She slid into the chair opposite him and quietly noted that no one had ever sat at this table with her. Certainly no one of the opposite sex. She was fiercely protective of her private space, and up to this point, she'd never felt the need to change that fact.

But now Zak, the beautiful bodyguard with the soulful eyes and the wonderful physique, was sitting across from her as if they were buddies.

Or lovers.

A shudder traveled her spine and she covered it by reaching for the weird squash masquerading as pasta. "Okay, so how does this work exactly?" she asked, grimacing a little as she tried to scoop the stuff onto her plate. *Just pretend that it's pasta. Don't think about it being squash, which you hate. It's pasta, delicious pasta.*

Zak smiled and ladled some marinara on her squash for her. “Just like that. Now sprinkle some cheese on that bad boy and you’ve got yourself an amazing, delicious and healthy meal.”

“You sound like an infomercial.” Caitlin cautiously forked some squash with a generous helping of marinara. “Here goes nothing…” She stuck it in her mouth with as much courage as she could muster. She only hoped it didn’t come back up, because that would be terribly embarrassing. She waited for the inevitable message from her brain rejecting what was in her mouth. But it was actually very good and the texture of the squash didn’t make her want to vomit.

“Well?”

“It’s not disgusting,” she admitted, forking another bite. “But I’m not going to break into song about it.”

He laughed. “High praise. I’ll take it.”

She risked a smile before taking another bite. “So you like to cook?”

“I do,” he admitted, even blushing a little as if being handy in the kitchen was something he usually hid. “But to be honest, I just like to eat, and seeing as I’m on the road a lot, figuring out how to make something I’d like to eat seemed the logical thing to do.”

“Family recipes?” she asked.

“Hell, no. My family wasn’t exactly *Full House*. Not a lot of happy memories in that photo album.”

“I’m sorry.” She thought of her own childhood. While it wasn’t particularly exciting, it hadn’t been traumatic, either. Her childhood had been adequate. That was the best way to describe how she’d been raised. Two busy, very smart parents, an average high school experience and a stellar university education, which had then transitioned to a career she was proud of. “My parents weren’t much on the kitchen scene, either. Not because they were bad or anything but because they were super busy. Research scientists. We ate a lot of TV dinners."

"Your parents are pretty big deals in their fields, right?"

She supposed he'd done his homework. "They are well respected," she confirmed but couldn't quite help the frown.

"Something wrong?"

"I'm not used to people knowing my backstory before I'm ready to share it," she admitted.

Zak understood. "Probably feels pretty invasive."

Caitlin nodded. "I know it's your job but I'm naturally a private person. Knowing that you're probably aware of everything in my past makes me feel more exposed than if I was standing in front of you naked."

He choked a little. "Sorry, sorry," he said, his eyes watering as he reached for his water glass. "Wrong pipe."

But her heart rate tripped a little. Did he like the idea of seeing her naked? Had she fallen down Alice's rabbit hole? Men like Zak did not fantasize about seeing her in her birthday suit. She wasn't a curvy seductress by any means. In fact, she'd always seen herself as built like a boy, straight up and down, no hips and barely any breasts. She'd long ago given up any hope that she'd wake up one day with a figure that stopped traffic.

"What's happening here?" she asked, unable to stand the questions in her head. "I… I'm not good with subtlety. Are you attracted to me? Because I'm getting some weird signals that I don't know how to process. If I'm offbase, I apologize for making things more awkward than they need to be but I need to know which way the wind is blowing so I can decide how to proceed."

And, just like that, she'd ruined a perfectly lovely dinner.

Chapter 8

Say no.

Zak knew the right thing to do. He knew protocol like the back of his hand. Messing around on assignment was a no-no.

And for the most part, unlike CJ or Xander, he played by the rules.

But he wanted to break rules with Caitlin.

There was something about her that lit him up like a Disneyland parade. He couldn't explain it but he knew enough to know that he had to shut whatever was happening down.

He swallowed and forced a smile. "Um, I like you. You're fascinating, for sure, but it's always best to keep things professional, you know?"

He hadn't exactly refuted what she was picking up but the message was clear enough. Even though two high points of color in her cheeks betrayed her embarrassment, she nodded stiffly and agreed. "Excellent. I feel the same. My mistake. I'm not very good at social cues. I apologize for misreading the situation."

"No worries. How's your dinner?"

"Good. Very good," she answered but he could tell she wanted to disappear. *Damn it.* He should've kept whatever was happening with him on lock. It was his fault for making the situation uncomfortable. "Good stuff."

"Better than box pizza?" he coaxed, trying to make her smile.

"I wouldn't go that far," she said. "Squash will never be pasta no matter how hard it tries but it doesn't make me want to throw up, so there's that."

"Fair enough."

A moment of silence passed between them and Zak knew he was losing her fast. Just when he'd started to make some inroads, he had to go and screw things up.

"Tell me about your project."

She looked up, question in her eyes. "What do you mean?"

"Well, I mean I've got intel but I'd like to hear from you what we're dealing with."

She seemed relieved at having something solid to hold on to and said, "Oh, of course. Yes, well, Tessara was charged with reverse engineering a cure for this nasty biological agent that had the potential of destroying entire populations in record time."

"Yeah, I don't know about you but...that's scary as shit."

"It was magnificent." At his confused frown, she clarified with a blush. "Yes, it was very scary but there's something incredible about how efficient it was in its ability to destroy. I know it's hard to understand but the beauty in its deadly efficacy was astounding. I was quite impressed with the genetic makeup. You know, people think it's so easy to engineer viruses because of what they see on TV but creating a new virus on this scale isn't like putting together a stew. Most times the genetic code collapses in on itself."

He cast a rueful glance her way. "All that aside, leaking out my insides isn't my idea of beauty in action."

Her blush deepened as if she realized she came off sounding like a psychopath. "Oh, goodness, no, of course not. The host dies in a most horrific way," she agreed, shoveling a healthy bite into her. "Internal organs liquefying is really gross and painful, too," she said around chewing. "I'm not saying that anyone should ever be subjected to such a horrible thing but from a scientific standpoint, it's really impressive."

He grimaced but he was amused at how nonplussed she remained while talking about something really awful in a clinical setting. "What was your first thought when you started working on the assignment?"

Caitlin leaned back, remembering with a sparkle in her eyes. "I thought, 'This is a game changer. This is the kind of work that makes or breaks careers.' I was excited," she admitted.

"You weren't scared?"

"Not even for a second."

"Don't take this the wrong way but you're a little scary yourself."

She laughed. "Me? How so?"

"Because most people would run from a situation that potentially puts them in that kind of danger. Yeah, there are safety protocols but mistakes happen. We've all seen *Outbreak*. All it takes is a rip in your hazmat suit and you're a goner."

"That's why we're very careful. Being OCD, as you put it, and being Type A has its benefits."

"I'd rather face down a firing squad than walk into a lab with that shit on the slides."

Caitlin chuckled, reminding him quietly, "People are far scarier than any virus. Viruses act according to their programming. Humans are unpredictable."

Couldn't argue with that logic. People were shifty as shit. "How close were you to finding the cure?" he asked.

At that her smile faded, replaced by consternation. "Not nearly close enough." She met his gaze. "Do you really think whoever stole the sample is going to release it to the public?"

"I hope not." He released a heavy sigh. "Experience tells me that whoever took the sample has plans but those plans likely have a dollar amount attached. They're going to sell to the highest bidder and then run off to some country without extradition."

"But without a cure, money means nothing. Eventually, the virus would find them, too."

"Sometimes criminals are blinded by their own ambition."

"What if money wasn't the motivating factor? What if whoever took the sample plans to destroy humankind? Some people kill for fanatical reasons that have nothing to do with the accumulation of wealth."

"Let's hope greed is the motivating factor," he said, his frown deepening. "In my experience, fanatics are the worst kind of people. They are motivated by internal conviction and there's no reasoning with someone who feels they are doing something for a higher purpose."

She nodded, agreeing. "Now, *that* scares me."

Zak nodded, his gut clenching with the same fear. "Me, too."

Caitlin digested Zak's quiet admission, becoming aware that the previous levity had evaporated. There was a lot at stake here. She bore a lot of guilt for the break-in, even though she'd been completely cleared of any wrongdoing. It was still her lab, still her project that'd been compromised.

She didn't understand people in general, but she was truly baffled by why someone would want to kill an entire population. For what? She couldn't fathom a reason strong enough to justify such a drastic action.

Chewing her lip, Caitlin lost herself in her thoughts until Zak started clearing the table. "I'll help," she offered, rising to bring the dishes to the kitchen. "If you cooked, it's only fair that I clean up."

"I don't mind. Keeps my mind moving," he said but she wouldn't hear of it.

"I might not be able to cook but I can run a dishwasher."

Zak cast a smile her way and she had to look away quickly. That smile was too seductive, even if he wasn't trying to be. Her body reacted in ways that she couldn't control. It was disconcerting. She wasn't going to embarrass herself by panting over a man who'd made it clear that the lines would remain professional.

Which she preferred!

Hadn't that been her biggest worry? That she'd have to suffer awkward advances that had no business happening between them? *Yes, exactly.* Except she hadn't anticipated Zak affecting her in this way. She'd never been the type to pine for someone. Or fantasize. Her sex life was decidedly clinical.

She refused to acknowledge how dissatisfying those quickly rubbed-out orgasms were during quiet moments alone in her bed at night when she needed release.

Orgasms by their very nature were good for a better night's sleep.

And a well-rested scientist was more efficient.

More effective.

She turned abruptly and ran into the solid wall of Zak's chest. "Oh!" The plates in her hands dropped from her hands to shatter on the floor. "Damn it, I'm sorry," she muttered, irritated with herself as she bent to pick up the shards.

"I'm sorry, I should've been watching more carefully. Let me help," he said, bending to join her. Together they picked all the broken pieces and he swept up the tinier pieces, dropping everything into the trash. Teasing, he looked to her, saying, "Maybe you're right, this kitchen isn't big enough for the two of us."

"Well, you're, like, ten feet tall and wider than the doorframe," she grumbled. "Compared to you, I'm practically a hobbit."

"Are you trying to tell me you have tufts of hair on your feet?"

She cracked a reluctant smile, surprised he knew anything about hobbits. It seemed more of a nerd thing than a buff-soldier-type thing. She would really be impressed if he started speaking in Klingon, though.

Caitlin rose and Zak followed. They were too close again. He was in her personal space.

And she liked it.

Of course, all that previous talk about keeping the lines drawn and whatnot flew right out of her head, and all she could breathlessly hope for was that he'd grab her and kiss her stupid. Maybe kiss her so hard that she'd forget it was a terrible idea and probably ranked in the top three most reckless things she'd ever do in her life.

Okay, twist her arm, it would be *the* most reckless thing but she didn't want to pull away or remind him that they'd agreed it was a bad idea.

But how often did opportunities like this drop into a

woman's lap? She wasn't dead below the waist. Zak was very handsome and he smelled like citrus and male skin, something that had never really made her quiver but it certainly did now.

Oh, God, he was moving in, his lips were tantalizingly close to hers.

This was happening.

Zak was going to kiss her.

Holy Madame Curie...

She lifted her lips, ready to feel his mouth on hers.

Her eyes fluttered shut but before Zak could seal his lips to hers, a sharp *tink* sound interrupted the moment. Suddenly Zak wrapped his big arms around her and took them both to the floor. He took the brunt of the impact but the drop clacked her teeth together.

Caitlin's mouth popped open on a gasp but he shushed her quickly with a motion to remain on the floor. What the hell was happening? It took a full five seconds before she realized with dawning horror that the sound had been a bullet puncturing her kitchen window, narrowly missing her head.

Fear squeezed her throat. A bullet! Nearly hit her head!

Zak carefully made his way out of the kitchen to melt into the night with the stealth of a trained killer. *Holycrapholycrapholycrap!* The word jumble in her head was on a repetitive loop as the realization that she'd been seconds away from meeting her maker kept her on the floor, paralyzed with fear.

It was jarring to see Zak go from teasing and laughing to a hardened soldier, gun drawn and eyes sharp and cold.

But if there was anyone out there, Zak would find them.

Suddenly, she was so grateful Zak had been there with her. If he hadn't, whoever had tried to put a bullet in her brain probably would've succeeded. She rested her forehead on the cold wood of her kitchen floor, saying a silent prayer to a God she didn't necessarily believe in for second chances.

Moments later, Zak returned to do a search of the house. When he was satisfied the house was secure, he allowed Caitlin to rise but he kept his body between hers and any open windows.

"Did you find anyone?" she asked, her teeth beginning to chatter. It was something that happened involuntarily when she was scared. It was also the biggest reason she didn't watch horror movies.

"Whoever took the shot is gone but we're not safe here anymore. Your house has been compromised. Grab your stuff, we're leaving."

"Leaving?" she gasped, horrified. "Going where?"

"Anywhere but here." He gestured curtly, all business. "Ten minutes. Go."

Ten minutes? To pack? Pack for where? For how long? But she didn't have the option of arguing. A second look at that tiny hole in her kitchen window put her feet in motion.

She'd pack light.

While Caitlin packed, he texted his TL, Scarlett.

House compromised. Need safe location. ASAP.

Scarlett responded a moment later.

4100 Old Hawk Road. Location secure. Await further instruction.

Caitlin appeared, pale and shaken, with a small suitcase in her hand. "I'm ready," she said, her eyes big. "Are you sure it's safe to go outside?"

"Whoever it was took the shot and split when they didn't hit their target."

She gulped, knowing full well that she'd been the target. "I guess we shouldn't look a gift horse in the mouth, right?"

He nodded, grabbing her suitcase and leading the way. "Stay behind me, just to be safe."

Zak went to his rental and tossed the suitcase inside as Caitlin climbed into the passenger seat. Punching the address into his GPS, he quickly left Caitlin's little cottage behind and hit the road.

"Are you okay?" he asked once they were clear.

"I think so."

The shake in her voice gave her away. "It's okay not to be."

"I've never been shot at. I don't like it."

"Not many people do. I never like getting shot at."

"Have you dodged many bullets?" she asked.

"A few," he lied. He'd been shot at more times than he cared to remember. It was definitely the less awesome part of his job. "I don't want you to worry. I will keep you safe, okay?"

"I know you will," Caitlin said, nodding. "I guess this blows my argument out the window about Tessara overreacting, doesn't it?"

"Pretty much."

She chewed her lip for a moment before admitting, "I'm really glad you were there. If you hadn't been… I might be dead on my kitchen floor right now." Caitlin shuddered. "And I would've ruined my hardwood floor. I spent a lot on that flooring. My entire Christmas bonus last year, actually."

"Hardwood is expensive," he agreed just to keep her

talking. Shock had a way of sneaking up on a person. "It was a good choice. The dark wood is nice."

She bobbed a nod. "Yeah, I thought so, too. More expensive but it was worth it." Caitlin drew a halting breath as if she just realized the gravity of everything and the reality that was staring her in the face. "I almost died. Someone almost killed me. Why would anyone want me dead? I don't understand. I'm just a scientist."

"You're the only person who currently has a chance of deciphering that cure code. Apparently, someone wants to make sure you don't get to figure it out."

Or they wanted to scare her, keep her on edge, which would affect her ability to think.

But with an attempt on Caitlin's life now in the mix, everything had changed.

No more was this a simple babysitting gig—shit had just got real.

"Where are we going?" she asked, her teeth clattering.

"Are you cold?" He reached to turn up the heat but she stopped him.

"My teeth chatter when I'm scared," she admitted. "I'm not cold."

A smile wasn't appropriate given the circumstances but that single thing seemed the most adorable quirk he'd ever heard of. Somehow he doubted she'd find his amusement adorable. Smothering his urge to grin, he said, "All right, well, if you change your mind, feel free to adjust the thermostat."

She nodded, seeming relieved that he didn't make a big deal out of her reaction. "So where are we going?" she asked again. "A hotel or something?"

"Can't trust a hotel. Red Wolf has access to safe houses throughout the United States. We're going to a secure location until I can regroup with the team and discuss our next course of action."

"Sounds very *Jason Bourne*."

He chuckled at her comment. "Yeah, pretty much. But we'll be safe. I can promise you that."

"I never realized how I've taken 'not being shot at' for granted. I won't do that again." She made a second realization. "Oh, man, I've been a real pill to you. It's a wonder you didn't bolt within the first ten minutes of meeting me, which, by the way, I would've been okay with. And if that'd happened, well..."

"I'm kind of a stickler for details, such as not bailing on an assignment, no matter how prickly they get," he said, winking. He was trying to keep things light. It was heavy enough to realize how close she'd come to death; he didn't need to make it worse.

Caitlin peered over at his phone, where the map app was directing their course, and read the address. "Old Hawk Road? I think I know where that is. Talk about the boonies. Well, one thing is for sure, I don't think anyone will find us."

"Sounds perfect for what we're needing for the night."

Caitlin settled against the seat and fell quiet. He wanted to keep her talking but her teeth had stopped chattering and she seemed to be in control of the situation. He didn't have to worry about shock anymore but he wanted to reach out and hug her. It was an irrational urge that he didn't dare act on but he hated that someone had gotten the drop on him. Made him feel like he'd let her down. He should've had the surveillance cameras mounted on the house already but he'd known Caitlin was going to squawk about it and he'd been trying to ease her into it.

His reluctance had almost cost her her life.

And that was unacceptable.

No more cut corners, no matter how much Caitlin squawked.

Although, when he spared a quick glance at Caitlin as she leaned against the window, something told him she wasn't going to squawk quite as loud as before after this incident.

But it never should've happened in the first place.

Chapter 9

As safe houses went it wasn't very exciting but there weren't a lot of windows to defend and there was great line of sight around the most vulnerable exits.

And that was just how he liked his defensible space.

"I've always wondered what a safe house looked like." After a small pause, she admitted, "It's a little anticlimactic."

"It's not going to win any *Architectural Digest* awards but it'll serve our purpose." The door was reinforced with steel and the windows were shatterproof glass. On the outside it might look very nondescript and bland but it was actually a very safe place. He grabbed her suitcase and headed for the front door. Zak keyed in the code for the electronic lock and opened the door, stepping inside to look for the light switches.

Soft light flooded the living room and Caitlin peered around their new digs, chewing her bottom lip with uncertainty. "Are you sure it's actually *safe*? What if there are spiders? Or even worse, rats?" She shuddered. "Do they keep regular maintenance on places like this? I don't believe I've had my most recent tetanus shot."

He chuckled. "Well, I can't say they've kept up maid service but I'm sure it's clean enough."

But there was a fine layer of dust on everything and his nose was already twitching with the urge to sneeze. It wasn't the best but it wasn't the worst, either.

"I'm not saying I expect to stay at the Taj Mahal but, um, well, I don't want to pick up a disease, either."

"You aren't going to get a disease," he assured her, double-checking the locks on the windows. "It's just a little dusty. Your allergies might act up but other than that, pretty safe."

Caitlin didn't seem so sure. She stood in the foyer looking forlorn and lost. The quicker he could establish some kind of normalcy in a screwed-up situation, the better. "Stay here. I need to check all the exits and rooms."

"Gotta make sure the safe house is safe," she said, wrapping her arms around herself.

He was beginning to figure Caitlin out. She had a tendency to fall back on sarcasm when she was nervous.

After determining they were indeed alone, he grabbed Caitlin's suitcase and showed her to the bedroom.

The queen-size bed was nothing to look at and probably felt as comfortable as sleeping on a plank but he would sleep just fine knowing that no one was getting into that tiny fortress without him knowing.

Caitlin's gaze strayed to the bed and narrowed. "And where exactly are you sleeping?" she asked.

"I'll stand watch."

"You can't stay awake all night, that's ridiculous. How are you supposed to be an effective bodyguard if you fall asleep on your feet?"

"I require very little sleep. I'll be fine."

"Are there no other bedrooms in this little house?"

"There is another bedroom but I'm not leaving you alone. If I need to catch a couple winks I'll do so in that chair over there." He gestured to the singular chair against the wall. It looked as comfortable as the bed. But he wasn't lying when he said he didn't need a lot of sleep. Probably a throwback to all of his time in the military. He had trained his body to operate efficiently with very little. Be it food, sleep or creature comforts. "Don't worry. I'll be fine."

"I don't understand why you have to stay in the same bedroom."

"Because I'm not taking any more chances."

"I appreciate your dedication but I don't want you sleeping at my feet."

This was the squawking he'd been avoiding earlier but she would just have to deal with his methods. "Look, I understand this makes you uncomfortable. I promise you I am not going to do or say anything that is inappropriate. But your safety has been compromised and I'm no longer going to second-guess my training just to save your feelings."

"What do you mean second-guess your training?" she asked, offended. "I haven't had any say on how things have been done thus far."

"I never should have allowed you to stay at your house. It was stupid and won't happen again."

"Where else was I supposed to stay?"

"It doesn't matter. What *should've* been done and what was done—none of that matters. All that matters is what we are going to do *going forward*. Your home is no longer an option. Likely you aren't going back to the lab, either."

Her jaw dropped. “How am I supposed to do my work if I can’t go to my lab?”

“Look, I suggest we sit on this topic for the moment, get some sleep and come back to it tomorrow morning. I have to talk to my superior and figure out what the next step is. Until then let’s just sit tight and try not to make each other too uncomfortable.”

“I’m not staying here for days on end.”

“You will, if that’s what is safest.”

“You are not my jailer. You were supposed to be protecting me. I have important work to do. You are not keeping me in this little house hidden away from the world.”

“I will, if it’s keeping you safe.”

“Has anyone ever told you that you are ridiculously stubborn?”

He smiled. “It’s not the worst I’ve been called.”

They were at an impasse but she would learn that he wasn’t going to budge.

“Do you recall that feeling in the pit of your stomach when you realized someone had tried to kill you? The realization that the bullet that shattered your window was meant for your head? Yeah, hold on to that. When you’re feeling as if you can’t stomach the idea of being sequestered away for your own safety, remember how much you enjoy breathing.”

Maybe he was being a dick, being so harsh, but Caitlin was nearly as obstinate as he was and he had to get through her thick little head.

“So if that means we’re stuck here for a week until my TL can figure out the next move, that’s what we do. Maybe if we’re lucky we can find a deck of cards to keep ourselves busy.”

Caitlin didn’t like that idea at all. It was written all

over her face that she wanted to poke him in the head with a sharp stick, but she grumbled, “Fine, but I am not happy about this.”

“I suspect you aren’t, but at least you’re alive.”

Caitlin seamed her lips together as she spun on her heel and disappeared behind the bathroom door. Once she was out of the room Zak let out a deep breath. Caitlin needn’t worry—he didn’t want to be stuck any longer than possible in this tiny house, either. But not for the reasons that Caitlin thought.

There was something about Caitlin that made him soft, and softness was weakness. He wasn’t about to ruin a great career over a girl he didn’t know and who didn’t really care to know him. This was just a job, and at the end of it he would deliver her safely to the lab once the crisis was over, and he would move on.

He just had to get through whatever it was that was clouding his judgment.

Including thoughts that involved kissing those pouting, sassy lips of one really difficult scientist.

Caitlin leaned against the door, her heart hammering. Her anxiety was at a zenith. First, an almost-kiss with Zak—inappropriate as hell, but that didn’t seem to stop her half wishing it had happened—and then the delicious real food followed by the near-death experience of dodging a bullet.

And now this? She wasn’t equipped with the right tools to handle this kind of duck and weave. Nothing in her life had ever prepared her for anything remotely close to this situation. She wasn’t a spy or a soldier. Tears burned her eyes. How was she supposed to deal with all this? *Damn, why did she have to be so awkward?* Everything about Zak made her jumpy and anxious—most of which had nothing to do with the current situation. She was attracted to him.

She startled at the soft knock. Wiping at her eyes, she answered, "Just a minute," and went quickly to the sink where she splashed some water on her face. The cold water washed away her tears but didn't provide any clarity. Okay, so she'd have to start looking at the situation with logic and reason.

Zak was keeping her safe. He wasn't looking to sex her up. Once the job was done, he'd leave and her life would return to normal.

All she had to do was get through each moment as a singularity and soon enough this would all be over.

Blowing out a deep, measured breath, she nodded to the reflection in the mirror, affirming her logic. *You got this. Don't be a baby. All things are temporary, even discomfort.*

Measurably calmer, she opened the door and went to her luggage with purpose. It was late enough for bed. Thankfully, she'd had the forethought to pack pajamas.

"Are you sure you're okay?" Zak asked as she pulled her suitcase and plopped it on the bed.

"I'm fine. I mean, as fine as the situation will allow, of course. The situation isn't ideal but anyone can handle anything when they know it's temporary. We're both adults. We can handle this without any further awkwardness. Thank you for keeping me alive."

Even to her own ears she sounded like someone sitting in on a job interview—professional, perfunctory and totally devoid of personality—but she didn't know how else to ignore the roaring in her ears whenever he was around.

She could smell his skin.

Pheromones were powerful.

He smelled like rain and thunderstorms, an aroma she never realized was incredibly sexy.

Was he really going to stay awake all night? That wasn't fair or safe. In the end, wasn't safety the most important factor? She had to ditch whatever reservations she was clinging to if she was going to get through this ordeal in one piece. *So, with that understanding...*

Lifting her chin, she said, "Look, let's be smart about this. You can't do your job if you're not well rested. We can share the bed if you're hell-bent on remaining in the room. But first, a few ground rules."

"This ought to be interesting," he said with a subtle, intrigued smile. "Please feel free."

"Okay, I think we should just admit that there's some kind of connection between us and acknowledge that nothing is going to happen. So with that said, I think it's understood that there will be no cuddling, right?"

"Probably a good idea," he agreed, still amused. "But you needn't worry. I'm not going to try to cop a feel or anything. Even if, as you say, there's a connection between us."

She faltered. Was she imagining their chemistry? Entirely possible—she sucked at these kinds of things. Caitlin was thankful for the dim lighting in the room, for her cheeks were pretty hot. "Of course, if I'm off-base, I apologize but I feel it's best to be up front and honest about expectations when faced with high-stress situations."

Zak's amusement faded for a brief moment. What she wouldn't give for a peek into his own internal dialogue. Finally, he nodded, saying, "I appreciate your candor and your offer to share the bed. The chair should be fine. Like I said, I can sleep anywhere and I don't need a lot of it."

She accepted his answer. "I guess that's settled, then." Grabbing her pajamas, she returned to the bathroom to change. A quick look in the mirror confirmed the blush in her cheeks could warm a small country. Patting her cheeks lightly, she blew out a small breath, trying to calm her heart rate. *Okay, focus on the important points—you're alive.* Yes, that was certainly important. She and Zak were adults; they could handle a little misplaced attraction, if that was what was happening. *There, much better.* Straightening her nightgown collar, she exited the bathroom to find Zak gone and her newfound hold on her confidence slippery. Had she scared him off? Where'd he go? Should she go find him? Oh, goodness, chase him? *Hell, no, that wasn't happening.* Besides, what was her plan when she found him? Shake him down for answers? "Hey you, why'd you leave me to feel vulnerable and rejected?" A question that would only leave her to feel more of the same, except amplified by a factor of ten?

No, thanks.

On that note, time for bed.

Sighing, she returned the suitcase to the floor and climbed between the starchy sheets. It smelled of dust and old linens. *Please, no cockroaches or bedbugs*, she prayed as she scooted down into the bed. Shivering a little, she snuggled more deeply into the cold bedding, wishing she were home in her own bed and definitely not in a strange house with a hot stranger, trying to stay alive.

She supposed nothing was perfect.

Chapter 10

The following morning Zak awoke early, his bones protesting the chair he'd slept in, and quietly left Caitlin sound asleep in the bedroom.

He took this time to call Scarlett.

"The dark web is eerily quiet," Scarlett said. "I have a bad feeling about this."

"The bio-agent isn't as valuable without the cure. Unless whoever wants it is planning a total extinction event," Zak said. "Which is possible if we're dealing with a psychopath rather than your typical greedy bastard."

"You know the world is going to hell in a handbag when the lesser of two evils is still pretty damn bad."

He drew a breath. "Okay, so we can't hole up here for too long and we have to assume that the lab is compromised, as well, but Caitlin has to be able to finish her work. Any ideas?"

"I'm working on it. Tessara has labs all around the world. I'll connect with Tessara today and find Caitlin a new lab to do her research. In the meantime, are you secure?"

"Yeah, for the time being. We're going to need supplies."

"We'll drop in some food for a few days. Watch for the drone."

"Roger that."

"Keep your head on a swivel. I don't feel good about this situation. Something feels off."

Yeah, he felt that, too. "Same. I'll sit tight until I hear word."

Scarlett clicked off and he went to the kitchen to survey the food situation. The cupboards had a few canned goods, stuff that would survive an apocalypse without spoiling but he wouldn't enjoy putting in his mouth, so he knew for a fact that Caitlin would balk at the prospect.

Not much for breakfast but he did find an old coffee maker and the right stuff to brew a batch.

He watched with satisfaction as the coffee began to percolate. He grabbed his pack and pulled a few protein bars he always carried with him for emergencies, a habit he learned while in the service, and went to see if Caitlin was awake yet.

He found Caitlin on her side, staring out the window, watching the sun crest the horizon. "Did I wake you?" he asked.

She shook her head. "I'm used to waking up early. Usually, I'm already dressed and heading to the lab by now. Feels weird to still be in bed." She rolled to her side to regard him. "Did you sleep at all?"

He nodded. "The chair is more comfortable than it looks. I caught more than enough winks."

If she didn't believe him, she didn't call him out.

Maybe she realized there were bigger issues than catching him on white lies. "What happens now?" she asked.

"My TL is working on a plan but for now, we sit tight."

"I hate that idea," Caitlin grumbled. "I'm not good with idle time on my hands."

He identified with that statement more than he cared to admit. "I'm sorry. Not much I can do about that right now."

"I understand. I'm not asking you to entertain me. I'm just stating a fact."

Someone was cranky in the morning. She sniffed at the air. "Is that coffee?"

"I can't vouch for how good it is but it's something," he said. "I came to see if you wanted a cup."

"God, yes," she answered, throwing the blankets free and padding to the bathroom in her Victorian nightgown that covered her from neck to toe. Why did that look sexy? He looked away as the door closed.

He called out, "I'll just fix you a cup. Hope you like it black."

"That's fine," she said from behind the door.

Zak turned on his heel, mildly baffled by the tingle of arousal in his gut, and quickly focused on that cup of coffee.

When she emerged, Caitlin was dressed and he was grateful. How was he supposed to explain that seeing her in that prim and proper getup had fired up his engine like nothing he'd ever experienced? Especially when he couldn't make head or tail of it himself? No one got horny from something that looked plucked from the pages of an 1800s' Sears and Roebuck catalog.

Except his immediate erection told a different story.

Caitlin slid into the worn chair at the breakfast table

and gripped her hands around the mug with an expression of gratitude. "I need this. I didn't sleep well at all."

"Don't count your chickens yet, it might taste like ass," he warned, lifting the mug to his own lips for a tentative sip. He grimaced at the burn on his tongue, but otherwise, it was serviceable. "Not bad, I guess. Could use some cream and sugar."

She chuckled, teasing, "The big bad soldier needs a little sweetness in his morning coffee?"

He grinned at the ribbing. "Guilty. I can drink it black but damn, I do like my sweet stuff." He could only imagine how sweet Caitlin tasted beneath that nightgown. Good Lord, what was wrong with him? Clearing his throat, he asked, "Well, what's the verdict?"

"Not bad. I've tasted worse but I'm more about the caffeine than the flavor. At the lab, I practically exist through the power of black coffee."

The lab. He sighed, hating to be the bearer of bad news, but there was no sense in sugarcoating what was inevitable. "Okay, so here's the reality. You can't go back to the lab. At least not that lab. Tessara has locations around the world. Scarlett is going to rendezvous with Tessara and find a new location for you to work your magic but until then, we're stuck here."

"What about my team?" she asked. "I need my team with me."

"That'll be up to Tessara to determine who comes along for the ride."

"Well, you need to stress that I need my team with me," she insisted. "To get someone new up to speed would take time we don't have."

It made a certain amount of logic but he hadn't had the chance to vet her team yet. It might not be feasible to bring everyone along. "I'll do what I can," he said, hoping to smooth the anxiety from her forehead. "What matters most is your safety."

"No, what matters is finding the cure," she reminded him. "If someone wants me dead…then they must not care about a cure, which means it's that much more important to find one before the psycho who stole my sample decides to unleash it on the world."

God, he loved how her brain worked. She was right, of course, but he hadn't expected her to come to that conclusion on her own. "The attempt on your life does call into question the theory that whoever took the sample is looking to sell it to the highest bidder. It also seems to explain why there's been no chatter on the dark web for a buyer."

She shuddered, understanding the implication. "Who could possibly hate humanity so much that they'd want to annihilate the world?"

"You'd be shocked and horrified by how many people would be willing to pull that trigger," he said. "I've seen the absolute worst of human beings out there who don't give two shits about their fellow humans. I'd much rather deal with greedy bastards than the crazy mofos who just hate everybody and everything."

"I can understand greed. I can't understand the other."

He agreed. "Red Wolf will figure out who's behind this, but keeping you safe is paramount."

Caitlin ducked her gaze, her teeth scraping her bottom lip. "I can't believe how close I came to biting the big one. Kinda puts things in perspective real quick."

"That it does. I remember the first time I got lucky. Just wasn't my time, I guess."

She looked up. "Yeah? What happened?"

"Sniper with a bad eye. It was my fault. Early days in my service. Wasn't paying attention to my surroundings. The next thing I knew, mortar was exploding near my head and a bullet was buried in the wall next to me. If I'd had time I would've shit my pants."

She cracked a reluctant smile. "I'm guessing your guardian angel has put in some serious overtime."

"I'm fairly certain my guardian angel is a full-blown alcoholic by this point."

Caitlin laughed, her eyes sparkling with amusement. "But you still manage to keep your sense of humor. That's an accomplishment. I'm not sure I'd be able to laugh about the things you've been through."

"Sometimes your sense of humor is what keeps you sane," he admitted, remembering plenty of times when he and his buddies had burst into laughter simply to keep from breaking down. Too many dark memories. He probably needed a shit-ton of therapy, just like everyone employed by Red Wolf. Hell, they couldn't do what they did without being a little screwed in the head. "At the end of the day, life goes on and you have to find a way to put the day's events in its place."

"So, basically, the secret to your success is compartmentalizing," she said.

He barked a short laugh. "Yeah, I guess so. Don't spill my secret."

She made a locking gesture in front of her lips. "Your secret is safe with me." However, she added, "You know, eventually that stuff rises to the top and comes out twisted. You should probably deal with your emotional trauma at some point."

"Probably," he agreed, but that wasn't happening today. "When I have time, I'll sit down with a therapist and unload everything I've been packing around. Until then, it's gonna have to wait."

Red Wolf had the best therapists on staff, not that any

of his team members enjoyed making the appointment. Only when mandated did they grudgingly step into that office but he supposed that when he was ready, he'd brave that emotional avalanche.

Thankfully for him, the timing was never right.

Caitlin peered around the small safe house, feeling oddly disassociated from the situation. She imagined this was what an out-of-body experience felt like, if she believed in that sort of thing, which she didn't. But in theory, this was how she imagined it would be.

She no longer recognized her life. Everything had been tipped upside down within the space of forty-eight hours. Right now, she should be in her lab, already working on her second cup of coffee.

Instead, she was in a strange house with a virtual stranger, hiding.

Hiding from someone who wanted her dead.

Caitlin suppressed a shudder as the implication ricocheted down her spine. Adventure was overrated. How had she ever thought wistfully about a little more spice in her life? Clearly, she'd had no idea what that actually meant.

Dodging bullets had not been on her radar.

Taking a second chance on a dating profile might've been more her speed, or accepting an invitation for drinks and appetizers with a fellow scientist more in line with her expectations.

Of course, two days ago, even doing that would've felt like a wild departure from her usual self.

Now?

It seemed absurdly tame.

Boring, even.

"I need to know a little more about you," she said, trying to find some semblance of normalcy in this messed-up situation. "I'm not in a habit of spending large blocks of time with a stranger and it's making me anxious. Perhaps if I knew more about you, I'd feel less awkward."

"What would you like to know?" he said, settling in his chair, seeming open to the idea. "I'll share whatever I can. Though some stuff might be confidential."

"Right. Um, well, do you have family?"

"No."

"No?"

He cleared his throat, clarifying, "I had a sister. She died when she was sixteen. Suicide."

"Oh, my heavens," she murmured, distressed at having inadvertently stumbled on something so personal with her first question. "I'm so sorry. That must've been devastating."

"I was overseas when it happened. My sister struggled with depression. Given our upbringing, it wasn't surprising."

"Your upbringing?"

"Shit parents, bounced from foster home to foster home. We never knew any stability. Zoey was more affected by it than me. I guess it got to be too much for her."

Caitlin didn't have any siblings but she couldn't imagine losing someone she loved to suicide, especially one so young. She struggled to find the appropriate words. Everything that came to mind felt trite and not nearly sincere enough. She couldn't imagine how horrible it must've been for him to lose his only family like that. "How did you cope being so far away?" she asked.

"Well, if you ask the Red Wolf shrink, I haven't dealt with it in any healthy way," he answered with a slight, self-deprecating smile. "I'm a simple guy. Give me a bad guy to shoot and I'm good."

She heard the pain behind the glib answer. "You must miss her."

"It was a long time ago."

She sensed his sister was a topic that he didn't invite conversation about but she appreciated his attempt at putting her at ease by answering her questions. Something told her he didn't let anyone touch that subject.

That tiny sliver of vulnerability touched her in a way she wasn't ready for. The moment felt important, as if they were suddenly standing at a crossroads together. *Pull back, you've already gotten too personal.* But she wanted to know more. She craved more. All her life she'd listened to that little voice telling her to pull away, to keep to her own bubble but maybe it was time to step outside of her comfort zone, especially given the current circumstances. "Do you have a girlfriend back home? Someone waiting for you after each mission?" she asked boldly. A brush with death had the uncanny ability to muzzle that pesky internal voice most effectively.

Caitlin held her breath, waiting for him to politely defer an answer—it's what she would've done—but he chuckled, shaking his head. "Nope. I'm not really cut out for long-term, if you know what I mean."

She wasn't sure what answer she was hoping for but that wasn't it. "Ah, you like to play," she inferred, disappointed. "Monogamy must seem terribly boring to someone like you. I mean, someone in your profession."

"No, not at all. I'm a one-woman kind of man but I work long hours. Sometimes I'm gone for months at a stretch, to different counties. There aren't a lot of women who are willing to sign on for that gig."

Caitlin smiled against the ridiculous relief she felt at his clarification even though she had no skin in his game. Clearing her throat, she asked, "Do you ever get lonely?"

He straightened his legs beneath the table, shrugging. "I mean, yeah, I guess sometimes. I keep busy enough, though. I don't have time to worry about finding someone to grow old with. Chances are I won't grow old anyway, so why waste the energy thinking about it?"

"That sounds like you have a death wish. Are you hoping you'll die out there?"

Zak hadn't expected that blunt question. "Not presently," he answered with a subtle quirk of his lips. "But there are some who might think that I have a death wish based upon the dangerous nature of my job."

"Okay, I think I understand. You crave the adrenaline rush," she said. "But you don't necessarily have a death wish. In fact, I think it might mean the opposite. You do these dangerous things because it makes you feel alive."

He liked the way she broke it down, much better than a few shrinks, actually. "There's nothing that feels better than that rush of heading into the unknown to face down a threat," he admitted. "Better than any drug out there."

Caitlin peered at him with curiosity. "Have you done many drugs?"

He sobered quickly. "No. My parents did enough. I saw how it ruined lives. I didn't need a refresher course."

"You said your parents weren't exactly the best."

"I called them shit parents," he reminded her flatly. "You can say it."

She blushed. "Okay, shit parents. Are they still around?"

"They did me a solid and died of overdoses when I was in my early twenties. They were both holed up in crack dens somewhere in Detroit. The only reason I found out was because they'd listed me as an emergency contact on my mother's driver's license and I'd been too caught up with my own life to switch numbers."

"Did you go to their funeral?"

"Hell, no. I got drunk and celebrated."

He sounded harsh but he felt absolute nothing for those shitbags. They hadn't cared when their daughter offed herself, so he couldn't bring himself to care when they'd effectively offed themselves. Seemed kinda poetic, to be honest. He rose from the table to stretch his legs. Too much real sharing made him antsy. "Stay put. I'm going to walk the perimeter, check the surroundings and make sure we're secure."

He didn't wait for her to agree; he just needed space.

Unlike Zoey, he'd written off Barbara Jane and Robert Ramsey a long time ago, right about the time he'd realized Robert was eyeing little Zoey as a potential way to pay for his fix.

Yeah, his dad had been a real treat.

Thankfully, Zoey didn't remember much about the time before they'd been taken by the state out of their parents' care.

Or, if she did remember, she sure as hell had never been willing to talk about it.

And he'd never been brave enough to ask.

Some things were better left unsaid, right?

Hell, what did he know? He was just a broken guy trying to avoid getting cut on the jagged edges.

Chapter 11

Later that afternoon a drone dropped a package of supplies down to them. Even though science and technology were her jam, she was a little geeked out by the futuristic delivery method.

"Does Red Wolf have an army of delivery drones at their disposal?" she asked, half teasing as they unpacked the food and other items, such as toiletries and practical items. "Or did Red Wolf ring up Jeff Bezos for the use of the Amazon drones?"

Zak smiled but answered with a cheeky "Classified" before exclaiming with happiness at his find. "God, I love these. CJ must've packed this for me."

"CJ?" she asked, interested.

"A colleague, my buddy. We're all pretty tight at Red Wolf but CJ knows that I love SpaghettiOs, so I know he threw these in."

"You? Like SpaghettiOs?" The revelation tickled her funny bone. "I thought you were a heath nut?"

"Oh, it's all about balance, sweetheart," he said with a grin but admitted, "Okay, this is not good for you but it tastes so great that I make an exception."

"Do you make deals with yourself when you eat a can, like, *if I eat this, I'll eat extra kale tomorrow*?"

"I make deals with myself all the time but they rarely involve kale," he said.

"You don't like kale?"

"No one likes kale."

She smiled, inordinately pleased with that information. "There's hope for you yet," she said, reaching for the can. "Now, the true test is this—do you eat the SpaghettiOs cold or hot?"

"Right from the can, baby."

She might have met her soul mate. Grinning, she said, "I guess I know what we're having for lunch."

Caitlin went to the kitchen, found a can opener and two spoons, and returned, handing Zak a spoon. His expression of bliss at that first bite was a bit arousing. She ducked her gaze and focused on her own bite. "Earlier you'd mentioned that I was always surprising you. Well, it goes both ways," she admitted.

"Yeah? How so?"

Her cheeks heated. She probably should've kept that to herself but it was out there and now she had to follow through. "Um, well, the more I learn about you, the more I realize you're not easily put into one category. Up until I met you, I always had a pretty easy time putting people into their boxes. You make it difficult to find a good box."

"I'm difficult to put in a box? I consider that a good thing."

She laughed. "I didn't say it was bad. I'm just not used to being around people who are openly complex."

"Openly?"

She explained between bites, “Well, everyone is complex at some level because humans are inordinately weird in their own way. But usually people hide the parts of themselves that are different. You don’t seem to do that, which I find intriguing.”

He chuckled. “Why do I suddenly feel like a lab rat under a microscope? Are you studying me?”

It was meant as a joke but he might’ve been onto something. Maybe she had been inadvertently studying him. He fascinated her. And she was attracted to him. Completely inappropriate, of course, but it didn’t change the facts. Now, what to do about it was the question she struggled with. Drawing herself up, she licked her spoon after a final bite, saying, “I’ve never met anyone like you. I’m sure it’s the novelty of being around someone like yourself that has me preoccupied, or it could be that my brain is focusing on you as a coping mechanism to deal with the fact that I’m in real danger. But either way, it will fade eventually so I’m not overly worried.”

His face crinkled in a smile that lit up his eyes. “You are an odd duck but I likc it,” he declared.

Not the first time someone had called her odd but somehow he’d made it sound, dare she say, *adorable*, and she found herself smiling a little bigger. Was this flirting? Good lord, she was terrible at this stuff. A woman accustomed to heterosexual banter would probably say something cute or witty, but her brain—her genius brain—just short-circuited, causing her stupid mouth to blurt out, “Have you had that mole checked out?” before she could stop it.

“What mole?” he asked, his expression faltering into confusion. She gestured at the tiny mole on his cheek and he found it with his finger, shaking his head. “Why, does it look like something I should be worried about?”

No. It was completely harmless but if she admitted that, she'd have to admit that she was way more awkward than he realized and completely challenged when it came to speaking to the opposite sex when attraction was present. "I'm sure it's fine but best to be sure. They have physicians at Red Wolf, right?"

"Yeah, some of the best."

"Well, then you're in good hands. Anyway, it's not my expertise, but you know, always good to check. I had a mole removed from my back that was questionable. Turned out to be benign but those things can turn bad quickly."

Why was she rambling about her mole? *Real sexy. Super. Fantastic. He's probably fantasizing about your medical procedure right now.* "All right, then, I think I'll just go find something to read or take a nap, if you don't mind."

She didn't wait for an answer and popped off her chair to disappear behind the closed door of the bedroom.

Heart thundering as if she'd just run the Boston marathon, she wondered if she'd ever be some semblance of normal.

And if so, when would it start?

Now would be good. A large, healthy dose of normal would be *friggin'* fantastic right about now.

Squeezing her eyes shut for a brief moment in exquisite embarrassment, she bit back a moan.

She was utterly hopeless. If the fate of the world hadn't rested on her shoulders, she'd wish for a nice lightning bolt right to her head.

Zak sensed the change in Caitlin—something behind her eyes that pricked at his senses—but she'd clearly wanted to be left alone, so he wasn't going to press.

He was beginning to see why she was single.

Most people would be put off by the awkwardness of her social interactions but he found her weirdness endearing. There was something so guileless about the way she blurted things out and the immediate color in her cheeks that gave away her embarrassment. No doubt she'd spent her life dealing with the aftermath of people who simply couldn't connect with her intellect or her quirky nature.

He remembered his sister struggling in the same way.

One day after school, he'd come home to find Zoey crying in her closet. She had always hidden in her closet; it was the only place she'd felt safe when faced with a world she couldn't understand.

"Zo?" He'd knocked on the closet door softly. "Zo? You in there?"

The sniffling behind the door answered his question. Zak had slowly opened the door to find Zoey curled in a tight ball amidst discarded shoes and boxes of whatever their foster parents had thrown in there for storage. He climbed in beside her, though it was a tight fit for his gangly sixteen-year-old legs. "What happened?" he'd asked.

"It doesn't matter," Zoey had replied in a small, tear-choked voice. "Same thing that always happens. I don't understand people."

"Someone teasing you?" he'd asked, ready to pound a kid into the dirt. "What's their name?"

Zoey shook her head. "It'll just make it worse."

He'd known she was right but he hated feeling helpless. "Okay, so tell me what happened. Maybe just talking about it can help. I mean, you can't sit in the closet for the rest of your life." That cracked a small smile. He relaxed a little. "Was it that dickhead Karen again?"

"No, it was the whole class. They all laughed at me

because I didn't understand the joke. Then, the joke was on me."

"Jokes are stupid," he'd said, wishing his sister could understand the subtleties of humor. She was always so literal. She'd frustrated more than one pair of foster parents and the foster siblings were worse, which was why he'd always pitched a fit whenever there was talk of separating them into different homes. Without him, Zoey wouldn't survive. "Look, you're way smarter than all those kids, so what do you care if you don't understand their dumb jokes? Someday you're going to be their boss and then the joke will be on them, you know?"

Zak closed his eyes at the memory. When would the pain of her death end? Zoey had been gone a long time but sometimes his grief rose up to slice his heart all over again, leaving the wound fresh and raw.

Caitlin was so much like Zoey. Wicked smart, socially awkward and completely unaware of how beautiful she was.

Zoey hadn't lived past sixteen. Caitlin had pushed through life to grab her opportunities but she'd retained that quirkiness that made her special. If life had turned out differently and their paths had crossed, Zak liked to believe that they would have hit it off. Two peas in a pod.

When he couldn't sleep and his mind wouldn't rest, the questions often hounded him without mercy. If he'd been around more, would he have caught the signs that Zoey was hurting? That she was in a dark place? Could he have stopped her from hurting herself?

Too many people had cautioned him against going down that road but how could he not? He was the big brother, he was supposed to keep her safe—and he'd failed.

He had to keep Caitlin safe.

Stop being so damn maudlin. Can't do shit about the past. Focus on the now.

Irritated with himself for his chaotic thoughts, he put his feet in motion, doing another perimeter check. At least if his mind was engaged, it couldn't wander into places it didn't belong.

His cell rang and he answered when he saw it was CJ.

"Hey, man, you cool up in the wilds of Vermont?" CJ joked.

Relieved to focus on something other than his own bullshit, he said, "Yeah, it's a damn picnic. Thanks for the treats. You ruined my diet, though, bro."

"Diets are for pussies. Eat the crap, live forever. Don't you know that it's the preservatives that keep us alive?"

He laughed. "God, you're an idiot. Okay, so aside from the food drop, what you got for me? Scarlett told me there's been zero chatter on the web about the sample. No one bidding?"

"Naw, man, quiet as a church after hours. Whoever took the sample isn't looking to get paid. That's kinda worrisome."

"You think?" Zak said with a dose of sarcasm. "Jesus, I was really hoping for greed over crazy on this one."

"Where's the fun in an easy job?"

"None of our jobs are easy."

"Right, which is why we get paid the big bucks. Stop your bitching. You sound like a pussy."

Zak barked another laugh. God love CJ for being a dick at the right moments. "Okay, so what's next? I can't keep Caitlin holed up here for days. She's already going stir-crazy."

"You or her?"

"Both. I can't shake the feeling that we're being watched. Something just doesn't feel right, you know?"

CJ sobered quickly. They knew enough to never discredit a gut feeling. "Yeah? I'll light a fire under Scarlett and see if we can't get you out of there sooner rather than later."

"Thanks, man. Anything else going on back at HQ?"

"Man, you must be bored to tears if you're asking about office gossip."

Zak chuckled. "Let's just say I could use some distractions."

Reading between the lines, CJ was immediately interested. "Yeah? Is the doctor hot?"

"Uh, well, she's not hard on the eyes," he hedged, not sure he was ready to explain the feelings Caitlin aroused. "But that's not the issue. I'm keeping it professional."

"Of course. You never break the rules," CJ said in a bored tone. "You're always whitey tighty. Keep those briefs pristine. God, you're such a human yawn."

"Just because I don't believe in crashing through every gate, breaking everything in the process, it doesn't mean I don't sidestep a few rules." Why was he justifying being a good guy? Jesus, CJ had a way of getting under his skin sometimes. "Look, Caitlin is a great chick. Supersmart, cute as hell, but I'm on the job and you know there's good reasons for keeping that shit straight and apart from each other."

"Yeah, yeah, I know. But chemistry, man. Sometimes you just can't fight that shit."

"You can, you just don't."

"What can I say? I'm a lover."

"You're a walking STD."

"That's why they have meds. Gotta love science." CJ laughed at his own joke but then sobered, saying, "Okay, in all seriousness, I'll see if we can't get you moved to a more secure location than that safe house. Stay tight, man."

"Always."

They clicked off and he knew he had to return to the house. He had to face another night with Caitlin. Another night of sleeping in a chair beside her, listening to her breathe, fighting the urge to climb in beside her so he could smell her hair and wrap his arms around her petite form.

Please hurry, CJ.

He could only hope his fervent prayer was heard and they were moved soon.

He didn't want to make a liar out of himself.

Chapter 12

Caitlin was going crazy, stuck in this tiny house with Zak. It was probably a bad idea, but she needed to talk to someone familiar, someone who could at least give her insight as to what was happening in her lab without her. Good God, not being able to go to the lab was like having an itch she couldn't scratch. Zak couldn't possibly understand how excruciating it was to be on the outside of her own research.

Frankly, she was surprised Zak had allowed her to keep her phone, but since he hadn't expressly told her to refrain from contacting anyone on her team, she quickly dialed Rebecca's number.

Rebecca picked up on the first ring. "Caitlin, oh, my God, are you all right? Nobody will tell us anything about your whereabouts and we have been worried sick. Where are you?"

Her first instinct was to share that she was in a safe house with Zak but she held her tongue. Something told her that it was probably a bad idea to go broadcasting her location. It wasn't that she didn't trust Rebecca but she didn't know if her phone was compromised and she wasn't going to take the chance. Instead, she focused on the true intent for her call. "Is everything okay at the lab? Have you made any more progress on the cure?" Her heart actually contracted with misery at being so far away from the action. "Please tell me you guys have made some progress."

"Girl, slow down. What is going on? Stan won't say where you are and I know you're not at your house. Are you okay?"

She was touched by Rebecca's concern, seeing as they'd never been what she would call friends, but rather simply work colleagues. "I'm fine but there was an incident at my house and I've been moved for my own safety."

Rebecca gasped. "Are you kidding me? An *incident*? What does that mean? This is like some serious spy stuff going on. Were you terrified? Tell me what happened."

"I can't really go into details. I don't know if my phone is being tapped. All I can say is that I'm safe."

"Wow, you are living quite the double life. Who would've thought that you, of all people, would be caught up in some international intrigue."

"We don't know if it's international. For all we know this could be some sort of domestic terrorism. Or it could be just some crazy fruitloop who has a death wish for the entire human race. But let's not go jumping to conclusions," she reminded Rebecca.

"Of course. You're right. I shouldn't draw conclusions without adequate information. To answer your question, no, we haven't made much progress. We keep running into the same walls as we did before. Frankly, as much as I hate to admit this, we need your brain."

It was the closest Rebecca would probably ever come

to admitting that Caitlin was the team leader for a reason, but Rebecca was no slouch; she was brilliant in her own way. Still, Caitlin was disappointed to hear that no progress had been made. "There's really no room for ego when the fate of the world is at stake," she murmured. "I'm going to see if I can get back to the lab soon. But I don't know if Zak is going to be willing to do that."

"Well, how is that going to work? We need you here," Rebecca insisted. "I mean, I get that your safety is important and all but as you mentioned, we are dealing with the fate of the world, so concessions might have to be made."

"I know that. I'm just saying Zak isn't willing to compromise on certain things." As frustrating as it was to be cooped up, Caitlin respected that Zak followed a certain set of rules and wouldn't budge. Okay, so she found his being a stickler for protocol sexy. Or maybe she just found Zak sexy. Hard to tell.

"So what's it like being locked up with tall, blond and handsome?" Rebecca asked.

Caitlin blushed, thankful it wasn't a video call. "It's no big deal. He's the perfect gentleman."

"Still? Good grief. That's a shame. If I were locked in a house with that hunk of burning love I'd be recreating the *Kama Sutra*."

Oh, not that she hadn't had those kinds of thoughts but she couldn't rightly attack her bodyguard for sexual attention. That would be the height of inappropriate. Not to mention she wasn't going to admit such thoughts to her assistant. "Well, Zak is here to do a job, not to be pestered by me with inappropriate sexual advances."

Even to her own ears she sounded like a stuffy old prune, so she wasn't surprised when Rebecca made a sound of annoyance. "Do you ever loosen up? Tell me, what do you do for fun? Go through your penny jar and make coin rolls?"

Actually, that was very soothing but Caitlin kept that to herself. "I do plenty of fun things. Right now isn't about fun. Right now is about saving the world. And it seems someone isn't on board with that plan and wanted to put a bullet in my head."

Rebecca gasped again. "Are you kidding me? Like, as in, a serious bullet? You must've been terrified."

"Yeah, it wasn't a great feeling knowing that somebody had tried to end my life but thankfully Zak was here and he took care of the situation."

"Oh, my Alpha Male, did he just seriously get hotter? C'mon now, you feel nothing for this guy? Evolutionarily speaking, that protector gene should be awakening that primal feminine core that's hardwired into our ape brains and turning you into goo. What gives?"

Caitlin was accustomed to Rebecca pushing the boundaries of their professional relationship but Caitlin's nerves were a little too shot for that right now. "Can you act your age for two seconds, please?" she snapped. "There's more at stake than knocking boots with the hot bodyguard. I was freaking shot at, I'm holed up in a strange house, hiding from only God knows who, and I have no idea what's going to happen next. I need you to act like a grown-up for once."

"Oh" was all Rebecca said in response and Caitlin actually felt bad for a moment until Rebecca added with a sniff, "I'm just trying to keep things light. You're about as fun as a poke in the eye. Fine, back to almost dying. Did Zak catch the guy who took the shot?"

Caitlin drew a deep breath before asking with mild suspicion, "How do you know it was a guy?"

"Oh, good grief, okay, let's keep it PC—*the person*—male or female, who took the shot."

Caitlin could only imagine how she must sound on the other end. Paranoid much? "Sorry, this whole situation has me on edge."

"You're forgiven."

"Thanks. Okay, well, whoever took the shot realized that he hadn't accomplished his mission, and he took off running. Once Zak realized the house had been compromised, we were out within ten minutes."

"So I'm guessing you were moved to some kind of safe house? Boy, you are living in a spy movie."

"Yeah, except it's not that fun and I wish I knew there was going to be a happy ending at the end of this movie."

And, predictably, Rebecca giggled. "I can think of a few different kinds of happy endings I'd be open to, hint, hint."

Caitlin's cheeks heated even more. "Good Lord, woman, you have got to be the most perverted person I've ever met in my life. You should probably get a boyfriend."

Or girlfriend. She didn't actually know which way Rebecca swung in her sexuality, not that she cared.

"So here's the thing. Zak is probably not going to let me return to the lab, but I need my lab to do my work and I'm going to need my team. So you need to be prepared to leave at a moment's notice."

Rebecca sounded giddy. "Are you kidding me? Are you asking me to go on an epic adventure with your hot bodyguard? Hell, yes! Where do I sign up? I'll pack my bags right now."

Caitlin smiled even though Rebecca's enthusiasm was a little unsettling. "Rebecca, this is very serious. You're not coming on board to flirt with Zak. I need you with your brilliant IQ to work on the problem at hand, not imagine my bodyguard tied up in some kind of sex dungeon."

"Caitlin, you dirty bird. I didn't realize you had it in you." Rebecca laughed. "Calm down, I'm not going to harass your bodyguard. However, what I fantasize about on my own free time is my business. You can't stop me from doing whatever I choose on my own time."

Rebecca was kidding but it made Caitlin a little uncomfortable knowing that Rebecca was likely touching herself while thinking of Zak. In fact, a ripple of possessiveness sharpened her tone as she said, "Well, just try to keep it professional when you're on company time." Even though it went without saying that Rebecca would always be professional when push came to shove, Caitlin took some comfort in voicing her expectations.

Rebecca was a flirt but she was also a bright scientist. Bottom line, Caitlin needed her, which was why she put up with her nonsense. It wasn't because Rebecca was the only person who seemed to take an active interest in her in spite of her lack of reciprocity. Now that she thought about it, why was that?

"Okay, so when is this big, secret move happening?" Rebecca asked. "I want to make sure I'm ready."

"I don't know. We're still waiting to find out where Red Wolf wants to put us. Zak's TL is coordinating with Tessara to find out which lab we'll be using."

"Do you think it'll be a lab in the States or out of the country?" Rebecca asked.

"I have no idea but in the interest of expediency I'm guessing that it's going to be here in the States."

"Good point. All right, I'll let the rest of the team know and we'll get our notes ready for travel. Is there anything else that you need from the lab that I should grab?"

Caitlin wanted to do the work herself but she knew that Zak wasn't going to let her be out in the open. So she gave Rebecca instructions on what to bring if and when the time came to mobilize.

Breaking character, Rebecca asked with genuine care, "Seriously, though, are you okay?"

Caitlin fumbled with the knowledge that Rebecca actually seemed concerned and wasn't feigning it like people did when they remarked upon your summer cold. The solicitude in her voice appeared to be real. Given the fact that Caitlin had never been particularly chummy in return, it made her feel like a jerk. "I'm okay," she reassured Rebecca, deciding she needed to make a better effort to be less prickly in the future. "Just a little bored and a little anxious to get back to work."

"Well, be careful what you wish for. As soon as they locate a suitable lab I'm guessing you can forget about sleep and eating until a cure is found or until we freaking die because some maniac has decided he's had enough of humanity."

Caitlin shuddered. "God, I hope not. We just need to find a cure."

"We will. I'll wait for your call."

Caitlin clicked off just in time for Zak to knock softly on the bedroom door. "Come in," she called out.

Zak stood with a deck of cards in his hand. "I thought you might be bored and I found these in a drawer. Are you up for a rousing game of rummy?"

She smiled, shaking her head. "I don't actually know how to play but I suppose now is as good a time as any to learn. Are you a good teacher?"

His lips formed a sensual line, probably without Zak

being aware of how that one tiny gesture sent ripples of awareness down her body. "Girl, I'm the best," he said.

Her heart fluttered an odd beat and she scooted off the bed. "All right, then, but don't get butt-hurt when the student surpasses the teacher. I'm a freakishly fast learner."

Zak stared at Caitlin's hand, amazed and, frankly, annoyed that she'd won again. "Seriously, you weren't lying. You're good."

"I catch on fast. This is fun," she said with a bright smile as she prepared to shuffle for another hand. "I've always enjoyed the concept of card games. There's something very quaint about playing cards. Something left over from a bygone era."

He laughed. "Card games are not that archaic. People still play cards all the time. You mean to tell me your parents never played rummy or pinochle to pass the time?"

"My parents were research scientists. They often had their noses stuck in books, completely oblivious to one another or me."

He felt a wave of sadness for the lonely girl Caitlin had been. He couldn't imagine how life would've been for him without Zoey. Even thought they'd been four years apart, their bond had been unbreakable. She'd been his best friend. Swallowing the lump that rose in his throat, he smiled through the sharp pain and said, "Well, they must've done something right. You're a pretty dope chick."

She paused to regard him with a quizzical smile. "Yeah? You think so? I never considered myself anything but different and strange. I had difficulties making social connections. I always attributed my challenges to being an only child but now as an adult I realize I don't think it would have made a difference to have a sibling.

In fact, I probably would've found a sibling incredibly annoying."

"Well, that's how they're supposed to be. Annoying your sibling is a given but there's a lot of love there, too. My sister, Zoey, could push my buttons like nobody's business but she was my world. For a long time, it was just she and I against the world, bouncing from one foster home to the next. Our bond was the only stability we knew."

"Was it awful?"

"At times."

"Why did you go from different homes?"

He drew a deep breath, admitting, "I got into a lot of trouble. Had some issues with authority. I was usually the one who got us bounced. Some of those places, though, it was a blessing to get moved, but there were some nice ones, too. I feel most bad about that."

"What do you mean?"

"Sometimes at night when my brain won't shut off, I wonder if maybe we'd stayed in one of the good places, if Zoey would still be here."

"You can't think that way. As much as it hurts, what Zoey did was her own choice. From what I've read of suicide, when someone makes the decision to go, there isn't much anyone can do to stop them."

"She was a kid. She just wanted some stability in her life and I kept taking that from her because I was selfishly just thinking about my own bullshit."

The stark truth had a tendency to burn. He blinked back sudden tears. God, this wasn't how he envisioned the evening. He wiped at his eyes, gruffly muttering, "Sorry," before rising and disappearing to the bathroom to get a hold of himself. What was his deal? He wasn't one to break down in front of strangers but somehow

Caitlin didn't feel like a stranger. She felt like someone he'd known his entire life and it was a relief to share that terrible burden of his guilt with someone.

But Caitlin wasn't his therapist and now wasn't the time to go all soft and weepy about the past. *Get it together, Ramsey. Package that shit where you normally stuff it and get back to work.* After taking a moment to rinse his face and to piss, he returned to the game. Caitlin waited with pursed lips as if contemplating how to move forward after such an awkward moment of sharing. "You hungry?" he asked, breaking the silence.

She looked up and shook her head. "I'm not sure what the right social interaction is for what just happened, so I'm going to just come right out and say what's on my mind and let the chips fall where they may. Is that okay?"

This ought to be interesting. He gestured with a nod. "Go for it."

"You loved your sister very much and I'm sure she loved you just as much. You can't carry the burden of her death on your shoulders forever. I didn't know your sister but I can't imagine that she would've wanted that for you. You need to forgive yourself for not seeing what she needed. You were a kid, too. She'd want you to move on, not use her death as some catalyst for destructive behavior."

"What destructive behavior?" he asked, stiffening slightly.

"You challenge death to feel alive. Your guilt drives you to court danger because deep down there's a part of you that thinks you deserve whatever happens to you. That's destructive behavior—eventually your luck is going to run out and then you'll just be gone."

Zak sat dumbstruck. Had she just accurately psychoanalyzed him? What the hell? How was he supposed to respond? He forced a chuckle, trying to find his footing. “Well, Doc, that was pretty adept shrink stuff. What do I owe you for our session?”

Caitlin made a face at him and rose, going straight to him, her hands resting on his shoulders. The warmth of her hands seeped through his cotton shirt and he was suddenly spellbound. “Sometimes what we know deep down is the thing we are terrified to admit,” she said, bending to brush her lips against his in a tentative but sweet kiss. Everything in him melted like hot wax. She pulled away slowly, her gaze meeting his, and added, “But it’s always the thing that holds the key to our healing.”

Holy hell, Caitlin had just made a move on him.

And he was shaking with the need to follow up with more.

Chapter 13

Caitlin knew kissing Zak was a bold move but it felt right. She couldn't explain it; nor did she want to. The minute her lips touched his, something inside her ignited and took her breath away at the same time.

She'd never been an advocate of chasing after broken men. Broken people tended to hurt those who tried to help them. But Zak's broken pieces weren't dangerous to her. She sensed his pain, which was deeply rooted in his grief over his sister's death, and all she could imagine doing was trying to ease that suffering in the only way she knew how.

And she didn't regret it for one second.

Maybe she was stupid and kissing Zak was the worst mistake she could've made but it was done and, honestly, judging by the way his gaze softened, he wasn't about to push her away.

In fact, his arms circled her waist and pulled her closer. "Why'd you do that?" he asked, almost desperately. "I'm not complaining, I'm just... Hell, I don't know, but I don't want you to feel that you owe me something or any shit like that."

Caitlin smiled at his bumbling attempt to put her at ease. "I kissed you because I wanted to," she said. "Are you okay with that?"

"Yeah," he answered, bobbing a short nod. "Yeah, more than okay, actually."

A giddy warmth filled her up as she allowed him to plant her on his lap. She'd never sat on a man's lap before. It felt perfect. "Can I kiss you again?" she asked.

"I'd like that."

This time she kissed him a little more deeply, her tongue slipping in to explore his mouth. He tasted of peanuts and apple juice. His hands dipped down to cup her behind. The subtle squeeze of her butt made her mouth pop open a little more, which he fully took advantage of, sliding his tongue more deeply into her mouth.

She shifted to straddle Zak, feeling as if someone else had taken over her body—someone far more sexually experienced than she—and she was just happy to enjoy the ride.

A tiny moan followed as he pressed her against him, grinding the hard ridge of his erection against the seam of her jeans. Her nerve endings danced with pleasure, blotting out reason and logic. She knew they ought to stop but she didn't want to, and judging by the way his kiss became more urgent, he didn't, either.

"Are you sure?" he asked, his hands roaming her backside as if he couldn't get enough. "I don't want you to do anything you aren't comfortable—"

Caitlin shushed him with a gentle finger against his lips. "I get it. You don't want me to feel taken advantage of. I want this. As long as you won't get into any trouble…"

Clearly, his expression said he shouldn't be kissing her but he also wasn't going to stop. His recklessness thrilled her in a dark, private place. Everything about her life had been tipped upside down, so why not enjoy this moment? She didn't want to question what was happening; she just wanted to savor the pleasure of feeling another human being against her skin.

Zak hoisted her up as if she weighed nothing. She gasped at the sensation of being carried to the bedroom, aroused by the sheer masculine energy Zak put off like a pheromone as he gently laid her down and began stripping his shirt.

The saliva dried up in her mouth as every hardened ripple of muscle went on display before her and she had to clench her fingers tight to keep from petting him like a dog.

"My God, you're a perfect male specimen. Have you ever considered donating your sperm?" She blushed, realizing too late that her comment was probably weird but Zak didn't seem to mind. If anything, he just rolled with it, the light in his eyes burning holes in her soul. "C-condom," she blurted out, suddenly very aware that they didn't have any protection. "You don't happen to have condoms in your jeans pocket, do you?"

"I don't," he admitted, advancing toward her with a sensual smile. "but there's more to sex than just penetration. Besides," he said, plucking at her jeans, revealing the creamy white of her hips and belly. "I wouldn't be a gentleman if I didn't let my lady come first."

Come? Caitlin's mouth dropped open as the import of his promise dawned. She gasped as he shimmied her panties free and gently parted her legs to gaze at her womanhood.

"I have a confession," she blurted in a breathy whisper as he settled between her legs, looking like a man who'd just found the promised land and couldn't wait to put down roots. He looked up, patient but ready to taste her secrets. She swallowed, not quite sure how to communicate that her sexual experiences were not exactly robust. *When in doubt, go with the truth.* "I—I, well, I'm not the most experienced and, uh, I've never, well, I mean to say, I know what an orgasm is because I've given them to myself but I've never reached that, you know, moment with someone else. So I don't want you to feel bad if it doesn't happen."

His low, deep chuckle sent tiny electric snaps up and down her nerve endings as he drawled, "Oh, baby, did you just throw down a challenge? I believe you did. Well, sweet girl, I accept. Now, lay back and let me do my work."

This was really happening.

Oh, sweet heavens, it was happening.

And it was happening over and over and over.

Her last coherent thought before tumbling into a sexually induced exhaustion was *What the hell have I been missing out on?* Immediately followed by *If Zak could reduce me to a quivering ball of flesh with only his tongue and fingers, what else could he do?*

Was she a terrible person for desperately hoping to find out?

Zak listened to Caitlin sleep. A lot of firsts had just happened between them.

First, he'd made sure Caitlin came so many times that by the end she'd started begging him for mercy, but the sound of her coming had become its own aphrodisiac. He smiled as he gazed at the soft swell of her exposed hip—a spot he'd quickly discovered was a wildly effective erogenous zone—and inhaled a short breath as his manhood threatened to jump to life once more.

No penetration but he could still feel the touch of her hand curled around his shaft as she'd helped him find his own release.

It'd been worth it.

The sweetness of Caitlin in the throes of passion was something he hadn't anticipated but he wanted more. God, he wanted so much more.

Of course this was all wrong. Couldn't exactly put in his report that he'd shagged the scientist he was supposed to be protecting.

CJ would never let him live this down.

This was something Xander would've done back in the day but not Zak.

Xander was known for playing fast and loose with the rules, not Zak.

So what was his next move? He could already hear Scarlett's irritation at his situation. How was he supposed to remain sharp, impartial, unmoved by emotion when he felt a certain level of possessiveness with Caitlin? He'd kill anyone who tried to hurt her.

But what happened when the job was over?

Would it hurt Caitlin to leave her behind?

He couldn't deal with the thought of Caitlin hating him, believing he'd taken advantage of the situation.

Even though she'd assured him that everything was consensual, his guilt nagged at him.

This was why you didn't mess with people on the job.

Solid advice that he usually abided.

What was it about Caitlin that spun his top?

She was blunt, yet, at the oddest moments, shy. The disparity was probably something that appealed to him but he didn't really have the luxury of puzzling things out. The best thing to do would be to sit down with Caitlin and explain how he'd stepped out of line and it wasn't going to happen again.

Would that hurt her feelings? He flexed his hands, wincing at the aches and pains that lingered from a lifetime of being on the receiving and giving side of a beat-down.

Hell, they all joked that by the time they were in their fifties, they'd be unable to move.

Of course, none of them actually believed they'd make it that far, so why worry?

But he thought of Xander—the one they all thought would eat a bullet first. Now Xander was in the FBI, running shit like a boss. Hell, he now wore suits when before he couldn't be pressed to wear a clean shirt—and he was all responsible and shit like a normal Joe.

And "normal Joe" was never something that could be applied to anyone within Red Wolf.

Yet Xander had found his center and a respectable career that didn't include killing people, so maybe that meant there was hope for all of them.

Except CJ. God love him but he was batshit crazy.

Caitlin stirred and opened her eyes. A sleepy smile curved her lips and it took everything he had not to taste that smile.

"You sleep okay?"

"Like the dead," she admitted. "How about you? Did I snore?"

"If you did, I didn't notice," he answered. "You want some coffee?"

"That would be amazing," she said, yawning and rolling to her back to stretch like a kitten next to a warm fire. "I know this isn't a vacation by any means but I'm more relaxed than I've ever been in my life. You can infer whatever you like from that statement."

He laughed. "I think you just gave me a pretty nice compliment."

Her smile curved with Cheshire cat accuracy. "So you're not just a dumb jock."

"Oh, don't go filling my head with smoke, now," he teased before climbing from the bed. "I'll make the coffee. Meet me in the dining room for a chat."

"That sounds ominous."

He didn't want it to seem that way but he knew the conversation was likely to be awkward. Best to do it over coffee.

Within minutes the coffee was ready, and, carrying two steaming mugs over to the table, he settled in a chair, trying to ignore how beautiful she looked in the morning.

Particularly when he could smell her on his body.

And he wanted to taste her again.

Actually, he wanted to do more than taste—he wanted to be inside her. Shaking off where his thoughts were going, he focused on the job.

"Okay, I know you're a straight shooter so I'm just going to come at this in a straight line. I shouldn't have done what I did. I take full responsibility. I should've been the one to put the brakes on and I didn't. I'm sorry but we shouldn't do that again."

She sipped her coffee, regarding him with quiet interest. He'd half expected a show of tears but when none came, he actually felt more anxious. "Okay," she agreed.

That was it? *Okay?* "You're not hurt, I hope," he said.

"Why would I be hurt?"

"Well, I don't want you to think that it's something

you did wrong. I'm the one who was in the wrong. I'm here to protect you, you know? I mean, lines get blurry when you don't keep things on their own side."

"I understand."

"You're making this entirely too easy."

"Would you like me to make it difficult?" she asked with a mildly perplexed look.

"Well, no, of course not but…are you sure you're okay?"

She shook her head, sipping her coffee. "I'm not sure what the right response is if you're disappointed that I'm not falling into hysterics because you don't want to engage in sexual activity with me."

"Don't get me wrong, I want to," he blurted, immediately blushing, but he couldn't have her thinking that she wasn't desirable. "Hell, you've got me all twisted up in knots. The question isn't whether I want to, because, damn, girl, I want you so bad."

Her tiny gasp reminded him too much of how she came so sweetly beneath his tongue. His cock hardened almost instantly, causing him to growl with frustration and need but it wasn't going to happen. Still, he wanted her in the worst way.

"I'd gladly lock us up in the bedroom and spend all our time getting our cardio in the old-fashioned way but that's against the rules. More important than the rules is the fact that it puts your safety at risk and I'm not willing to do that."

"Rules are important," she murmured. There was a spark in her eyes that he didn't trust, but, damn, it was seductive as hell.

"Yeah, exactly."

"I respect your position."

"I'm glad."

But then she leaned back in her chair and said, "Here's the way I look at it—you've awakened something in me I never knew existed and I'm not ready to put it back to bed just yet. Particularly when, let's get real, the danger I'm in makes every moment worth seizing. I've spent my life on the outside staring through the window at the party. Well, if the party is about to end, I'm not going to stand outside anymore."

He understood where she was coming from but he didn't want her to get hurt. "If I do my job right, once the threat has been resolved, I go back to Virginia and you stay here. I'm not the staying kind, you feeling me?"

"Who said I wanted to keep you?" she countered with a quizzical smile.

Okay, ego blown, but yeah, he supposed he'd assumed she'd cling to him.

"So you're okay with just getting your groove on for the time being and then kicking me to the curb when the time comes?"

"Well, I'd probably strive for a little more tact but let's be real for a moment. We are nothing alike and have little in common. I wouldn't expect a fairy-tale happily-ever-after, nor would I know what to do with such an obligation. My work is everything and I don't see that changing."

This was the most surreal conversation he'd ever had with a woman but it made a certain amount of sense. However, his ego was howling. "Easy to say but I'm not so easily forgotten," he replied with a sure smile that probably came off as cocky but she didn't seem to mind.

"I never said I'd forget." She smiled. "But I will move on."

The tension in the room crackled. He would've given his left nut to be that coffee mug as her lip dragged across the rim, her tongue darting to catch a tiny drop of liquid. "Are you sure?" he asked, almost desperately.

Her smile widened with a sexy coyness that he'd never thought he'd see on Caitlin. Where'd his awkward scientist go? The woman who tripped on her own feet and walked into doors because she was too focused on her work to pay attention to such little details? He liked this newfound confidence, even if he wasn't sure he liked the idea that walking away from him was going to be easy.

And there it was, a slightly tremulous quality to her smile that gave her away even as she said, "Don't worry Zak… I'm sure."

Maybe she was right, now wasn't the time to sit outside the party, waiting for it to end. Now was the time to grab on to every moment available to them and live it to the fullest because who the hell knew what tomorrow would bring.

Chapter 14

She was being reckless. Foolish, even.

She didn't care.

Everything she'd said was true. Caitlin understood the risk, the danger that awaited her outside these walls. That bullet whizzing past her head had erased any doubt of the stakes, and a sudden clarity she'd never known had taken over her brain.

Zak was hot and unavailable for anything long-term. What better way to work out the nervous energy she had coursing through her body than to lose herself in the dizzying pleasure of multiple orgasms? Physiologically, she knew orgasms provided a number of benefits, including stress relief. And right now, she needed something to allow her to relax.

Otherwise, she might go insane.

But it was more than that. Since meeting Zak something that'd been bubbling beneath the surface had finally burst. For so long she'd secretly craved adventure.

She'd taken the job with Tessara knowing full well that the company had a history of dangerous associations, because it'd felt far more exciting than a regular lab job. With her qualifications, she could've had her pick of any lab in the United States but the truth of the matter was, she'd sought out Tessara. That was the one thing she'd conveniently left out when breaking the news to her parents that she'd been offered the job.

In some small way, working for Tessara had been her way of walking on the wild side but now that she'd experienced real danger, what she'd been doing seemed silly and childish. Worse, the life she'd been living seemed stunted and abbreviated.

So she was ready to take advantage of everything Zak had to offer.

Suddenly, she understood the saying that rules were meant to be broken, because she wanted to break them all.

She didn't need to tell Zak she was behaving out of character for him to know that this wasn't her average Thursday but then her life wasn't usually in danger, either.

That one factor had a shocking tendency to change one's perspective.

Caitlin rose, pushing a chunk of hair behind her ear, offering one final piece of information for Zak to help him decide his next course of action. "While I appreciate the need for condoms to prevent disease, I'm reasonably okay with taking the risk that you are free from anything communicable, and I'm on the pill, which means I'm not getting pregnant. So if you're ready to throw caution to the wind… I'll be in the bedroom."

Caitlin turned to walk away but Zak was on her in a flash, scooping her up, his eyes hot as he carried her.

"You do make a damn persuasive argument," he said in a low, sexy growl that thrilled her to her toes.

She grinned. "That one semester of Debate has suddenly paid off."

"You took Debate?"

"It was excruciating. I nearly had a panic attack every time I had to present my argument."

"You adorable little bookworm," he chuckled before tossing her to the bed, her squealed laughter echoing through the room as he wasted no time stripping. She hastened to do the same when he indicated, with a gesture, that it was her turn.

Being naked with Zak felt completely natural. His skin against hers was sublime.

Flipping her to her belly, he pressed kisses down her back, sending shivers down her spine and goose bumps rising. A groan escaped as his tongue dared to dip between her twin clefts and a trickle of moisture wet her thighs.

Her nipples hardened against the coarse bedding as the heat of Zak's body grazed hers. His mouth was at her neck, nibbling at the sensitive shell of her ear while his hand dipped down to rub between her legs, seeking that wet heat.

"You're so damn sexy," he growled against her skin, nipping at her neck. She shivered with a groan as he rolled her over, gazing at her with eyes that practically glowed from the sexual hunger radiating from his body. "Do you know what? Sexiest woman I've ever seen and that's no lie."

When he eased himself inside her, splitting her open, feeding that shaft into her opening until she was filled with him, she closed her eyes with pure ecstasy, knowing in that moment that she'd made the right choice. Maybe it wasn't the smart choice, maybe in hindsight she'd rethink it, but for now, it was fantastic and that was all that mattered.

Well, that and the freaking second orgasm that was curling her toes.

So much for ending things before they began. As they lay there, exhausted and sated, and the sweat dried on their skin, Caitlin traced designs on his chest, her finger playing with the tiny tuft of chest hair on his sternum. "Tell me about Red Wolf," she said, snuggling against him. "What is a paramilitary organization?"

"We do the jobs that need to get done when the government needs a high level of deniability. Shadow ops, black ops, that kind of thing."

"So you're all military?"

"Former military, yeah. We also provide high-level security when a specialized training is required."

"So why was Red Wolf called for this job? I mean, as much as I think you're pretty awesome, this seems like an easy one."

"After the last mission we finished, I was actually looking forward to a laid-back gig," he admitted with a rueful chuckle. "The last job was a doozy."

"What happened? Can you tell me? Or is it classified?"

"I probably shouldn't but what the hell, I'm living dangerously right now," he joked. He liked having someone to talk to about his work. He found it oddly comforting. "Okay, so I had this colleague, Xander Scott. He was a real firecracker, kind of a loose wire. He got himself framed for a bad situation, and knowing that his goose was cooked because he had some personal issues, he ran instead of coming to us and letting us help him through it."

"What kind of personal problems?"

"Let's just say he had some demons, but he and our TL, Scarlett, had a thing going on beneath the radar. So when the FBI was gunning for Xander, Scarlett was going to be the one to bring him in."

"Ouch. That had to be a conflict of interest."

"Well, she kept her feelings on the downlow. None of us really knew for sure—I mean, they had sexual tension, but hell, you can't trust that, especially in our field where adrenaline is pumping through your veins at any given moment. So Scarlett chased Xander all over the country, trying to see if he was innocent or guilty and, of course, we never doubted him. But as it turned out, some real bad people at the highest level of government were behind the Tulsa City bombing and we were able to prove it."

"Wow."

"Yeah, right? So I was kinda hoping for an easy gig after that."

"I should say so."

A beat of silence passed between them as Caitlin digested the information. Then she ventured to ask, "So is that how your jobs always go? Like life-or-death situations?"

"Mostly."

"Oh. That's rough. I hope you have really good life insurance."

"I don't have anyone to leave anything to, so I figured I didn't need to bother."

Why did that sound way sadder coming out of his mouth than it had in his head? Time to change the subject. "Tell me about this bioweapon we're dealing with. How bad is it?"

"Honestly, it's the worst I've ever seen. It grows like

a supervirus and attacks every major organ, liquefying the insides of the human body within forty-eight hours. It's nasty."

He shuddered. "That sounds about as horrific as the briefing suggested. To be honest, I was hoping it was a little more hype than fact."

"No, it's the real deal. Since it's a virus, I'm not even sure we can manufacture a cure. You know there's no cure for the common cold, right?"

"With all our technology, we can't cure the cold?"

"Nope. All we've learned how to do is manage the symptoms. With this manufactured virus, there's no time to manage anything once its course is set. It's one hundred percent fatal."

"So how do you know this? Was this tested on humans?"

Caitlin rose up, tucking the sheet around her, a frown forming. "Before Tessara acquired the sample, we were given intel on what had been observed from the facility it was taken from. The pictures were…beyond anything I'd ever seen."

"Where did the sample come from?"

"North Korea."

"I didn't realize they had the technology to make something like this."

"Well, it's probably not something they like to advertise but they made one helluva scary bioweapon."

"Here's my question—why? Why the hell do scientists get in their little labs and go crazy, whipping up this shit that's end-of-days level of destruction? Can't we all just stick to the classics and shoot at each other with missiles and shit?"

She chuckled but shook her head. "If you don't have missiles, you find different ways to level the playing field.

I say we end war altogether and then no one will feel the need to one-up the other."

"Yeah, that may be true but it'll never happen. Not in our lifetime anyway."

"Well, if whoever took that sample releases it out into the public, war will be the last thing anyone is thinking of."

That was a savage truth. "Let's say, for the sake of scaring the piss out of me, that does happen—how quickly are we talking?"

"Based on what research we were able to get…we could have extinction-level death tolls within months of the original contagion. It was my opinion that once Tessara had been compromised, we should've gone straight to the CDC to alert them of the situation but Stan put a gag order on my team. He said the last thing we needed was a terrified mob rushing the hospitals thinking they've been infected when they've just got the flu."

He understood the logic. Large masses of people easily whipped up hysteria but he also saw Caitlin's point. "How close were you to finding that cure?"

"Not close enough," she admitted. "That's why I need to get back to the lab. This has been an adventure—and please, don't take this the wrong way, you're super fun in bed—but in the back of my mind, I'm always thinking about the ticking clock."

"Ouch, my fragile male ego," he said, pretending offense but he got where she was coming from. Even earth-shattering orgasms were no match for the fate of the world hanging in the balance.

Caitlin smiled and leaned forward to brush a kiss across his lips. "I'm willing to make it up to you, if you like."

"I do like," he said, grinning. "What did you have in mind?"

Caitlin slid down his body and her mouth closed over his semihard erection, sucking the tender flesh to sudden life. And he forgave whatever fake transgression he'd been pretending to hold on to.

Girl had skills.

Well, if the world was slated to end soon, at least he'd go out with a smile.

Chapter 15

Caitlin had never spent a day in bed her entire life but then she'd never had the opportunity to spend it with someone like Zak, either. However, at a certain point, showers were needed, so while Zak went to throw together something to eat, Caitlin used the time to rinse off.

The water pressure was good, better than at her place, but there was precious little in the way of toiletries, so she had to make do with what was available. She grimaced at the industrial-size two-in-one shampoo-conditioner bottle—obviously a man did the shopping for the safe house—and lathered up.

Zak was hoping that by tomorrow they'd have their next location, which would include a lab, so she knew it was likely they'd be heading out of state. She wasn't much of a traveler—to be honest, flying was her least favorite mode of transportation—but she did it when it was required.

However, usually she didn't fly without the help of a

light sedative to calm her nerves, but now she didn't want Zak to see her so weak.

There was probably nothing that scared Zak. He was like Superman.

Or Batman.

Or Thor.

She smiled at her own silly humor even though guilt poked at her. She shouldn't be cracking jokes when the stakes were so high. But like Zak said, sometimes humor helped defuse the tension and helped a person to cope.

Yes, she'd go with that. She was operating so outside her comfort zone that she didn't know which end was up any longer. She was half under the spray when she thought she heard something. Pausing, eyes closed, she called out with a smile, "You're supposed to be making us something to eat."

Suddenly, the loud crash of bodies hitting the floor, grunts and obvious scrabbling popped her eyes open as she frantically tried to see through the blur of shampoo bubbles and the water streaming down her face. She screamed when a knife went flying across the floor, as Zak grappled with a stranger dressed in all black and a ski mask.

Sweet mother of God, who the hell was that?

She watched, frozen in fear, as Zak and the stranger—who really seemed to take a page out of the Bad Guy Handbook—traded blows in a real, live fight to the death.

The assailant got the upper hand for a brief moment before Zak slammed his fist into his junk, rolling him off, but the intruder rebounded quickly, landing a kick straight to Zak's head.

"Zak!" she screamed but Zak took the hit and charged the man like a bull, knocking him down. The goon fell, his head hitting the tile floor with a hard thud.

She turned the water off and grabbed the first thing she could find to hurl at the attacker. She got lucky, hitting him in the face with a can of shaving cream.

It was a heartbeat long enough to give Zak the chance to get the guy in a headlock. Within seconds Zak had choked him out. "Are you okay?" Zak asked, rising, breathing hard. He handed her a towel, which she quickly wrapped around herself.

She stared in horror. "Is he dead?"

"No," he answered tersely, grabbing the man to hoist him over his shoulder. "But he's going to wish he were."

Zak strode from the bathroom, leaving Caitlin to start to trail after him until she realized she was still clutching a towel to her body. She dressed quickly and found Zak in the garage. The attacker was tied to a kitchen chair and was slowly coming to.

She held her breath as Zak shook the man fully awake. "Wakey-wakey, asshole," he said, getting right in his face. When Zak was in work mode, he was scary but she was so grateful he was on her side. "Hey, wake up. Got a few questions for you."

"Eat me," the man muttered, wincing as he rolled his neck, cracking a few bones with a groan.

"Look, I'm going to skip the part where you pretend to be a badass and then I proceed to beat the ever-loving shit out of you because unlike you, I actually am a badass, so let's cut to the chase. Give me the name of who sent you and I'll consider not cutting your balls off."

Blood trickling from a cut in his mouth, the man just grinned with a "Screw you" and Caitlin knew this guy was going to get his goose cooked.

"Okay, have it your way." Zak rolled up his sleeves, pausing to say to Caitlin, "Hon, you might not want to watch this," but when she indicated she wasn't going anywhere, he just shrugged and returned to the guy with a quick rabbit punch to the ribcage that had enough force to shatter bone.

Caitlin gasped, realizing she was out of her depth. She'd never watched a human being beat another and she didn't think she should. Zak was right. "I'll just be inside," she murmured before practically running from the garage.

She didn't want to see whatever Zak was going to do to that man.

Her instinct was to beg Zak to go easy, to not beat him within an inch of his life, but her logical brain told her that they wouldn't get answers going soft. Not to mention, as she returned to the bathroom, she saw the knife the man had been clutching and she realized with dawning horror that the knife had been meant for her.

Being knifed seemed even worse than dying by gunshot.

Whoever was coming after her didn't seem to care about doing it humanely.

When did poisoning go out of fashion?

It seemed like forever before Zak returned from the garage, his knuckles bloody and his demeanor hard. She was afraid to know if the guy was still alive or if he was dead.

If he was dead…well, it freaked her out to think there was a dead body in the garage, and if he was alive, she was worried that he might need medical attention.

And how did that work?

Were they legally responsible for his medical care? What if he didn't have medical insurance? Was Red Wolf responsible? Caitlin nibbled at her fingernail, her nerves strung tight. "I don't understand how this works," she blurted, looking to Zak for answers. "Is he…dead? Are you allowed to kill people? I don't know... Are we supposed to take him to the hospital if he's not dead?"

Maybe she was rambling but she had no precedent for handling the interrogation of a person who had come to kill her.

She swallowed the lump in her throat. "Is he...dead?" she asked again in a fearful squeak.

"He's not."

She sagged with visible relief. "I'm glad. I guess I'm not as bloodthirsty as I should be given the fact that he'd been willing to put that knife in me," she said, gesturing toward the knife on the table. "I made sure to protect the fingerprints. I used the towel to pick up the weapon. I saw that on an episode of *CSI Miami* once."

Zak nodded with a briefly held smile, pausing to press a hard kiss to her forehead. "Are you okay?" he asked.

She was touched by his instant tenderness even though he still had murder in his eyes. "I'm okay," she assured him, even though little tremors had started shaking her limbs. "What happens next?"

"Red Wolf is sending a retrieval team."

"What the heck is that?"

"Exactly what it sounds like. We can't have this guy floating around. So he's going to be taken to a secure location until he can be properly processed."

"Processed?" She envisioned a firing squad. "What does that mean?"

He must've sensed where her mind had gone, for he chuckled and said, "After we've determined he's of no more use to us, he'll be handed over to the proper authorities."

"Oh," she said, relieved and yet finding the answer a little anticlimactic. "I guess I thought you might kill him."

"Too much paperwork."

She laughed, but she wasn't entirely sure Zak was joking.

"Are we safe? I mean, what if he tries again before your retrieval team gets here?"

"He ain't going nowhere," Zak said with a small smirk. *What did that mean?* Her perplexed expression prompted him to add, "Somehow in the scuffle to subdue him, he seems to have suffered a few injuries that will affect his ability to walk."

Caitlin's mouth dropped open. "Did you—"

But Zak silenced her with a kiss before saying, "Hey, are you hungry? I'm starved." He returned to the kitchen with a seemingly light heart in spite of the savagery that had just happened.

She suppressed a shudder. Was this her life now?

She didn't know what normal was anymore.

And no, she wasn't hungry.

Caitlin was freaked out. If the blanching of her face wasn't a total clue, the fact that her eyes seemed permanently stretched in the wide, OMG look since he'd emerged from the garage was a dead giveaway.

"You should eat something," he told her, watching her push her pasta around without having eaten a bite. "Gotta keep up your strength."

She dropped her fork with a clatter. "This is not my regular Thursday night. I'm not accustomed to having strangers burst into my shower and try to murder me. I don't know how to process this. And to make matters worse, said potential murderer is tied up in the garage in some disabled state awaiting this mysterious retrieval team. You can pretty much ascertain that this is some messed-up shit and it's screwing with my brain—the brain, I might add, that is supposed to save the world. Yeah, not exactly hungry."

Yep. She was freaking out. He wiped his mouth and said, "Yeah, if I were in your shoes, I'd be pretty overwhelmed, too. I wish the situation allowed time for you to slowly come to terms with the situation but honey, time is a luxury we don't have. I know you're not digging my methods—totally fair—but that guy in the garage might be our first real lead."

"How'd you disable him?" she asked.

"I broke his ankles."

She gasped, her hand flying to her mouth. "You what?"

"Best way to ensure he ain't running anywhere," Zak explained with a quick grin but when he realized she didn't appreciate his humor, he sobered quickly. He had to handle this situation more delicately. Caitlin wasn't like his buddies at Red Wolf, who should be arriving any minute, by the way. He could sense she was wavering on the edge of information overload. "Okay, that was a bad attempt at smoothing things over with humor," he admitted. "But you're right, that guy is dangerous and I couldn't take the chance that he might get free before the team could get here. Your safety is everything. I'm sorry you think it's savage but I'd do anything to keep you safe."

She was more than just a job—helluva time to catch feelings, right? But when he'd seen the guy in the bathroom, knife in hand, he'd gone berserk. If Caitlin had suffered a single scratch, Zak would've ended him. Plain and simple. Yeah, bad time to catch feelings. He needed to stay focused. Now more than ever.

"I'm just struggling with everything right now," she admitted with a scowl. "I need a minute to figure out where my head is at. Everything is mixed up and jumbled. One minute I understand the rhythm of my life and the next, I'm Alice in Wonderland falling down a hole and rabbits wearing ski masks are trying to kill me." She sniffed. "Ski mask, so original. And whatever happened to poison as an acceptable way to kill someone? He was going to put that very large knife in my body. That seems a little more vicious than necessary. I mean, I can tell you there are a million different ways you can kill a person using science that are way more effective and less messy than stabbing a person."

"You seem to have very strong feelings about the method in which your assailant chooses to kill you."

"Well, yes, actually, I do. If he had managed to get past you and finish what he'd started, then it would've made a terrible mess and what if there was a struggle? What if I was poked full of holes and then my family had to arrange for a closed casket? My parents would want to see me one last time. I'm their only child. I know they would not agree to a closed casket."

This was the weirdest conversation ever. "I guess it's a good thing I prevailed," he said, struggling to hide his laughter. She glared at his poor attempt as a chuckle escaped. "Look, this is some heavy shit to deal with. I get it. So you do whatever it is you need to get through it. Ramble on about your murder bias or worry about the potential of your murderers messing up that cute face. But at the end of the day, I'm not letting anything happen to you, so you can rest assured about that."

Her glare softened as she said, "I guess I haven't thanked you for saving my naked ass."

His smile widened as his mind wandered. "And what a fine ass it is."

She blushed with a small smile but waved away his praise. "That's not the point, but thank you for that, too. Anyway, I'm glad you were there to save the day. Again."

"Anytime, gorgeous."

Caitlin melted a little. When he leaned forward, she met him halfway, their lips brushing for the sweetest kiss, which Zak was more than ready to take to the next level but the sound of tires crunching gravel ended whatever might've happened.

"The team is here," he said, returning to business. "Wait here and when the team comes in, say nothing about you and me. Got it?" She had a small frown but nodded nonetheless. "It's complicated," he said and then returned to the garage where he found CJ, Scarlett and Laird, heavily armed and looking like they were ready to party.

His kind of party.

"Break his ankles?" CJ asked, regarding the man tied to the chair, who was breathing heavy and trying not to move.

"Went full-on *Misery*-style."

CJ approved. "Nice."

Scarlett looked at the man without a shred of mercy before turning to Zak. "One assailant?" Zak nodded. She returned to the man in the hot seat. "Ready to talk yet?"

"Nothing to say to you." He spat, missing Scarlett's booted foot by an inch. "Screw you."

Scarlett didn't so much as blink at the insult. If the man didn't have the sense God gave a goose to know he was staring down a highly efficient killer, he didn't deserve to live anyway. A little respect could go a long way but then idiots didn't often realize how close they were to checking out until it was too late.

The man's labored breathing did nothing to soften the rage in his eyes. CJ peered at him, saying, "You're an ugly mofo, aren't you? No wonder you went with a mask. I'd cover that shit up, too."

"Screw you," he panted again, refusing to give an inch.

"Pretty much the response I got, too," Zak said, folding his arms across his chest. "I say we put a bullet in his skull and bury him in a field. Let him become fertilizer. At least then, he'd serve a purpose."

CJ frowned as he straightened. "I ain't digging no hole. Dump his ass in a chipper. Let him become fertilizer without the need for a hole."

"You got a chipper handy?" Laird drawled. "'Cuz I left mine at home."

"Fair point." CJ turned to Zak. "Think we could rent one?"

"Enough," Scarlett commanded, returning to the man listening with dead eyes. Nothing shook him, apparently. Whatever cause he was following, he was dedicated. "We're going to find out who's behind this, and when we do, you'll have zero leverage. You're looking at hard time with really bad people. If you cooperate, we can put in a good word for you, maybe find a way to soften your time."

"You're wasting your time. I have nothing to say but this: judgment is coming for you."

"Judgment? So this is a religious thing?" Scarlett said. "Refresh my memory, in what scripture does the Almighty call for the total destruction of mankind at the hands of some crackpot lunatic with a God complex?"

"Religious nut," CJ muttered, irritated. "Why is it always the self-righteous idiots who somehow get their hands on the real dangerous stuff?"

To Laird, Scarlett said, "Start searching up the usual fanatics and see what they've been up to. Time to switch gears and start looking beyond people hoping to make a quick buck."

"You won't find shit," the man said, chuckling. "We

are right beneath your nose and you'll still never see what's coming."

"Yeah? And why is that?" Zak asked.

"Because God is on our side. He wants this to happen."

"He wants his most kick-ass creation to go down in a hail of shit and piss as everyone leaks out their insides? Yeah, naw, dude, I don't know what God you're praying to but it ain't what was taught to me in Sunday school," Zak said, disgusted.

CJ looked at Zak. "You went to Sunday School?"

"A time or two."

"And you didn't burst into flame?"

Zak laughed. "Kiss my ass. No, but the holy water did make a slight sizzle sound when it touched my skin. Is that bad?"

All joking aside, Zak knew, just as Scarlett knew, that religious conviction was almost impossible to shake.

They could violate the Geneva Convention six ways from Sunday and still come up empty with this guy because he believed in the cause he was willing to die for.

Zak sighed. "Screw this. I need a beer."

Scarlett checked her high-tech watch. "We can take five minutes. I want to talk to Dr. Willows." To Laird she said, "Prepare him for transport," before exiting the garage. Now the real fun began. Caitlin was going to love Scarlett.

Or not.

Only one way to find out.

Chapter 16

"Well, that was a bust," Zak said, irritated. "There could be hundreds of religious crackpots out there. There's no way to narrow down which one was responsible for breaking into Tessara and stealing that sample."

Caitlin's eyes widened as two men and a woman entered the kitchen through the garage with Zak, all looking as dangerous as vipers with a bad attitude and equally as good-looking. Was Red Wolf also known as the Hot and Dangerous Squad?

The woman stepped forward with a no-nonsense expression. "You must be Dr. Willows. I'm sorry we had to meet under these circumstances. My name is Scarlett Rhodes." She thrust her hand out. Caitlin acknowledged the greeting with a nod and shook her hand. "Pleasure."

"Likewise," Caitlin murmured, her gaze darting to the other men. "This must be the team Zak has mentioned."

Scarlett nodded, gesturing to the men. "This is CJ Lawry and Laird Holstein."

"What kind of food you got around here?" Laird asked. "Did CJ pack you anything good?"

CJ grinned with the smug assurance of a job well done. "Only the best. SpaghettiOs, Twinkies, Pop-Tarts and gummy worms, basically the four food groups."

Laird quipped, "How is it that you don't weigh four hundred pounds?"

CJ answered with an angelic smile, "Blessed with the metabolism of a twelve-year-old boy. Don't be jealous."

Their camaraderie didn't disguise the disappointment in their eyes. The interrogation hadn't gone well, if she were to hazard a guess. The man had given up nothing and they were back to square one.

Caitlin asked, "What happens now?"

CJ winked, popping a dimple in his cheek as he assured her, "Don't you worry, we'll find out who the Big Bad is. By the way, Zak didn't mention how cute you were."

Scarlett barked, "Knock it off, CJ. This isn't the 1980s. Sexual harassment isn't cute." Looking to Caitlin, she softened slightly to ask, "How are you feeling?"

Caitlin appreciated the gesture from the hard-as-nails team leader. She was a little intimidated by the GI Jane but she figured there was nowhere safer than behind the Red Wolf wall of muscle and ammo. "I'm not sure what the appropriate answer is, but I'm alive, so I guess everything after that is a bonus. What's going to happen to him?"

"We will transport him to a holding facility where he'll be properly processed."

"I'm a little weirded out by this whole interrogation situation. Do you all usually do this kind of thing in your line of work?"

Scarlett was judicious with her answer, not that Caitlin

expected anything less. "We do what we have to do to get the job done. However, I can definitely say there have been extenuating circumstances when it comes to this case."

"So you're telling me you've never had end-of-the-world scenarios happen before?"

Scarlett had the grace to chuckle. "Not like this. This case is definitely keeping us on our toes."

At that, Zak said, "Now that we're pretty sure we're dealing with a religious cult of some kind, we know why the dark web has been silent."

"Yeah, for once, greed isn't the catalyst."

"Yeah, that's just our luck."

"What do you mean?" Caitlin asked, worried. "What religious cult?"

"Whoever took the sample feels they have a righteous cause. They aren't in it for the money, like we thought. Usually when big-ticket items are stolen—priceless art, large sums of cash, etc.—the dark web lights up with talk about the theft because usually an auction will follow. Most money wins the prize," Zak explained.

"And because you can't put a price on faith, that's why no one's been nipping at the bait."

"Why does that sound so much worse than greed?" Caitlin mourned, worrying her bottom lip. "So now what happens?"

"Well, it's obvious this location has been compromised. The fact that they were able to locate you so quickly means either they're watching 24/7 or they're tracking you somehow." Scarlett looked to Zak. "Did you confiscate her phone?"

"I didn't," Zak admitted with a pursed frown. "I should've."

"My phone?" Caitlin repeated. "What's wrong with my phone?"

"All smartphones are equipped with location trackers. It's a very easy thing to hack into a SIM and hijack the GPS. Dr. Willows, will you please retrieve your phone?"

"What are you going to do with it?"

"Smash it to bits," Scarlett answered simply.

Caitlin gasped. "You can't do that. I have important notes in my phone. Notes I need."

"Sorry. No compromising."

Caitlin looked to Zak for help but he was backing his team leader without a second's hesitation. She had all of her contacts, her notes, her passwords… She'd never be able to remember everything she had stored in her phone. "There has to be another way," she protested.

"Sorry, it's just the way things have to be done," Zak said.

Caitlin made a small sound of frustration as she reluctantly handed over her cell phone to Scarlett, who promptly smashed it on the ground, just as she'd promised she would.

Caitlin yelped as the phone shattered, feeling just as broken as that phone. It was stupid—cell phones could be replaced—but there was so much in her life that had spiraled out of control that this was just one more thing to remind her that she was well and truly screwed.

Ridiculous tears pricked her eyes. She refused to cry in front of strangers. Lifting her chin, she said in the strongest voice she could muster, "If you'll excuse me, I'd like some time by myself," and then left them in the kitchen to disappear behind the bedroom door.

"She was real attached to that phone," CJ said with an arched brow but Zak knew it wasn't about the phone.

"She's been through a lot. Hard to process."

CJ shrugged. "Feelings. I get it. I mean, I don't get

it, because *feelings* aren't exactly in my wheelhouse but yeah, I get it." He grabbed a package of Twizzlers and ripped them open. "I really outdid myself on the grub."

"The fact that you don't have diabetes yet isn't fair," Laird said.

Zak and Scarlett walked out of the kitchen and into the living room. She gave the place a quick once-over before declaring, "It's not the best, not the worst." Zak agreed but he was still replaying the scene in his head where the knife-wielding religious wack job had been too close to Caitlin.

Naked Caitlin, at that.

He knew that streak of possessiveness revving up his testosterone wasn't appropriate to the situation but it was there, juicing up his veins, all the same.

"I screwed up. Got sloppy."

"Don't let this get in your head," Scarlett warned. "It happens to the best of us."

"No excuse. If I'd been a second late, she'd be dead."

Scarlett didn't argue. Nor did she waste time trying to soothe his pride. She simply moved on. "Tessara has a lab on standby but we need to move out by 0600. We'll take turns taking watch until we can move out. You good with that?"

"Yeah, sure." He immediately hated the fact that he would be sleeping in the chair again but there was no way in hell he'd climb into Caitlin's bed with his TL standing guard. For one, he wasn't interested in getting the lecture or "the look" because he knew it wasn't right. He also knew he didn't care. He was already getting grumpy at the knowledge that he couldn't have the sweetness of Caitlin's body against him but he'd shove that down deep because nobody had time to dig deeper into that issue.

"Laird will drive the prisoner to the airfield where

he'll be picked up for processing and—" she slid a slightly amused look Zak's way "—medical attention."

Zak shrugged. "He resisted."

"Yes, I'm sure he did. Odd injury, though."

"Isn't it, though," he agreed with a nod. "Where's the lab?"

"Tessara wanted to stay on this side of the States, even though the California lab was the next best choice as far as equipment goes. Apparently, they have a small lab in New Hampshire that's adequate. It has a smaller footprint, so it should be easier to secure than the Vermont location."

"All this lab business, I don't know, makes my head spin. Reminds me of high school chemistry. Unless I could blow stuff up, I wasn't interested."

Scarlett chuckled. "Not much of a school nerd, huh?"

"Not really," he admitted. The nerdiness, if he were being honest, was one of the things that intimidated him about Caitlin. She wasn't only smart, she was genius-level smart, which meant they had next to nothing in common.

Aside from the epic sex. Yeah, that was pretty good. He caught the smile before it appeared but Scarlett, damn her intuition, knew something was up right away.

"Are you into the doc?" she asked, her gaze narrowing.

"Of course not," he lied. "Why?"

"Because you've got a dopey look on your face."

"Sorry, that's just my face."

Scarlett looked annoyed. "Seriously, Zak? I've never had to worry about you dipping your wick where you shouldn't. Do I need to start worrying?"

"Calm down, TL. I'm fine. I feel protective over Caitlin because she reminds me of my sister."

"Your sister? How?"

"She's smart like Zoey and a little socially awkward.

She doesn't have much of a filter. Maybe if Zoey hadn't checked out early, she might've ended up a brilliant scientist like Caitlin. So yeah, I feel a certain sort of way about her but it's not like you're thinking."

It sounded like good copy but Zak knew he was spinning tales for his TL's benefit. The thing was, he did feel a certain sort of way about Caitlin and he wasn't sure what to think about it so until he could figure things out on his own, he'd just keep that intel to himself.

Whether Scarlett bought his bullshit or not, she didn't pursue the topic. That was what he appreciated about Scarlett. She didn't play Twenty Questions; she simply got down to business. "We'll all head to the New Hampshire location to give you more support. Now that we know we're dealing with a religious faction, we're going to need more eyes on this, which means more eyes on your scientist."

He knew Scarlett was making the right call but it didn't make him happy. "I'll tell Caitlin. She wants to bring her team. Have you spoken with Tessara to see if that's possible?"

"If the team is necessary for her to finish her job, then, yes."

"She says they are but we need to do more checks on them before that happens. I still feel this was an inside job."

"Copy that."

CJ joined them. "Laird left to transport the prisoner," he reported. "And while you two were yapping, I made some food. Thought you might be hungry."

"Twinkies are not considered food," Zak retorted.

"Shut your ungrateful piehole, Mr. I-Only-Eat-Veggies. I made burgers. I found an old grill and some briquettes outside. Cooked up real fast and easy. You can even wrap your meat in a piece of lettuce."

"I'm impressed, CJ," Zak said, laughing. "I'll go get Caitlin."

Scarlett chuckled and followed CJ back into the kitchen to grub up.

Zak knocked once and then entered the bedroom, where he found Caitlin hastily wiping her face.

"Are you okay?"

"Stop asking me that," she said, glowering. "No, I'm not okay. Nothing about this situation is okay. I've been shot at, knifed at, shipped from one place to another, been witness to a man tortured for information and now, playing hostess in a house that isn't mine to a bunch of people I don't know. So yeah, things are not okay."

"I told you not to watch," he reminded her. But he received a dour look, so he stopped. "Look, I know this sucks. Everything is crazy and I can't promise it won't get worse before it gets better. But I can promise on my life that I'll do everything humanly possible to keep you safe."

She cast a frightened look his way. "What if that guy had hurt you? I was so scared when he kicked you in the head. I thought he might've killed you."

"Takes more than a kick to the head to put me down," he said, knuckling her cheek softly. "Come here," he instructed. When she stepped forward, he pulled her to him and brushed a tender kiss across her lips. He could practically feel the anxiety vibrating off her in waves. Touching her seemed the right thing to do. Immediately he felt her soften against him. He drew her closer, savoring this stolen moment because he knew it would be their last, with the team surrounding them. After a long moment, he reluctantly broke the kiss, meeting her gaze. "You're pretty damn cute, you know that?"

A shy smile followed a rueful look. “I think you’re blind or that kick to the head did more damage than you realize.”

He shook his head. “Nope. I thought you were pretty cute the moment we met. There’s a whole lot of spunk hiding under that shy-girl facade.”

“It’s no facade, I can promise you that. I’m a card-carrying introvert but you make me braver than I normally am,” she admitted. “Watching you in action…it’s pretty impressive.” Then she whispered, “And super hot. God, you are hot,” before lifting on her toes to kiss him again. Only this time her hand went straight to his groin, where she cupped his hardening erection.

He bit back a groan and covered her hand, squeezing before gently removing her grip. “It’s not that I don’t want to, because, damn, girl, I want to do all kinds of dirty things to you right now, but there are rules and I’ve broken them. I’ve gotta keep this on the DL, you know?”

“I understand,” she said with a small sigh. “So I’m guessing you won’t be sleeping next to me tonight?”

“No, but I’ll be in the chair so you can sleep safe.”

“It’s better than nothing but I want you next to me.”

“Me, too.”

She gazed up at him with hope. “One last kiss?”

How could he resist such a sweet request?

Zak gathered Caitlin into his arms, holding her tightly, his hands roaming her backside to land at her cute tush. He filled both palms and squeezed. She gasped and melted against him, her mouth open, her tongue meeting his, tasting, exploring. He was quickly becoming addicted to her smell, her taste. Everything about Caitlin turned his crank. His erection was nearly bursting through his jeans. Irrational thoughts crowded his brain as he envisioned bending her over the bed and sliding himself inside her for a quick and dirty romp but he knew they didn’t have time.

Questions would be asked.

Scarlett would see through any excuse he could give.

CJ would call him out for smelling like sex.

It was almost worth all the risks.

But he wouldn't put Caitlin through that kind of invasion into her private business.

With a groan he pulled back, taking a mental snapshot of Caitlin as she was in that moment—lips plump and red, cheeks pinked, breathing hard, and pupils dilated. "God, you're sexy," he murmured. He pushed at his erection, trying to make it less obvious. "This is what you do to me."

Her pleased yet sweetly sensual smile was like heroin.

"Uh, CJ made burgers," he said, running his hand through his hair, trying to get his mind right. "He's a decent cook. Not as good as me but decent. Are you hungry?"

"Yes."

"For food," he clarified.

She laughed. "No. But I'll eat."

"Good girl." He couldn't resist and brushed a quick kiss across her swollen lips. "Let's go. Scarlett's going to start asking questions if we stay in here much longer."

Caitlin giggled, admitting, "It's kinda exciting to be the secret."

Zak grinned. "I love your sense of adventure." He lightly slapped her ass as she walked by. "Now get your game face on."

"Or what?"

"Or I'll find a way to spank you, little girl," he promised.

That final look she sent his way was hot enough to melt metal.

And suddenly, he was hoping for bad girl Caitlin to make an appearance.

Chapter 17

Caitlin had gone to bed but Zak and the team spent some time researching various religious groups they knew were whacked in the head.

CJ snapped his fingers as he triggered his memory. "You know that group out of North Carolina, the Congregation of the Eternal Light? They've got to be involved. That's some weird-ass shit they're preaching."

Zak chuckled but he didn't think they were big enough to pull off this coup. "They're a ragtag bunch of hillbillies. They don't have enough money to pull off something of this magnitude. Keep looking."

Scarlett agreed with him. "The group that pulled this off has deep pockets, deep enough to have connections in high places. The intel on the production of the sample had to come from our own government. No one else knew that North Korea was cooking up this nasty thing except a privileged few. The op to get the sample had been strictly black ops, off the books."

"So we've gotta tap our FBI contacts," Zak said. "What's Xander know about this case?"

"I haven't talked to him about it. He's not going to know much—it's way above his pay grade," Scarlett retorted.

"But he might know someone who does," Zak countered. "I know you don't want to involve Xander but this is bigger than any justification that you might have not to."

Scarlett shot Zak a sharp look. "The last time I used an FBI contact who had a personal connection to me, he died. I don't want Xander facing the same threat."

He hated to play hardball but Scarlett was being soft. "I get it. Conrad was a good guy. Without his help, we wouldn't have been able to clear Xander's name, and Conrad paid the ultimate price for helping us out. But Xander isn't Conrad and he's sharp as hell. Besides, if this whole deal goes sour, we're all biting the big one anyway."

Scarlett conceded Zak's point grudgingly, saying, "I'll see what he can poke around and find out."

"Good. Okay, so we need complete background checks on all of Caitlin's team before we can allow them to follow to the new lab. I had just started vetting the team when all hell broke loose. My gut still says it was an inside job. I don't trust any of those people until they've been cleared."

"Does Caitlin have any idea who might've compromised the lab?" Scarlett asked.

"No, she's not willing to believe anyone on her team is capable but she's lived a fairly sheltered life. It's one of her best qualities but it's also her weakness."

CJ nodded. "I'm on it. Give me the names and I'll run them down."

"Thanks, man," Zak said, throwing in a compliment. "Those burgers were actually edible."

"Don't front, they were Gordon Ramsay–good."

"I wouldn't go that far."

Scarlett rolled her eyes. "You two are like children."

CJ scoffed. "He started it." Then, he said, "Hey, about your scientist, what's she like?"

Instant prickles rose on his arms. He sensed CJ's interest and it didn't sit well with him, but he needed to tread cautiously with Scarlett around. "She's fine. A little on the prickly side but she's ridiculously smart, so small talk is difficult for her."

"She's cute."

He shrugged as if he hadn't noticed. "Her looks don't matter. She's just a job."

"I've always said you've got the patience and the virtue of a saint. I couldn't ignore that little cutie right beneath my nose."

"Well, that's why you weren't picked for this job," he returned with an easy grin. "Too easily distracted."

Scarlett chuckled. "You walked right into that one."

CJ conceded with good humor. "Yeah, yeah. Okay, so back to the religious wing nuts. I'll check with any newly registered nonprofits with a faith background or those with even a whiff of faith attached. If we're looking for deep pockets, we need to look where money is flowing."

Zak yawned. "Good idea."

CJ looked incredulous. "Are we tapping out already? It's barely midnight."

But Scarlett did Zak a solid and said, "CJ and I will take first watch, you and Laird, second. That work?"

"Yeah, sounds good." He rose and headed for the bedroom, saying, "I'll take the chair in the bedroom. Caitlin is nervous with all the new people."

Scarlett gave him a thumbs-up and he went into the bedroom, softly closing the door. He pulled his shirt off and tossed it but he was going to sleep in his pants. Still, he went to Caitlin and pressed a soft kiss to her forehead, smiling when she made soft little sleepy noises as she moved toward him. He regretfully grabbed a spare pillow and returned to the chair.

Settling in for a few hours' sleep, he tried to get over his need to cuddle up to Caitlin. Being so close yet unable to touch her was a different kind of torture.

He'd never felt this way about a woman, not this quickly.

He wasn't sure if he liked it but he knew there wasn't much he could do about it, either. Whatever Caitlin was, she was firmly buried in his brain and there to stay.

He'd figure out the rest once she was safe.

Until then, he'd just have to make sleeping on the chair work.

He'd also have to figure out how to hide his reaction to CJ sniffing around his girl. Scarlett was too sharp to miss the signals for too long—and he had a pretty good idea how that conversation was going to go.

Get your head out of your ass, Ramsey. Yep. That was exactly how it would go.

Caitlin woke before dawn to a cup of coffee thrust into her hand and instructions to rise and shine before she was even coherent. Luckily, she'd gone to bed at a decent hour and she was an early riser but the events of the recent past had left her discombobulated.

She gratefully clutched the mug and sipped at the coffee, watching as the team moved in coordinated action to clear the house.

At some point Laird had returned and they were all

gearing up to vacate the house. An odd pang of sadness followed the realization that she'd miss this little house. Not because it was particularly show-ready or filled with hospitality but because this was where she and Zak had made love.

She smothered the immediate shiver that followed her internal dialogue.

Made love.

It'd felt like that—not simply sex.

Was that possible? To love someone within such a short time period? They'd only known each other for days but their connection had been off the charts.

And the way their bodies moved together, like a perfectly orchestrated symphony, had to mean something, right? She'd never been much of a die-hard romantic but it was hard to ignore the facts as she knew them.

There was so much to process that perhaps she was jumping the gun. High-stress situations could trigger chemical reactions in the brain that mimicked the intense feelings of attraction. Maybe all of this would fade as soon as the danger was over and she'd be left with the realization that they had zero in common.

He was rough and masculine to a fault but he smelled like heaven and made her dizzy when he was near.

He had a way of twisting her insides until she was a melty piece of butter on a hot pancake.

He was an excellent cook and he actually made vegetables palatable.

But he worked for a company that routinely put his life on the line and she didn't have the temperament for constant anxiety.

Did she mention that he smelled like sex and warm shortbread cookies fresh out of the oven?

No, that wasn't right. It wasn't cookies, exactly, but

the way his skin smelled was the way fresh cookies made her feel when they were in her mouth.

Loved.

She'd had a great childhood and Zak wasn't anything like her father, so take that, Freud. *Imagine bringing home Zak to Mom and Dad.* One word: awkward. She pictured her parents, both vociferous supporters of gun control and steeply entrenched in academia, science and other dusty, cerebral subjects, trying to find common ground with an alpha soldier who could assemble a gun blindfolded within seconds.

Zak had probably played sports in high school.

Her parents had both been science club geeks.

Zak had probably been prom king and Mr. Popular.

Caitlin had been blissfully forgotten, spending most of her free time in the library.

They were polar opposites.

Opposites attract—or they completely baffle, leading to huge chasms impossible to cross.

"Are you ready?" Zak asked, breaking into her ridiculous internal debate. She perked up and nodded. "Good. We leave in ten."

She finished her coffee, quickly dressed and brushed her teeth.

"Zak, you and Dr. Willows will follow behind us to the airfield. A plane is waiting for us," Scarlett instructed, all hard edges and sharp lines. Caitlin wished she had that kind of presence. The Red Wolf team leader looked like the kind of woman who didn't take any crap from anyone. What kind of boss did Scarlett have? Who would dare to give her orders?

Caitlin climbed into Zak's vehicle and they fell in behind Scarlett's rig, leaving behind the safe house and its memories.

"Where are we going?" she asked.

"Tessara has a small lab in New Hampshire. We're heading there."

"And my team?"

"When we've determined your team is safe to join you, they will. Until then, it's just you and me and the Red Wolf team."

"What about my research?"

"You'll be able to access all your research from the computers at the new lab. All the servers are connected."

"Except the notes I had on my phone," she grumbled.

"Except the notes on your phone. Sorry."

She understood but it was just so *Jason Bourne* that she couldn't quite wrap her head around it. "So…a religious cult, huh?"

"Seems that way."

"It probably goes without saying that I'm not a huge believer in a man in the sky who dictates our lives. I'm a Big Bang believer. Where do you land on that debate?"

"Hard to say. I wasn't given much encouragement to believe in an all-powerful being who had my back. Too much shit happened to make me doubt that anyone had my back but myself."

Her reasons for not believing in God weren't nearly as sad as Zak's. Hers felt more clinical, his more emotional. From being tossed around from one foster home to another to losing his sister to suicide, he'd had a life horrible enough to make even the strongest believers question their faith.

Then he surprised her by saying, "But as much as I don't believe for myself, a part of me hopes that I'm wrong."

"Why?"

"Because I hope that someone was there for Zoey up

in heaven because I sure as hell wasn't there for her when she needed me down here on earth."

Her eyes pricked with sudden tears even though it wasn't her tragedy. She could feel the buried anguish Zak carried, even after all these years, and it landed like a stone in her gut. In that moment, she wanted to believe for Zak, too. The words choked her throat as she said, "I hope so, too."

Zak cast her a quick look before ducking his gaze, as if the moment was too much for him and he hadn't meant to share something so deep. He cleared his throat a few times and finally said, "Anyway, yeah, the God thing, just never was my deal. Hard for me to understand people who do crazy shit in the name of an imaginary man up in the clouds."

"Same."

A beat of silence passed, giving them both a chance to collect their thoughts and take a step away from the ledge they were teetering on.

"Do you know the New Hampshire lab?" he asked, changing the subject.

"No. I've only ever been to the Vermont lab but I know they have labs all around the world. It was one of the reasons I wanted to work for Tessara. Unlike a lot of labs that are located in one spot, I liked the opportunity to transfer to a new place if I ever got bored of Vermont."

"Do you think you'd be willing to pick up and move your entire life like that?"

She shrugged. "I don't know but I liked having the option available. Somehow, it felt less stifling to know that I had options. My parents worked for the same lab their entire lives and even though they seemed very happy, it just felt stale to me. I wanted to be able to move around if I got bored with one lab."

He quirked a subtle grin her way. "Are you wishing for a little bit of that boredom you feared so much?"

"Yes," she admitted with a laugh. "I didn't expect this kind of excitement but I don't regret it."

"You sure?"

"Not one bit."

She wasn't talking about Tessara any longer. Getting shot at, attacked in her shower and whatever else might be coming her way was worth meeting Zak and everything that happened after.

His smile widened and he seemed to know that she wasn't talking about Tessara, either.

What were they getting themselves into?

Trouble—that was what they were getting into—pure trouble.

And she was down for it all.

Chapter 18

The lab was a gray square box of a building that sat back against a backdrop of trees, off a main road and away from through traffic. As they pulled into the parking lot, Zak felt it looked like something out of a sci-fi film where the government did secret experiments that resulted in something horrific.

As in something that nature would never spawn and would probably try to eat your face off.

"Home sweet home," Scarlett announced, immediately doing a perimeter scan, checking the visuals against what she'd already gathered from their intel. "Good defensible space, though."

"It looks haunted," CJ voiced what they were all thinking. "You sure this place is the right one?"

"Don't be such a pussy. No such things as ghosts," Scarlett said, though she didn't look happy to be calling this place home, either. "Tessara said the building is empty, no personnel, only security at night, which we've already vetted."

"Why does Tessara have an empty lab lying around?" CJ asked. "It's not like having an extra pair of shoes, just in case you get caught in a rainstorm."

"Deep-pocket companies can have whatever tickles their fancy," Laird said grimly. "Let's get inside and see what we're looking at."

Zak looked to Caitlin and she cast a giddy smile his way. "I'm excited," she said. "To be in a lab again will be the first semblance of normal I've known in days." She headed for the front door, excitedly calling, "C'mon, I want to see what I'm working with."

They went into the four-story building and took the elevator to the fourth floor, exiting onto BSL-4—Biosafety Level 4. "Whoa," CJ said, taking in the clean room and safety protocols. "This is some serious shit."

"This is state of the art," Caitlin agreed with unsuppressed awe. "Incredible. This is even better than the CDC labs."

"It looks like the kind of place where demons roam at night," CJ quipped.

Caitlin gushed, still starry-eyed. "I can't believe Tessara has this facility in its possession and it's not filled with research scientists, top to bottom. If I'd known this place was available, well, I would've put my résumé in. I don't even care what they're working on. This is fantastic."

"Be careful what you wish for. Tessara has its secrets and not all of them are nice," Zak said warily, walking past her to stop short of the clean room. He gestured toward the room and asked, "That where you're going to work on the sample?"

"When you're able to find it again," she answered. "In

the meantime, I'm going to boot up the computers and see if I can access the servers."

Zak followed her into the office adjacent to the research lab, similar to the layout in Vermont. She powered up the computer, and within seconds, she was in the mainframe. "I'm in. I love technology," she said. "Aside from the notes I lost on my phone, I have access to everything I had at the lab in Vermont. I have everything I need except one thing, my team."

"As soon as their background checks are complete, we'll bring them on. A few days, tops."

"Do you really think we have a few days to spare?"

"Nothing I can do about that. I still think the theft was an inside job and until we can clear each member of your team, they're not stepping within ten feet of you."

She smothered her immediate protest. He knew her irritation was based on her belief that her coworkers were innocent but Zak wasn't going to budge on what his gut was telling him.

Scarlett joined them. "We've sealed off the entrances to this level. The only way in or out is through the elevator, and we'll be posted there 24/7. No one is getting into this facility without our say-so."

"Thank you, Miss Rhodes."

"You can call me Scarlett," she offered with a brief smile.

Caitlin nodded and returned to Zak. "Well, I'm going to dig into my notes and refresh my brain. Maybe the forced break will reveal something I'd missed before."

"Smart thinking. You hungry?" At her disinterested shrug, he knew he'd have to slide food under her nose now that she was back in her element. Next time he wouldn't bother to ask. "I'll check on the food situation. Laird and Scarlett are here with you."

She nodded, already scanning her notes, focused on the task. He chuckled and left her to her work.

Zak and CJ roamed the halls of the facility, checking exits and entrances, making sure they controlled all points of entry. "This place gives me the heebie-jeebies," CJ admitted.

"Yeah, I know. Tessara has their hands on some scary shit. No telling what they use this facility for. I, for one, am glad we're only occupying the one floor. I don't even want to know what might be stored in the basement."

"Probably a doorway to another reality, like on that show, *Stranger Things*. Did you watch that?"

"Naw, you know I don't like scary stuff. I've seen enough in my lifetime to scare me for real. I don't need it for entertainment."

"True enough. Hey, so what's the real deal with you and the doc?"

"What deal?" Zak asked, being evasive. "My job is to keep her safe long enough for you guys to find that damn sample."

"Yeah, but there's, like, chemistry between you. If I didn't know better I'd say you guys were knocking boots. But I know you don't break rules like that, so I know it hasn't happened."

"Exactly. So why even bring it up?"

"Touchy. What's up with you?"

"This job has me on edge. I don't particularly like the idea of dying by shitting my insides out and bleeding through my eyeballs. Makes me a little grumpy."

"I get it, man. This is some scary shit but we'll find the wing nuts that are behind all this and it'll be business as usual like it always is. We save the day, man. That's what we do."

"Yeah, but what about when we can't save the day? What happens then?"

"Then the world is screwed," CJ retorted with a grin. "Hey, lighten up. No one is dying today, so let's just count our blessings and move on."

CJ, ever the philosopher when it suited him. "Let's check out the sleeping quarters. I want everything arranged for when Caitlin is ready to go to sleep."

They detoured, following the map, to the section of the building where several rooms were simply labeled APT 1, 2, etc. and opened up the first one.

They saw a small, utilitarian room about the size of a hotel room, with the same amenities, but without the charm. This was about efficiency, not comfort. "The Hilton it ain't but we've slept in worse," CJ quipped.

Zak agreed, noting the double beds. At least he wouldn't have to bed down on the floor. He looked to CJ, saying, "The doc will take this room with me on duty."

"Good thing there are two beds," CJ said with a hint of slyness that made his teeth grind. CJ was going to be on him like stink on dog crap. Hiding his feelings was going to be a bitch with CJ on his tail.

But Zak played along, barking a short laugh. "Yeah, tell me about it. I've been sleeping in a chair the last few days and my back isn't what it used to be."

CJ nodded. "Preach, bruh. Ibuprofen is my standard breakfast at this point. Every morning I think I might be getting too old for this job and then I think about getting a regular job and I want to jump off a bridge, so yeah, ibuprofen it is."

A regular job? What was that? But weirder things had happened. Their buddy Xander was wearing a suit and tie now as an FBI agent when a year ago he'd been on the run. "You think Xander misses Red Wolf?" he asked.

"Who wouldn't miss what we do? Hell, we're living the dream."

"I can't tell if that's sarcasm or not," Zak said.

"Me, either."

They laughed and left it at that. Neither had the answers and neither had the balls to ask the right questions.

After a half hour Caitlin glanced up to find Laird and Scarlett looking intensely uncomfortable around the protective laboratory equipment. No doubt it was pretty intimidating to the average person. Most people never had the opportunity to step foot on a BSL-4 because there were very few rated for the kind of virulent virology like that of the deadly sample.

Even her own parents, who were familiar with a lab environment, would find a BSL-4 environment daunting, simply because they understood that the scientists handled death with each dangerous pathogen. For that very reason, she understood why her parents were less than excited about their only child jumping at the chance to work in her chosen field but she found the genetic symmetry in virology mesmerizing, beautiful, even. Imagine trying to explain that to the average person without coming off sounding like a psychopath. Exactly why she kept those thoughts to herself.

Refocusing, she felt that familiar crick in her neck from staring at her computer for too long and leaned back to roll her neck from her shoulders, sighing as it popped and cracked. A thought occurred to her. Where were they staying? Here in the facility? As far as she knew there wasn't any barracks but then, what did she know about this secret place?

For all she knew there could be a suite located somewhere on the grounds.

As if reading her mind, Scarlett entered the office and said, "Your sleeping quarters have been arranged. When you're ready to call it a night, Zak will escort you."

Sleeping quarters? "What do you mean? Like a cot or something in the break room?"

Scarlett shook her head. "This particular facility has sleeping quarters for key staff. Are you fatigued?"

No, but she was very curious. However, her curiosity could wait. She was making progress and didn't want to stop just yet.

"Thank you," she murmured, returning to her work. "It'll be a while before I turn in."

"I understand." Scarlett returned to her post with Laird, and Caitlin lost herself in the work.

Zak returned with food. She smiled, her heart warming. "Is there a secret restaurant located on the premises, too?" she asked, eyeing the plate of food.

"That, my dear doc, is a government-issue MRE. Meatloaf and mashed potatoes, hot and ready. It even comes with a candy bar for dessert."

"An MRE? Wow, I've never actually eaten one of these. Are they any good?"

"I like them," he admitted. "However, they will land like a lead brick in your gut, so I wouldn't eat too many or else you won't be able to go to the bathroom for days."

"Oh, good to know," she said, eyeing the food with a different perspective. Giving the plate an exploratory sniff, she had to say it smelled good. Besides, she was hungry. She shrugged before taking a bite, declaring, "I've eaten worse," and braved the military grade meal. She chewed slowly, waiting for something weird to happen to her taste buds but when it simply tasted like cafeteria-style meatloaf, she happily took another bite, announcing, "I like it."

Zak chuckled and said, "I'll let Uncle Sam know you approve of his culinary skills." He took a seat on the edge of the desk, gesturing to the computer. "So how's it going?"

"Well, the good news is I'm back up to speed from a few days ago but the bad news is I haven't had any major breakthroughs. It's impossible to run theories against a sample that I don't have. Everything I've factored out is simply a theory. I have no idea if they will work or not."

"We're working on it. We've got a few leads to run down. Something will pan out. It always does."

"How do you stay so calm when we're talking about the end of the world if we fail?"

"Not my first rodeo."

Maybe she was exhausted and it was finally catching up to her but his dry comment made her laugh. "No? Well, I don't remember buying tickets to this show."

"You and me both." He gestured to her half-eaten plate of food. "You done?"

Caitlin nodded and pushed away the remains of her meatloaf. "Doesn't taste quite as good when it cools down."

"That's why the secret is to gulp it down while it's still hot. Once it cools down it returns to its original chemical state," he joked as he took her plate and stuffed it into a trash bag. "You look like you could use a hot bath, a massage and a good night's sleep."

"Is that available?"

"I can make it happen. Your room has a small bathtub and I've got pretty good hands." He leaned forward to whisper for her ears only, "And I've got a pretty good method for ensuring a deep sleep."

"I'm interested," she said, her heart rate jumping. Caitlin calmed her fluttering pulse with deliberate breaths and then resolutely flicked her computer off, saying, "I think I'd like to retire now. Can you escort me to my sleeping quarters?"

"I'd be happy to."

That solicitous offer belied the hot spark in his eyes.

And she couldn't wait to get behind closed doors.

Chapter 19

Zak made arrangements with Scarlett for the night before walking Caitlin to what would become her sleeping quarters for as long as they needed to be stuck in the facility.

In a sense, it would become his quarters, as well.

He closed the door and locked it, stalking her as he pulled his shirt free. "I've wanted to do this all day," he said, sealing his mouth to hers even as he helped remove her shirt. He filled his hands with her breasts and moved her to the bed. "This is harder than I thought it would be."

She chuckled deep in her throat as her hand reached down to cup his groin. "Oh, yes, seems pretty hard to me," she said and he nearly came in his jeans. Caitlin plucked at his buttons and released his erection, her hand curling around the hard staff. He groaned against her mouth as they tumbled to the bed.

He was mindless with the need to touch her. Pulling her jeans free, he made quick work of his own before descending between her thighs. Within minutes Caitlin's soft, breathless pants hit a crescendo and she shuddered with a muffled cry as she clutched a pillow over her own face. He appreciated her forethought but he loved the sound of her cries when she came. He growled as he climbed her body, grabbing the pillow to reveal her beautiful face. He kissed her hard as she wrapped her legs around his torso, his erection grinding against her soft, damp cleft.

He came fast and wild with the most jaw-droppingly powerful orgasm of his life and when it was done, he was left boneless.

Zak barely had the energy to roll off Caitlin, his breathing harsh as he tried to catch his breath. "I think I'm having a heart attack," he said, his chest heaving. "Holy crap, that was intense."

He felt her soft, exhausted laughter and knew she felt the same. This thing they were doing—it didn't make sense—but it was real and tangible and he didn't know how to quit it.

Not that he wanted to.

That was the problem. He was insatiable when it came to Caitlin and he suspected the feeling was mutual. What were they supposed to do with this?

They were both committed to going their separate ways when everything was said and done because—c'mon, him and her as a couple? Yeah, right, what a laugh—they had next to nothing in common and everyone knew relationships built on sex weren't meant to last. But when he envisioned that scenario, as in actually walking away, his gut cramped and a growl popped from his mouth. He spent more of his free time thinking about—God help him—*snuggling* than he did about what he used to enjoy thinking about, like new guns and hunting trips, and frankly, his head was a mess. But he liked her, as in *really* liked her and even if it didn't make sense, it was as real as anything he'd ever known.

Aww hell, the more he thought about it, the more confused and agitated he got.

He rose on wobbly legs and made it to the bathroom to splash some water on his face. He returned with a damp washcloth and gently cleaned Caitlin, taking extra care around her sensitive parts. But seeing Caitlin so exposed just made him want her again. His rebound time had never been so swift. There was something about Caitlin that changed everything.

"I just want you to know, this isn't what I do," he said, trying to put into words some kind of explanation. "I mean, I don't mess around on the job."

"You mean there isn't a girl in every city you've been in?" she teased, rolling to her side to regard him in the semidarkness. "Why are you telling me this?"

"I don't know. I guess I don't want you thinking that I'm easily swayed by a pretty face."

She smiled more brightly. "You think I'm pretty?"

He chuckled, shaking his head. "Of course I think you're pretty—hell, I think you're damn gorgeous. You've got to know that you're a looker, right? That smart girl vibe is hot."

But maybe she didn't know that, because he saw a flash of vulnerability in her eyes that told a private story as she admitted, "Zak, I've never been the girl who turned the cute boy's head. I was always hiding in the library or the science lab. Not many cute boys hanging out in the quiet zones."

"Boys in high school are blind, and college isn't much better. Yeah, you're pretty damn hot." He knuckled the soft blush in her cheeks. "Too damn hot, actually. This thing between us could burn us to the ground. It ain't going to end in a fairy tale, sweetheart."

"I don't believe in fairy tales."

"You say that now but what about when the job is over?"

She chuckled as if he were being a worrywart and rose up on her knees, drawing his face to hers. "Listen, I understand. This isn't a happily-ever-after situation. For all we know, this is the end for everyone, so why not enjoy a little pleasure while we can? We aren't hurting anyone and we're consenting adults so let's stop picking at the bright spots in this moment, okay?"

Good advice. "This is why you're the smart one and I'm the muscle," he said with enough self-deprecating humor to soften the blow. She wasn't looking for a *long* time, just a *good* time. He could work with that.

Except, he already hated the idea of goodbye.

That was a problem—a big one.

He supposed he'd deal with that when it happened. What other choice did he have?

There was something different about Zak, something that felt deep and important.

The way he'd made love to her, almost savagely, had been incredible but it'd felt as if something had clicked between them, leveling up the tension in a way that confounded her.

She'd meant everything she said—forever wasn't what she expected, even if it was fun to dream—but if she was his addiction, he was equally becoming hers.

But the stakes were high and neither had time to play this game. So she'd do her best to simply enjoy the stolen moments, the epic orgasms and the way Zak made her feel with a look from those soulful eyes. She'd live in the moment because she was beginning to realize those moments might have to be sweet enough to last her a lifetime.

A man like Zak only came along once. Birds of a feather flocked together, right? If she was a spindly-legged stork, hanging around a bunch of other storks in the science pond, Zak was the eagle soaring above them, being a majestic raptor, owning the skies, swooping down to murder field mice. Eagles didn't normally hang out with storks.

And they certainly didn't set up nests together.

The imagery alone was disturbing.

Pushing away her sad thoughts, she cuddled up to her eagle while she still could. "Shouldn't you get into your own bed?" she teased, fitting perfectly in the cove of his shoulder, her hand resting on his chest. "It might be a little awkward to explain if your friends decide to check on us."

"They won't. Door locks on the inside. Besides, I think CJ already knows what's up."

"Really? Will he rat you out?" she asked, worried.

"Naw, he's a good guy. More than likely he'll bust my balls about it in some way because he thought you were cute but he'd never poach on a man's territory. Bro-code."

"Bro-code. Blech, sounds very caveman-ish."

"I didn't hear you complaining about my brutish mentality a little earlier," he reminded her with a silky laugh and he could almost feel her blushing. When she remained quiet, he chuckled, saying, "Exactly."

A beat passed before Caitlin asked, "What happens if I can't reverse engineer a cure? What if I fail?"

His hold tightened around her. "Don't think that way. You're brilliant. You'll find the cure."

"I've never done something like this. Maybe Tessara put their faith in the wrong person."

"They didn't."

"How do you know?"

"Because I do. I can feel it in my gut. You do your thing and we'll do ours."

"I wish I had your confidence. I'm worried."

"I have faith in you."

Caitlin fought the urge to cry, not because she was scared or unhappy but because his belief in her shook her to her foundation. She'd never known someone like Zak and she had a feeling she never would again. He truly listened. He didn't try to offer solutions to her problem. He recognized that she had to process her own demons, in her own way, but he was there for her.

In another life, were they more than passing acquaintances? She didn't believe in past lives as a general rule, but how else could she explain the intense connection between them when anyone from the outside looking in would rightly call bullshit?

"What was your sister like?"

"Smart, like you."

"I wish I could've met her. She seemed like a cool person."

His voice was strained as he said, "She was."

"I'm sorry she's gone."

"Me, too." Zak kissed her forehead and closed his eyes. "Time to sleep."

She didn't want to sleep just yet, even though she was exhausted. Sleeping would bring the morning and with morning, the need to pretend that whatever was happening between them wasn't and that the world wasn't hanging on the edge of a blade.

For now, she just wanted Zak to hold her and pretend that everything was fine.

Even if it was just for tonight.

Chapter 20

Rebecca and Jonathan showed up two days later, while Robert stayed behind to run his data back at the Vermont lab.

Caitlin was inordinately happy to see Rebecca, which surprised her because she hadn't realized how much she'd come to appreciate her presence.

"This place is epic," Rebecca said in awe as she stepped into BSL-4. "How is it that Tessara has this place and nobody knows about it? Tell me I'm not wrong."

"You're not wrong," Caitlin agreed with a grin. Rebecca and Jonathan could appreciate how sweet the lab was, even if they also had questions as to why no one knew about it. "Everything is brand-new and state of the art. Almost as if it was untouched until now. Maybe plans were in the works to staff it but they weren't planning to share that information until later."

"Or maybe it's their secret lab where they perform off-book experiments," Rebecca supplied with a conspiratorial eyebrow wag. "Seriously, though, wow."

"Tessara isn't doing off-book experiments," Caitlin refuted with more conviction than she felt. Since becoming the lead scientist on this project, she'd found more questions than answers when it came to her employer but her excitement overrode her caution. "I'm so happy you're here. I've been banging my head against a wall trying to factor through some equations. A second pair of eyes would be great."

"I'm all yours—after I see my sleeping quarters," Rebecca said giddily. "This feels like something out of a movie. Like a sci-fi movie, you know? Pretty exciting stuff."

"I can take you. I need a break anyway," Caitlin said. "Follow me."

The halls were secure, so she had free rein to go from the lab to her quarters without an escort but she always had to check in with Zak before leaving his sight.

He'd been talking with Scarlett when Laird brought Jonathan and Rebecca through and now nodded when she said she was taking them to their rooms.

"Each room has key-card access but they also lock from the inside," Caitlin explained, feeling like a pro at this point. "Just like a hotel."

"Fancy stuff. Imagine if our lab had sleeping quarters," Rebecca said, impressed. "Where's your room?"

"Just down the hall."

"With your hunky protector?" Rebecca guessed with a sly grin and Caitlin just smiled and moved on. Surprisingly, Rebecca didn't press for more details but Caitlin supposed that the new lab was more exciting than Zak for the moment. "This is some wild stuff. My God, I knew Tessara had deep pockets but this is incredible. An entire lab at their disposal, like an extra box of crackers at the back of the pantry, and not just any old lab but a BSL-4 lab? Good gravy, this is like Christmas."

Caitlin giggled, pleased to share with someone who actually understood how exciting it was to be in a lab setting of this caliber. "It feels like our own private lab, doesn't it?" she said.

"Yeah, it does. We can be mad scientists here," Rebecca said, taking in everything with an expression of pure awe. "Except without the mad part." A beat of silence passed between them before Rebecca turned to Caitlin and said, "I'm really glad you're safe. I've been worried."

For the first time, Caitlin saw Rebecca showing genuine emotion, not overcompensating with over-the-top, hormone-riddled, pushy banter, but real talk, and it occurred to Caitlin that maybe this was the real Rebecca and not the persona she'd previously projected. "Thank you. I was scared," Caitlin admitted. "Being shot at is no picnic. I don't recommend it."

Rebecca responded with a small laugh. "No? Surprising. They make it look like such good cardio in the movies. All that jumping and dodging."

"It's mostly a lot of dropping to the floor, glass shattering and trying not to pee your pants. At least that's how it unfolded in my experience."

"Cardio is overrated anyway," Rebecca said. "Any news on who might've taken the sample?"

"No, not exactly but they think whoever took the sample is going to release it as a way of cleansing the earth of the sinners."

"Sinners? You're telling me this is a religious thing?"

"It looks that way."

"Good grief. That's a pain in the ass to deal with."

"You're telling me. Greed is easier to understand."

Rebecca sighed. "So that explains why they're trying to wipe you out. No need for a cure if they're not planning on curing anyone."

"Exactly. But that really puts the pressure on us to find that cure. The fate of the world—all of us unrepentant sinners—rests on our shoulders."

"Ah, great," Rebecca said.

"Yeah, exactly."

"How are you holding up?"

"Um, well, okay, I guess. I don't think I've had time to freak out but I'm sure if we survive, I'll have to schedule in a nervous breakdown."

Rebecca laughed. "That's the spirit. I love how your priorities are always on point."

"I wish my parents felt that way," Caitlin retorted with a wry laugh. "They've questioned my priorities ever since I accepted a position with Tessara."

"Can you blame them? I mean, let's get real. We both know Tessara is a mixed bag but you make sacrifices if you want to be involved on the ground floor of great things. I guess what I'm saying is, I'm okay with breaking a few eggs to make an omelette."

Caitlin chuckled but was she actually saying that? Maybe that was the issue. She was still clinging to a naive understanding of science when Rebecca had embraced the good, the bad and the ugly without blinking an eye.

Maybe she needed to be more like Rebecca.

"So how's things back at the lab?" she asked.

"Oh, it's a shit-show. Stan is losing what little hair he has left over this situation. He's getting some heat from the brass about the break-in but that's why he gets paid the big bucks—to deal with the bureaucratic bullshit, right?"

"Yeah, I guess so."

Rebecca went to the bed and tested it with a few exploratory bounces. "Not bad, firm but not too firm. I think I can make this work for the time being."

"The bed is actually pretty comfortable," she said, trying not to think about how much she adored falling asleep in Zak's arms. Her life seemed surreal. She worked all day in the lab while Zak and his team ran down leads on the various religious groups that might be responsible for this looming catastrophe, and at night she and Zak attacked each other behind closed doors, then fell asleep wrapped around each other. A new day dawned and they repeated the cycle.

It seemed weird but somehow she knew, when it was all said and done, she was going to miss this.

Zak frowned at the intel Scarlett had gathered. "Are you kidding me?" Scarlett confirmed the intel with a nod and he cursed under his breath. "This shit is getting ridiculous. So when is this lunar event supposed to happen?"

"In two weeks. According to what the followers of the Faith of the Chosen believe, a major lunar event will signal the catalyst required of the faithful to cleanse the earth of the unclean. And it just so happens that for the first time in hundreds of years, there will be a super blue moon eclipse, and these idiots think that by starting some kind of worldwide event it will bring on the apocalypse."

"Kind of like pushing the start button on a really big cosmic machine primed to destroy the earth," CJ put in. "I admire their conviction if not their total craziness."

"I can't with this bullshit," Zak muttered, rubbing his eyeballs because his brain hurt. "It doesn't surprise me that there are enough idiots out there that believe this crap but it does surprise me that there are supposedly smart people with enough money to fund this stupid plan."

"Yeah, this makes the flat-earthers look like amateurs."

"At least flat-earthers aren't trying to wipe humanity off the planet," Zak said. "Right? Jesus, Mary and Joseph, this gives me a migraine."

"So here's the plan. I'm going to send Laird and CJ to snoop around the top brass of the so-called Faith of the Chosen and see what we can't shake out of them. Maybe they'll break easily and we can end this nightmare fast and under the radar."

"Something tells me that's not in the cards. If they had big enough balls to steal from Tessara, they aren't playing around. They've got a contingency plan and they've got the money to hide."

"Well, this is where we start. In the meantime, keep the doc safe and working, and we'll do the rest."

"I hate sitting here like a lame duck," Zak muttered. "I'd rather be out there doing something useful."

"The doctor seems to trust you. We need her focused. In the event that this situation goes sour, we're going to need her to come through with the cure. So whatever, you're doing…keep doing it."

Zak flushed with guilt but managed to keep his reaction on the downlow. What was he doing? Aside from *doing* the doctor? Don't get it twisted, he enjoyed every minute with Caitlin but he was starting to get twitchy. He felt useless remaining behind when the real action was out there, outside this box.

"C'mon, TL, you know I'm better on the outside. I'm starting to go stir-crazy in here."

Scarlett's expression softened with understanding. "I know. This isn't anything like our usual operation but the stakes are so much higher. We're all just trying to save our own asses in this one, right? We're talking end of the world. Not just crooked politicians and screwed-up, greedy bastards trying to get rich on the backs of innocent people. This is the realest shit we've ever been in and what we're doing matters."

Zak ducked his head, ashamed. Big-picture time. "Yeah, you're right. I'll keep doing my part. I just feel like I'm not doing enough."

"Trust me, you have the most important job."

He was overwhelmed by the urge to come clean with Scarlett about Caitlin but he knew now wasn't the time. She had enough on her plate to add his issues, too. "When are they leaving?" he asked.

"Red-eye flight tonight. The Faith of the Chosen have one of their chief officers in New York."

CJ rose, saying, "Speaking of, I better freshen up. I want to look my best when I go to meet up with one of God's warriors."

Zak couldn't help the laugh. "Don't forget to wear your pentacle necklace."

"Already part of the plan, bruh."

"You two chuckleheads are going to be the death of me," Scarlett muttered as CJ and Laird walked out of the room, trading jokes and ideas about how best to get under the Faithful's skin. Zak rose to leave, too, but she stopped him with a question. "Are you sleeping with her?"

It was a blunt question. He could be honest or he could lie. Both options were problematic.

"Your silence is my answer," Scarlett said, sharp as ever.

He supposed there was no sense in lying now. "It just sort of happened."

She leveled a wry look his way. "What are you, fifteen? Your dick does not just happen to find its way inside a woman by accident. Take responsibility, man."

He bristled slightly. "Okay, yeah, it happened and I'm not sorry. We're not sorry. I think I might love her."

The "L" word. He hadn't meant to drop that bomb. It just came out but it felt right, even if he didn't know what to do with it. Maybe he wasn't meant to do anything with it because nothing had changed but he could admit to his feelings, right? Yeah, in a different life, maybe they did the white picket fence thing, had babies, got fat together and bickered over who got ownership over the television remote—no contest, he'd win—but in this life, he was a messed-up soldier with a head full of issues and she was a superscientist who was too smart to get mixed up with someone like him, so there was no sense in touching that hot stove.

But Scarlett was still going to bust his balls about it.

"Jesus, Zak, what are you doing?" she asked, exasperated. "You know this is against the rules."

"Yeah? And so was you and Xander knocking boots when you were his superior and he was a Red Wolf team member. Rules don't always apply evenly to people like us. We break rules for a living."

She couldn't argue that point but added a good one of her own. "She's a *civilian.* She's used to living her life by a certain set of standards. You're going to break her."

"She's stronger than you give her credit for."

"Seriously, Zak, I should do the right thing and switch you out. You're compromised."

"Or maybe I'm even more dedicated. I would die before I'd let anyone hurt her."

"Solid point," she conceded with a grumble. "So what does this mean? She knows about your past? About your work? What you do for a living?"

"A little but we don't really talk about that stuff."

"So it's basically just a sexual thing?"

"No, I can't say that's true. I feel things." *Deep things.* "It's different than anything I've ever experienced. Kinda scary, actually."

"Great," she said with derision. "That's just what we need. You falling in love for the first time in your life. Look, I don't have the time to lecture you on your stupidity because whatever you're doing seems to be working. She's calm and focused when before she was like a long-tailed cat in a room filled with rockers. However, this is going to blow up and it's not going to be pretty. I can only hope we're all alive long enough to deal with the fallout."

"She knows this is a temporary situation. No one is looking to buy in. For whatever reasons, it works between us and I don't want to question it right now. Not when the stakes are so high for all of us."

Scarlett nodded, giving in with a muttered expletive. "Fine. But we keep this on the downlow. I don't need Joshua finding out about this. My ass is still sore from the bite he took out of it when he found out about me and Xander."

Joshua Handler, the owner of Red Wolf, was the man behind the team. He was former military so he knew how things worked but his record was completely redacted. Whatever he'd done for Uncle Sam had been so deeply classified no one left alive was talking about it. He had connections in all the right places, had deep enough pockets from taking the right jobs and ran a lean, mean fighting machine. He took no crap and gave none, either. He was legit scary but if he had your back, you had nothing to worry about.

"Fair enough, TL." They were a true ride-or-die team,

no matter what. He should've known Scarlett would have his back. "I'm sorry I wasn't honest right away."

She waved away his apologies. "You had your reasons. We've all had our reasons, one way or another. Just as long as it doesn't interfere with the job, understand?"

"One hundred."

"All right, get out of my face. I need to go over this tactical plan before CJ and Laird ship out."

Zak didn't question. There was a reason Scarlett was the boss. She was freakishly good at her job.

Zak hustled to his quarters, where he found Caitlin curled up in bed, notes scattered around her like fallen leaves, softly snoring.

Yeah, saying goodbye was going to be hard.

But that wasn't happening tonight and that's all he was focusing on right now. He quietly picked up her notes and placed them on her nightstand, stripped and slid in beside her. Pulling her close, he listened to her breathe before falling asleep himself.

Chapter 21

Laird and CJ touched down into New York by 3 a.m. And by 6 a.m. they were showered and ready to hit the streets for some recon before they ambushed the reported head officer of the Faithful, Carl Browne.

CJ tossed back a few almonds along with a handful of M&Ms, waiting to see who came and went out of the stately brownstone. "Man, I went into the wrong business," he said to Laird, who nodded in agreement. "Fat cats getting rich with religion when we're busting our humps for change and risking our asses for nothing but bragging rights."

"Can't even brag about it," Laird reminded him. "All that black ops and shadow ops shit is off-book."

"Yeah, that's true. Good point. Hell, if it weren't for Red Wolf, I'd probably be homeless thanks to my shitty government pension."

"Politics, man. Nothing but crooks."

"Damn straight."

CJ offered a few candies to Laird. "Hungry?"

"If I eat that my ulcer will start acting up," Laird said, shaking his head, pulling a protein bar from his jacket pocket instead. "You ought to try this sometime. Actually something good for you."

"My liver wouldn't know what to do with that," CJ said. "I survive on a steady diet of sugar, caffeine and bad decisions. It's what's kept me alive. I don't mess with what's not broken."

"Not broken yet, dude. You're a ticking time bomb," Laird warned.

"So say we all," CJ quipped with good humor, then gestured to a woman walking hurriedly up the brownstone steps, ringing in. "A little early for visitors, right?"

"Too early by my estimation. Someone seems in a hurry, too. Should we crash the party?"

"Hell, might as well. I'd hate to have gotten dressed up for nothing."

Laird grinned. "Let's do it, bruh. I'm ready to bring the fun to this doomsday shindig."

"Amen."

They exited the car, bounded across the street and up the stairs, and forced the lock. Within seconds they were inside the historic brownstone. One look around and it was easy to see plenty of money flowed through the place. "Damn, definitely got into the wrong business," CJ whispered, pulling his gun and gesturing with his head for Laird to take the flank while he came around the front.

They had the element of surprise, which worked in their favor, not to mention it was doubtful the Faithful were gun-toting lunatics, judging by the decor.

CJ followed the sound of low-key talking and found

an older woman, hair twisted in a severe bun and dressed in an equally austere dress suit, arguing with the man CJ assumed was Carl Browne.

"We're behind schedule. This is unacceptable, Carleton," she said in a clipped tone. "As the chief officer, I expect more from you. The congregation expects more. We expect results."

"Regina, everything is well in hand. Trust that everything is as it should be." Carl's voice was calm and measured in spite of Regina's obvious pique. CJ hated to break up the party but he didn't have time to listen to their rich-bitch, first-world bullshit.

"Where can I make a donation to the Church of Crazy Mofos?" CJ asked, making his way into the room, his gun drawn and pointed straight at the two. "'Cuz I'm feeling generous."

Carl blanched at the sight of the gun and Regina actually wilted a little. "Good lord, an unrepentant!"

"Yes, unrepentant and feeling pretty good about it, actually. Now have a seat, would you please. My associate and I have some questions."

Laird rounded the corner, revealing himself, and Regina sank into the nearest chair as if ready to faint. "Call the police," she told Carl in a shaking voice. "Do something."

"Carl, you best have a seat so we can get this over with. I've been up for twenty-four hours and I'm nearing my cranky point. Would you mind?" He gestured to the chair and Carl dropped into it, his gaze never leaving CJ's, and it was creepy as all get-out. "Okay, so like I was saying, if I were interested in making a donation to the Church of Crazy, I'm sorry, the Faith of the Chosen, how would I go about that?"

"You are not one of us," Regina said, her lip quivering.

"You're right about that, lady. I'm not a lunatic. My original question stands." He paused to narrow his gaze at the older woman. "Excuse my manners, and you are?"

"Regina Burke, if you must know, and you'll be hearing from my lawyers, you uncouth ruffians!"

Laird moved to idly poke through drawers, riffling through papers, chuckling at the mention of lawyers. "*Oooo*, lawyers," he mocked with hands in the air. "Please, not *lawyers*. So scary. They might throw *paper* at me. Although, kudos for the usage of the word 'ruffians.' You don't hear that very often anymore. It's definitely deserving of a comeback."

"What are you doing? This is illegal search and seizure," Carl said. "Nothing you find here is admissible in a court of law."

CJ laughed. "Did you hear that? He thinks we're cops. Sorry, nope. Not the law. We could give two shits about the law. As far as the law goes, we don't exist, so shut your piehole about 'illegal search and seizure' because it doesn't apply. Tell me about the Faith of the Chosen."

"We will tell you nothing." Regina stiffened, the picture of indignant outrage.

"How about this? I'll tell you what I know and you fill in the blanks because we're short on time. Okay? Great. Okay, so you crackpots believe that the super blue moon eclipse is supposed to kick off some cataclysmic event that's going to cleanse the earth as God's will, leaving behind the Faithful. Is that the gist of it?"

"And if it is? Religious persecution is a crime," Carl said.

"Hey, I could give two shits about what you believe as long as it doesn't affect me. The minute it starts affecting me is the minute I care about your silly little religion. Okay, just exactly how are you planning to kick off this cataclysmic event?"

"That's privileged information," Carl said.

"Actually, if it involves releasing a deadly bio-agent into the general population of a crowded city, causing massive death and hysteria, that's no longer protected under the right to worship—that's called domestic terrorism, asshole."

"What are you talking about?" Carl said, looking baffled. "Who's killing who?"

"Nice try. I like the wide-eyed befuddlement, gives it a real authentic touch," Laird said, approving. "But we have information leading back to your organization that paints a real pretty picture of doomsday proportions. Start talking before I start cracking your soft kneecaps like hard-boiled eggs."

CJ whistled low. "Yeah, and that's just nasty stuff. I don't know if you've ever seen anything like that, but it will turn your stomach, especially this early in the morning."

"Carleton," Regina whimpered, her bun quivering. "What are they talking about?"

"Okay, let's start from the beginning since you're having a hard time remembering the facts. How are the Faithful planning on bringing about this cataclysmic chain of events during the super blue moon eclipse?" CJ asked with feigned patience. He'd really rather just start cracking kneecaps but Scarlett had told him to try to go the non-messy route first. Less paperwork. So he was trying his best to do as she'd asked.

But it was a pain in the ass.

And boring, too.

"Look, you're barking up the wrong tree. I don't know where you got your information from but it's bad. We're a peaceful organization. We help the homeless, for crying out loud!"

"Could be a front," CJ said, shrugging. "Not convinced."

"We organize a charity ball each February to help the less fortunate. W-we donated to a literacy campaign!"

"Tell me how the Faithful are going to kick off the big event during the super blue moon eclipse," CJ asked again in a bored tone. "I won't ask again. My friend is ready to start squishing kneecaps. I can promise you that if you keep testing my patience."

"I swear to you I don't know what you're talking about. We're a peaceful organization that just wants humanity to rise above the ugliness in the world to become better versions of themselves!"

"Then what were you talking about earlier when we came in?" CJ asked.

Regina answered, her lip trembling. "For the charity ball! We're supposed to have the party favors in by now but the shipment is late and the event committee wanted answers! That's all, I swear it."

Laird scratched his head. "Boy, lady, you came in pretty hot on those party favors. You sure that was all?"

Regina's cheeks heated. "I'm positive."

Laird and CJ exchanged looks. Was it possible they'd received bad intel? Hell, if so, this was embarrassing. But CJ wasn't ready to give up just yet. "Mind if I look around a bit?" he asked, even though he wasn't actually asking. He poked around drawers and cabinets and found nothing. He had a sinking feeling that someone had misdirected them.

Ugh. The paperwork on this one was going to be epic.

He holstered his gun with a smile. "False alarm. You can go about your weird church-y business. God bless

America." He gestured to Laird and they stalked past the horrified couple. Before they let themselves out, he said, "You didn't see us, we weren't here. Uh, have a nice day."

They bounded down the stairs and sprinted to their car. "How long before they call the cops?" Laird asked, sliding into the passenger seat.

"Shit, the old lady's probably got the cops on speed dial. Let's beat it out of here. I don't want to explain myself to a bunch of donut-munchers."

"Hey, my dad was a cop," Laird growled.

"Did he like donuts?" CJ asked, peeling out.

"Yeah."

"I rest my case."

And they left the Faith of the Chosen behind—as well as their only real lead.

Scarlett rubbed at her temples. "Shit," she muttered. Zak had a feeling their intel on the Faithful was bad.

"What happened?" he asked.

"The Faith of the Chosen are just a bunch of do-gooders with a goofy name for their cult. They're basically harmless but I think CJ might've made the two he interrogated crap themselves."

Zak chuckled. "Well, you did send a bulldog to do precision work," he reminded her.

"Yeah, well, I won't do that again. Anyway, we're back to square one but I have Xander running some names through the FBI database to see if anything pings."

"You brought Xander in? I thought you didn't want to do that."

"Yeah, well, we're out of options. Don't have the luxury of picking and choosing." She watched Zak grab a bottled water from the small fridge and crack it open. "You okay?"

"Something about this situation feels off. I can't put my finger on it. Bad intel about the Faithful, the radio silence on the dark web… It all feels like the calm before the storm."

"Like the shoe's about to drop," she said, nodding with grim agreement. "God, I hope we're wrong."

"Yeah, me, too."

She asked, "The doc any closer to the cure?" Zak shook his head. Scarlett sighed and rose on legs stiff from sitting too long. "Maybe things will look better in the morning."

But Zak knew where Scarlett's head was at and it wasn't just on the case—it was personal. He took a chance and broached a touchy subject. "Xander is smart. Nothing is going to happen to him," he assured her, knowing Scarlett was remembering the death of her FBI friend Conrad Griggs, who'd died trying to help clear Xander's name.

"Conrad was smart, too. One of the best," Scarlett reminded him. "And he got killed. I live with that guilt every day. Honestly, Zak, I couldn't function if something happened to Xander and it was my fault."

"We had to bring the FBI in at some point anyway," he told her. "The fact of the matter is, we work dangerous jobs. The people we love understand this. Xander understands this better than most."

Better than Caitlin ever could. How would she handle the stress of being attached to him, knowing that at any given moment he could eat a bullet on a mission? Her work was too important to waste on worrying about him. Zak forced a smile for Scarlett's benefit. "You're the lucky ones. You and Xander get it. Fighting about your job is never something that will become an issue."

She nodded, ceding his point. "I'm just on edge. Losing our first real lead has me second-guessing everything."

He got that. "We're all on edge," he agreed. "Something will come up. It always does."

"But will it come up in time?"

"We have to hope."

Scarlett blew out a short breath, her expression all but saying what they were both secretly afraid of—what if they were all out of hope?

Chapter 22

Caitlin awoke to Zak shaking her with an urgency she'd never seen, and her insides immediately cramped with fear. Oh, God, something had happened; she could feel it. "What is it?" she asked, holding her breath.

"The CDC reported an outbreak of something that sounds a lot like our bioweapon in New York at a local hospital."

"Oh, my God." Caitlin kicked the covers free and stumbled to struggle into her pants. "We have to get to New York. If it's the same viral agent, I can get a test sample from one of the victims and compare against the profile of what we had on our sample. This could be our big break!"

"Or this could be the beginning of the end," he countered, his mouth set in a dark line. "I'm not sure I want you anywhere near the contagion."

"Zak, this is what we've been waiting for. I can't stay

behind. You know that." Fear mixed with excitement as she shoved her arms through her shirt and pulled it over her head. "Seriously, nothing could keep me from going."

"I knew you were going to say that," he said, giving up. "We've got transport ready in an hour. The CDC has been apprised of the situation. They'll meet us at the hospital."

"Good. I need Rebecca, too. Also, we're going to need to bring some of the BSL-4 safety protocols for transport. Thankfully, this place is equipped with everything under the sun that we'll need. I'll go pack."

She left Zak behind, practically sprinting to the lab as Rebecca joined her, rubbing the sleep from her eyes. "You think this is the real deal?" she asked, fear in her voice. "I mean, our sample had a one hundred percent mortality rate."

"Are you scared?"

"Hell, yes, I'm scared and if you had the brains God gave a goose you'd be scared, too."

"Do you want to stay behind? I can take Jonathan if you prefer," Caitlin said, trying to be accommodating.

"That's not what I'm saying. I'm just saying… Hell, I'm just scared, that's all. But I'm excited, too. Is that weird?"

Caitlin broke into a nervous grin. "That's exactly how I feel, too. This is our chance to get the sample we need. There's a chance it's mutated but we can isolate the cellular structure and get to the original genome, and we can use it to reverse engineer the cure as we'd been trying to do before the sample was stolen."

"But the mutation could render the sample useless," Rebecca said, worried. "And we could become exposed for nothing."

"We're going to take every precaution necessary," she

assured Rebecca. "But we can't miss out on this chance. Besides, the CDC doesn't know what they're dealing with. They need our help."

"I guess we could be heroes if this pans out right," Rebecca said.

"Yeah, I guess that's one way to look at it," Caitlin said, chuckling wryly. "Okay, let's get packed up."

They loaded up the car with the supplies they'd need and prepared for the transport to New York by private plane.

Caitlin had never flown by private charter before but her anxiety didn't seem to care if it was flying in luxury or coach.

"You okay? You just went all pale," Zak said as they climbed the short staircase into the plane.

"I'm fine. I just don't like flying."

But Rebecca had no problems and exclaimed, "Holy moly, this is amazing! Red Wolf has its own plane? Talk about riding in style. Wow. This is nice. A girl could get used to this. You know what they say, once you fly first class, it's impossible to drop back down to economy."

Caitlin dropped into her seat and wiped at the sweat beading her brow, ignoring Rebecca as she oohed and aahed over the plane's amenities. Zak came over to hold her hand. "Do you need anything?" he asked quietly.

This was the scenario she'd been hoping to avoid but she risked a small smile for his concern. "I usually take a Xanax before a flight and fall asleep but I need my wits about me when we land, so I'll just have to tough it out."

"There's nothing to be ashamed of. A lot of people don't like flying."

"I know, but it's a real bummer when it happens to be you."

He chuckled. "True. How about this? I can't get you

a Xanax but I can fix you a whiskey neat. That'll settle your nerves a little bit."

She nodded with gratitude. "That would be awesome, thank you."

Rebecca overheard and said, "Make that two, kind sir!"

"Two whiskeys, coming up."

Scarlett took her seat while Zak returned with two whiskeys and handed them to Caitlin and Rebecca.

Caitlin murmured her thanks and quickly downed her glass, needing that liquid courage as the plane began to taxi.

"Are Laird and CJ going to meet us there?" she asked, trying to occupy her brain with anything other than the knowledge that the plane was taking flight.

"Yes. How are you feeling?" he asked.

"Better," she answered, which wasn't entirely a lie, but it wasn't truthful, either. Her hands were still shaking and she wanted to puke but she didn't feel the need to cry. She could use another whiskey but she'd try to close her eyes and make it work.

"I love to fly," Rebecca prattled on, oblivious to anyone but herself. "And this is definitely way better than flying coach like I normally do. Once I took an eight-hour flight to the Bahamas and spent the entire flight with a kid kicking the back of my seat. It was horrible. By the end of the flight I was pretty sure I never wanted to have kids."

Caitlin smiled wanly, which was the equivalent of saying, "Cool story, bro," but Rebecca didn't seem to mind. She was just tickled to be traveling in such style.

Thankfully, the flight was short enough and the whiskey did help dull the edge. By the time they landed at JFK in New York, her anxiety had lessened, replaced by the tremulous nerves of coming face-to-face with quite possibly the most dangerous bioweapon of today's age.

It could kill her.

It could kill them all.

Her hands were shaking like leaves in a stiff wind.

"Are you sure you're okay?" Zak asked, grasping her hand softly. "You're shaking pretty hard."

"I'm scared shitless but I'm not running away. No one can do this but me and my team."

Zak's mouth firmed with displeasure but he didn't argue. He simply shouldered the huge bag she required and they exited the plane.

It was go time.

Zak didn't like this one bit. It was one thing for him to rush headlong into the lion's mouth but entirely another for the woman he cared about to do the same.

But there was no telling her to stay at the lab. Hell, he could see the fear in her eyes when she stepped on board the plane and yet her feet had never faltered. He respected her guts, her grit, but goddamn, it scared the shit out of him.

A sleek all-black Tahoe awaited them at the airfield, taking them straight to the hospital where the patients were quarantined.

They came in through a service entrance and were greeted by some very pissed-off CDC officers.

Scarlett took point as she flashed her Red Wolf credentials.

"I don't care who you are, you're not authorized for this level of clearance," Roger Peterson, the lead CDC officer, barked. "I've done some research. Red Wolf is nothing but a bunch of mercenary thugs willing to do the dirty work for anyone willing to pay the price. What makes you think you're qualified to step into this investigation?"

"Because we've been hired by Tessara to protect the one woman who's smart enough to save all our asses from what you've got percolating in your quarantine right now," Scarlett answered, meeting the man's gaze without flinching. "We can sit here and measure our dicks all you want but I can guarantee you, mine is bigger, and how embarrassing would that be? Or we can work together and possibly prevent an epidemic that has a one hundred percent mortality rate. Factor that into how many people have potentially been exposed and you've got an inkling of the seriousness of what we're dealing with."

"Red Wolf also has the full cooperation of the FBI," a voice said from behind them. Zak turned to see Xander striding in, his dark suit and equally dark trench coat giving him a superhero look. *Damn, homeboy makes that outfit look good.* He'd have to bust his balls about it later. For now, Zak was happy to see him. Scarlett, on the other hand, didn't look so pleased.

Xander flashed his own credentials and Roger looked like he'd just been forced to choke down a shit sandwich. "What we want to remember is that we're all on the same side," Xander said. "We've got a potentially world-threatening event on our hands, so let's keep our egos in check."

Scarlett cast Xander a look that promised a conversation later but otherwise simply nodded in greeting and returned to Roger. "I understand you have questions, but the longer we wait around, the less likely Dr. Willows will be successful in finding the cure we all need to prevent a catastrophe."

Roger looked to Caitlin, his gaze shrewd. "This the doc?"

Caitlin stepped forward. “I am.” She showed him her Tessara credentials. “Please, Mr. Peterson, time is our enemy. The virus has a forty-eight-hour life span. It is quick and ruthless.”

Roger couldn’t argue that point. From what they knew, they’d already lost a few patients. By the time they’d realized they were dealing with something virulent, it was impossible to know how far the contagion had spread, which was exactly how whoever was orchestrating this nightmare wanted it to work.

“Follow me,” he said gruffly, turning on his heel and leading them down the halls to the cordoned-off area. He stopped them short of the plastic sheeting blocking off the doorway. “From this point forward, anyone going in must wear full-body hazmat suits. We have the quarantined rooms set up with negative pressure and their own lab capabilities but this is unlike anything we’ve ever seen. We’re taking every precaution possible.”

“That’s wise,” Caitlin said. “This virus is within the same class as Ebola but it is not Ebola. It is stronger, faster and more deadly. It also adapts to its environment with frightening efficiency. This virus was created in a lab, not by Mother Nature, and as such doesn’t seem to follow the rules.”

“Who in the hell would create such a terrible thing?” Roger asked.

“That’s a question for another day,” Caitlin answered, sharing a look with Zak. The details of where the virus came from and how Tessara came to acquire it were still highly hush-hush. Zak was proud of Caitlin for knowing what to share and what to keep quiet about.

He watched as Caitlin and Rebecca climbed into the sterile, white hazmat jumpsuits and zipped up, securing all entry points with duct tape so that nothing could get in. His heart rate was like a rabbit on meth. He didn't want her going in there.

Scarlett caught his anxiety and gave him a minute shake of her head. He wasn't going to stop Caitlin but it didn't mean he had to like it.

He couldn't even kiss her before she went into the hot zone. Couldn't hold her hand, couldn't pull her in tight in case it was the last time they were able to touch without neoprene between them.

"Be safe in there" was all he could say but she got it.

The wordless exchange between them was enough.

After one final look, Caitlin and Rebecca disappeared behind the door where hell awaited them.

And Zak was forced to wait on the other side.

Chapter 23

Caitlin and Rebecca, armed with their sample collection kits, walked into the patient's room, careful to walk slowly and cautiously. The room wasn't built without sharp edges, so anything that could tear the suit presented a potential hazard.

The patient, a young woman, didn't look good.

Blood wept from her eyes and nose as she stared, her gaze glazed from the massive doses of morphine given to keep the pain at bay as her insides liquefied. Her appearance gave Caitlin the creeps. This was horrific. How could anyone willfully set out to do this to another human being?

"I'm so sorry," she whispered, swallowing the lump in her throat. Her hands shook as she reached into her kit for a needle. Rebecca stopped her with a worried expression. "I'm okay," she assured her but she wasn't okay. Not by a long shot. It was one thing to read about the effects of a virus and even to see gruesome photos, but to be faced with the patient, to see their suffering first-hand, it was entirely different.

She sniffed back tears and refocused as she cleared her throat. To the patient, she said, "I'm going to draw some blood through your IV. You shouldn't feel anything." She might as well have been talking to a brick wall. The woman was practically in a medically induced coma but Caitlin felt obligated to say something. This wasn't a lab rat—she was a person. Prior to this moment, she'd been someone's daughter, possibly a sister or, God forbid, a mother.

She withdrew enough blood to test, labeled it and placed it in the containment box. She nodded to Rebecca, and they moved to the next patient. In all, they collected blood samples from eight infected patients.

By the time they left the quarantined area, Caitlin's previous scientific excitement was tempered by the reality of the situation. The virus in action was nothing that mere notes and slideshows could convey. Human suffering was visceral and it grabbed your soul in a way that stole your breath—that part was hard to accurately report with charts and graphs.

After a thorough decontamination bath, Caitlin exited the quarantine, shaken and ready to have a mental breakdown, but somehow she held it together long enough to make it to the bathroom.

Then, she broke down and sobbed.

That was how Rebecca found her—curled on the bathroom floor, knees hugged to her chest, crying into her folded arms.

Rebecca slid down beside her with a sigh. "Zak sent me in to find you. He was worried."

Caitlin could only nod.

"Man, that was intense," Rebecca said. "Who knew saving the world was so gross."

Caitlin agreed, crying a little. "So, so gross," she said with a hiccup, recognizing that Rebecca was using humor to defuse the awful situation. "That woman is dying. All of these people are dying. Some lunatic released a virus that could kill us all. Every single one of us could die exactly like they are right now if we don't figure out how to stop it. I don't know if we can. I'm freaking out right now." She sniffed back a wash of tears to peer at Rebecca. "Why aren't you?"

"Maybe I am and I deal with it differently," Rebecca said, rubbing her leg. "People deal with tragedy in different ways. Doesn't make it wrong."

Now she felt even worse. "I'm sorry, Rebecca," Caitlin apologized, wiping at her eyes. "I'm a mess. I shouldn't have said that. I'm just overwhelmed right now."

"Yeah, I get that. But to play devil's advocate for a minute…there's a grotesque beauty about the way the virus takes care of business. Even Ebola can take up to two weeks to get the job done. This virus is an efficient killing machine. Gotta respect the biology, right?"

"Of course. I've said that from the beginning. On paper, it's stunning. I just wasn't prepared to see what that efficiency would mean to a real human body. Maybe I'm not as analytical as I thought," Caitlin said, wiping at her eyes.

"Some might consider that a good thing," Rebecca teased.

Caitlin shared a watery chuckle, blowing out a long breath, finally catching hold of her runaway emotions. She was better than this. She hadn't risen to the top of her field by running scared every time a challenge bested her. "Sorry, I lost it. That was embarrassing," she said to Rebecca, climbing to her feet and helping Rebecca up. "Enough crying, time to get back to work. Do me a favor and promise me we'll never mention this again?"

"Oh, hell, no, this is leverage," Rebecca said with good humor.

Caitlin laughed. She wasn't sure but this was beginning to feel like a real friendship. "Fine. But I'll deny it."

"I would expect nothing less."

Caitlin grinned. "Just as long as we understand each other."

Rebecca gave her a sly look to ask, "Hey, since we're sharing and being all honest…tell me, are you sleeping with your bodyguard?"

Caitlin, hand on the bathroom door, returned the sly grin and answered, "Every chance I can get."

Rebecca's crow of laughter was the final boost her spirit needed to kick this virus's ass.

While Caitlin was doing science stuff—he wasn't going to pretend to understand what was happening in that head of hers—he, Scarlett and Xander were out doing what they did best.

Running down leads.

"Where was Patient Zero discovered?" Scarlett asked Roger, as they convened in a vacant conference room at the hospital.

Roger consulted his notes. "Patient Zero, Londa Jackson, forty-three, was brought into Lenox Hill at 0405, five days ago. She died within two days of being hospitalized."

"Who brought her in?"

"Unknown." Roger's irritation didn't stop Scarlett.

"Why not?" Scarlett pressed. "Isn't it CDC protocol to follow the chain of contagion?"

"The CDC wasn't contacted until after the body had been cremated. There was, admittedly, a breakdown in protocol."

"We need to find out who brought in Patient Zero. Londa Jackson could be our connection to who is behind all of this," Scarlett said.

"Or," Roger injected sternly, "she could simply be a victim. It wouldn't take much to infect someone with this virus undetected."

"Well, I guess there's one way to find out," Zak said, rising. "Let's find out where Ms. Jackson called home."

"Calm down, son, this isn't our first rodeo," Roger groused. "We already did the follow-up. Londa Jackson lived alone with a cat. She had no known relatives and lived off disability. For all intents and purposes, she was a recluse, which is a good thing because it limits how many people she was exposed to."

"Then how did she infect seven more people?" Zak asked.

"With an infectious agent like this virus, it can happen with a simple touch or shared air." Roger pulled another sheet of paper. "From what we've figured out, Londa came into contact with patient number 2 when she ordered takeout Chinese from Bamboo Sunrise. He passed it on to his two-year-old-daughter, LeeLee Sing, and so on."

Zak felt sick. "They're all dead?"

"Half of the infected are dead, but patient number 5, Simone Heland, is alive but not looking good. Hell, none are looking good. We can't seem to stop this thing, no matter what we throw at it," Roger said. "I want to know how a private company could, in good conscience, have something like this in their possession when the goddamn CDC doesn't even have knowledge of it. This is what happens when money overrides good sense." Roger shot up abruptly, kicking his chair out from under him, growling, "I need some air."

Zak waited for Roger to clear the room before he admitted, "I hate to say it but he's right. Tessara was playing with fire."

"It wasn't just Tessara. You know there are other factors at play here," Scarlett reminded him quietly. "The irony is not lost on me that the US government stole the sample from North Korea, who'd been hoping to use it as a weapon against the US, and then it was stolen by a domestic terrorist to use against its own people. In a sense, they're doing North Korea's dirty work for them."

"Damn politics. No one wins," Zak muttered. "I'm sick of fighting the wars of old men who hide behind their ivory towers."

Xander sighed, knocking his knuckles lightly on the mahogany. "Be that as it may, it doesn't change the fact that we've got a real situation facing us right now. We don't know who did this and we don't know how to stop it."

"Thanks, Captain Obvious," Scarlett muttered, turning to face Xander. "And about that—what the hell are you doing here? I never asked you to ride up to play the hero."

"Stow your pride, Scarlett," Xander said, cutting to the chase. "We don't have time to pussyfoot around your issues on this one. Look, you do need my help and I wasn't about to let you face this alone. This case affects everyone, not just Red Wolf."

She couldn't argue. God, Xander was probably the only person on the planet that could handle Scarlett so masterfully. Their sex was probably epic…and probably left bruises.

"Fine," Scarlett bit out. "But don't think for a second that when this is all over I'm not going to ream your ass over this."

"I look forward to it, baby."

Zak grimaced. "I think I need to wash my ears out."

Scarlett ignored him and moved on. "I want to know everything about this Londa Jackson. I want to know why the body was cremated. Find the person who signed off on that order. That body was evidence."

Zak nodded. "I'll take that."

"Good." Scarlett rose, along with Xander. "I'll follow up with the CDC and find out what else they've uncovered about Londa Jackson and her day-to-day. The answers are there, we just have to find them. I don't have to remind everyone the clock is ticking." She paused to add, "Oh, and make sure to wash your hands. You never know where that virus could be lurking."

Zak made a face. "That's a sobering thought."

"Right?"

"Just one more thing to add to my nightmares," Zak said. "Ah, what the hell, I was feeling too emotionally well these days anyway."

They broke off into separate directions and Zak detoured to Caitlin first. He had to see her, hold her, make sure she was okay.

This shit had a way of making everything else seem small.

He couldn't lose her. He'd lost Zoey—he couldn't lose Caitlin.

Chapter 24

Caitlin saw Zak from across the containment room and motioned for him to wait while she decontaminated. While impatience thrummed in her veins, she took the time to go through each protocol with due diligence until she could safely exit and go straight into his arms with a grateful sigh.

She needed to feel his lips on hers as much as he needed to feel hers. Maybe it was because they were surrounded by death, and the threat of dying was so very real that they needed that primal sense of life to remind them what they were fighting for. Or maybe they were just scared and touching reminded them that they were still alive.

They hadn't seen each other since earlier that morning when she and Rebecca had gone to the lab to process the blood samples, and it felt like an eternity.

"Are you okay?" he asked, a sense of urgency in his touch.

She nodded, so happy to see him again. "I'm fine."

His expression was tense as he admitted, "I hated watching you walk into that hot zone. It was like watching you walk into the mouth of hell and not being able to do anything about it. I'm not trying to be dramatic but that's exactly what it felt like."

Caitlin shared, "I lost it when we came out of the contaminated zone. Zak, you have no idea the horror of this virus. It's one thing to see it in photos but another reality entirely to see it in action. As we expected, the virus has mutated. We're still isolating the genome. It's a slow process and the victims don't have much time. This is the dangerous thing about this virus. It replicates so fast and it kills so swiftly that it doesn't give us much of a window. How about you? Have you found any leads?"

"We're following up on Patient Zero, Londa Jackson. Scarlett seems to think everything starts and ends with her. She was a recluse but somehow she was infected and she spread it to seven more people."

Caitlin nodded. "This virus is similar to Ebola in that it can be airborne, so it is very easy to spread."

A storm passed across his features and she sensed the tension gathering. Not that she blamed him—the situation wasn't ideal. "I don't like you being that close to the infected patients."

She stiffened in confusion. "You know that can't be helped," she said. "I have to collect the samples."

"Send someone else."

"You're being irrational. It's my project," she returned, frowning. "I can't do that. What's wrong?"

Zak shoved his hand through his hair, agitated. "This shit is getting real and I don't like you being right in the thick of it. Watching you walk through those doors… I can't explain how it feels. I hate it. Scares me. I'm not used to worrying about someone else like that. I want to wrap you in Bubble Wrap and I can't do that. The idea that I can't protect you is messing with me in ways that I can't explain."

Under different circumstances, his admission might've been sweet. She might've been able to overlook the vague sexist overtones but she was exhausted, her nerves were strung taut and her patience was thin. "There are bigger issues at stake than your feelings," she reminded him, struggling to hold on to those wildly happy feelings of earlier. However, she tried to remember that they were both operating on low reserves and adjusted her tone. "I don't want to fight, Zak."

"I can't let anything happen to you, Caitlin," he said, his voice dipping low. "I don't know when it happened but I have feelings for you, all right? I just can't deal with the idea of you getting hurt and do what I need to do to protect everyone else."

Caitlin's breath caught in her chest. Why did the most wonderful thing in the world have to hurt at the same time? And why was he doing this now? "You're being very selfish," she said, a scowl building beneath the hurt frown. "I can't believe you would spend the only free moments we have together to pick a fight over my career choice. For crying out loud, don't you think I get enough of that from my parents? I don't need it from you, too."

"I'm not picking a fight, I'm stating facts. You said you wanted me to be straight with you. Well, here it is—I'm scared and I don't like it."

"This is my job."

"Well, then, I don't like your job."

She gasped, blinking against his shocking statement before shooting back. "Maybe I don't like your job, either."

Zak muttered an expletive under his breath and stepped away, rubbing his jaw as if trying to stop himself from saying anything else, but frankly, Caitlin was already stung by his admission.

"Caitlin..."

What had she been thinking? That they were going to ride off into the sunset together? That after she solved this crisis they were going to go get married, have kids and go on exotic vacations together? Good grief. Get real.

Oh, the truth was that she'd lied to Zak when she'd said she didn't believe in fairy tales, because she'd been penning her own little masterpiece since falling for her ten-foot-tall bodyguard.

Somehow she'd glossed over the fact that they were wildly different in temperament, upbringing and background, but their happily-ever-after was going to happen, right?

Caitlin wiped at her eyes, angry at herself for being so embarrassingly stupid.

"Actually, I have to get back to the lab," she said, needing to get away from Zak before she broke down and sobbed. Ignoring his attempt to stop her, she pushed past him and went through the double doors, leaving him behind.

Only when she was safely back in the lab, within the privacy of the decontamination bathroom, did she allow the tears to fall.

The CDC had already cleared Londa Jackson's residence but it was still cordoned off with caution tape. Zak, Scarlett and Xander made their way into the small apartment, careful not to disturb anything as they took mental note of everything.

"Are you seeing what I'm seeing?" Zak asked, panning the apartment with a slow 360-degree perusal. Scarlett and Xander nodded as he answered his own question.

"No personal effects. No pictures, nothing of sentiment. The CDC said she was a recluse with no family, living on disability, but it doesn't even look as if she lived here. I've seen people staying in a hotel with more personal items."

Xander cautiously agreed but wanted to look around some more. "I'm going to check out the bedroom. Maybe she was just a fan of Spartan living. Not everyone is into knickknacks."

Zak went to the kitchen, put on gloves and then opened the fridge. Empty. He went to the cupboards. Also empty. He was starting to get a weird feeling. "Didn't the CDC say she had a cat living here with her?" he recalled. Scarlett nodded. "Do you see evidence of a cat anywhere?"

Scarlett searched high and low. "No, I don't. I don't smell a cat, either."

Xander exited the bedroom. "Clean as a whistle in here, too."

Zak frowned, meeting Scarlett's gaze. "I don't think she lived here."

"Something feels wrong," Scarlett agreed, looking to Xander. "Can you do a search on Londa Jackson? See what pops up on the FBI database?"

"Yeah, give me a few minutes." He grabbed his phone and made a call. Within minutes the details were sent to his email. He shook his head and said, "Well, the plot thickens. Londa Jackson doesn't exist. At least the Londa Jackson who died a few days ago."

"What do you mean?"

"The real Londa Jackson died in 1972, car accident. Whoever was cremated at Lenox Hill was not her."

"Well, that explains why someone was in a rush to make sure she was cremated."

"Yeah," Zak said, adding dryly. "A fake doctor by the name of Dr. William Travesky. No one thought to question the order, seeing as everyone had been so freaked out by the circumstance of Jane Doe's death. It'd been orchestrated pretty damn well, if you ask me."

"I hear ya," Xander agreed. "No one was going to think twice about cremating a body that was leaking hazardous, contagious fluids. Hell, they probably tripped over themselves to get her into the crematorium."

"So we're back to who the hell is our Jane Doe and why did the CDC sign off on their investigation here when it clearly was shady as shit?" Zak said.

"I guess that's a question for the CDC," Xander said.

"Damn right it is," Scarlett growled. "Take pictures of everything here. Mr. Peterson has some explaining to do."

Once back at the hospital, they found Roger Peterson and corralled him in the conference room.

"Did anyone from the CDC actually go into Londa Jackson's apartment or did they just cordon it off?" Xander asked.

"What are you talking about?" he asked. "Of course we went into her apartment. We did a standard sweep to determine if there was a threat and then we cordoned off the apartment."

"But did you see the inside of the apartment? Did you see a cat?"

Peterson did a double take as if they were nuts. "A cat? What the hell are you going on about? Don't you think we have bigger problems than a goddamn cat?"

"There was no cat," Scarlett said, making her point. "There was no Londa Jackson. Whoever died in that hospital bed was not the real Londa Jackson and that apartment was just a front. Our Patient Zero is part of this epidemic in more ways than accidental."

Xander leaned in. "Now the question we need to ask is this—are you a bigger part of this epidemic or are you just as duped as the rest of us? Think long and hard. We're not afraid of taking down big fish."

No doubt their reputation had preceded them. Before Xander had made the transition to the FBI, he'd been part of a huge criminal takedown that'd been responsible for outing a corruption ring at the highest government order at Capitol Hill. It'd been a big splash, with lots of coverage on the CNN and MSNBC. Even *The Onion* had done a parody, but suffice it to say Red Wolf had certainly made a name for itself as having balls as big as, well, you know.

"Hold on, slow down. If you think I had anything to do with this you're barking up the wrong tree. You're crazy if you think I'd release something as horrific as this virus on the general population. That's madness!"

"That's what I say but people do crazy things for less than compelling reasons," Zak said, not convinced. "Convince us or we're slapping you in handcuffs and taking you in for questioning."

Peterson turned red in the face as his jowls shook. "Look here, okay, maybe we didn't search the apartment as thoroughly as we should've. But we had more patients coming in and we didn't know what we were dealing with yet. I had them seal off the apartment and we were going to come back to it but we hadn't had a chance to yet. For God's sake, you've seen what we're up against. Are you really going to bust my balls because of a damn cat?"

"Did you not hear what I said? It's not about a cat. There was never a cat. There was never a Londa Jackson. We've still got a situation where a fake doctor signed off on a cremation order for Patient Zero, whom we couldn't identify, and we have you, taking shortcuts when people's lives are at stake."

"I swear to you, it wasn't that I was trying to take a shortcut. We are short-staffed and I made a judgment call.

I wasn't at the apartment myself. I went off the word of an employee."

"Which employee?"

"I…uh, I don't know. I'd have to check my notes."

"Go ahead, we'll wait." Scarlett leaned back, tapping the table with her nail. "My guess is that this little show was a test run. They wanted to see how it would work and they just got a report card with flying colors. So when they decide to put the full run into play there's nothing we're going to be able to do to stop it. So, please, Mr. Peterson, if you don't want to go down in history as one of the lazy jackasses who helped facilitate the end of humanity, please stop being part of the problem."

Peterson fumbled with his reading glasses and grabbed his papers, reading through to find what he was looking for. He scanned the reports until he found a name. "CDC official, R. Burke." Then, he double-checked the report and repeated the name to himself. "R. Burke, wait a minute—" he searched a few more papers "—I don't have an R. Burke on my team." He swore under his breath as his florid face paled. "I can't believe this is happening."

"You and me both," Zak muttered. To Scarlett, he said, "Didn't CJ and Laird say that the religious nut old lady in the brownstone was named Burke?"

Scarlett nodded. "Get CJ on the phone. I need an ID. I want to know what that old lady looked like. I think we've just found our first real connection and it leads us right back to the Faith of the Chosen."

Zak punched up CJ and texted him the intel. Within moments, CJ was on the phone with Scarlett, and in another five minutes had sketched a likeness of the woman. "The man probably missed his calling as a world-renowned artist," Scarlett murmured as the sketch came through.

"Yeah, lucky for us he likes to blow shit up more than

he likes to paint pretty pictures for a lot of money," Zak quipped and Xander smothered a laugh.

Peterson looked horrified by their humor. "This isn't funny. Someone infiltrated the CDC and passed off as one of my team. I don't find that funny at all."

"If we didn't laugh about half the shit that came our way we'd cry ourselves to sleep most nights," Zak retorted and that was the damn truth. Just another point in Caitlin's favor that she got it and didn't judge him for it. To Xander he said, "Think you can get your FBI buddies to put out a BOLO for Regina Burke?"

"Yeah, I think I can make that happen," he said.

"Great." Zak rose and said, "Send CJ and Laird to go pick up that Carl Browne for a few more questions. I need to make sure Caitlin is okay. I don't feel comfortable leaving her alone with a bunch of fake doctors and shit running around the hospital."

"Good point," Scarlett said. To Peterson, she said, "You, don't go far. We need to make sure Burke was your only leak. You need to do a check of your internals. We can't take the risk that more than one area was compromised of the CDC."

Peterson nodded, visibly shaken. Not only was his head on the chopping block for screwing up so royally but his screwup might've just cost the world more than they could pay.

Chapter 25

Caitlin yawned and stretched, her back popping in a few spots as she rolled her neck after being bent in one position for too long. Rebecca had long since left to catch a few winks but Caitlin couldn't sleep knowing the clock was ticking.

Everyone was working around the clock, no exceptions. She tried not to think about Zak. She didn't have the luxury of breaking down. Compartmentalizing had always been her strength and she was using every bit of talent she had in that department to keep her feelings boxed away.

The only saving grace—they might've found the chink in the virus's armor. She'd just discovered that if a serum was introduced to the infected cells during a certain window, eradicating them before they could infect the healthy cells, it rendered the virus impotent. But the window was incredibly small due to the aggressive nature of the virus itself.

If she could find a way to extend that window, she could effectively introduce the serum that would save lives.

In particular the lives hanging in the balance right now.

A family was hanging on for dear life.

Wes, Ellis and little Georgia. Georgia was only three. Statistically, she had the least chance of making it because her little body couldn't fight the virus like an adult but she was holding on like a champ. Still, it was just a matter of time.

Until this moment. Now, maybe she had a chance.

She blearily smiled at the empty lab, having to settle for celebrating silently. It was the first breakthrough she'd had since starting this journey and she was half-delirious.

She still needed to run some tests to double-check her findings but her preliminary tests were good and that was worth crowing about—especially when the stakes were so high.

Thirty minutes later, she was fresh out of the decontaminate bath and out of the lab when a new woman greeted her with a smile. "You must be the incredible Dr. Willows everyone has been talking about," she gushed, extending her hand.

Given the fact that Caitlin had just exited a level 4 hazmat room, she refrained from shaking her hand with an apology. "I'd rather not, if you don't mind," she said. "It's for both of our protection right now. The least amount of contact, the better."

"Of course," the woman agreed with an embarrassed expression. "How silly of me. I should know better. I'm just so verklempt to be in your presence that I've forgotten protocol. Forgive me."

Caitlin wasn't sure if she should know the woman, but it was very awkward, and her instincts were going off like a four-alarm fire bell in her head, though she couldn't exactly say why. The woman wasn't exactly threatening. She looked like a schoolmarm or a librarian. The bun was a particularly nice touch. Maybe she was one of the hospital's administrators. Either way, Caitlin was too tired to figure out the mystery. She just wanted some sleep.

"I'm flattered, thank you, but I'm just doing my part, like everyone here at the hospital," Caitlin said. "We all have the same goal."

"Well, you have a good heart. Your parents must be very proud."

Strange conversation. "I like to think so."

"Are they scientists, too?"

"Yes, actually."

"Hmm, I'm not much of a science person, myself, but thank goodness for people like you in situations like this."

Caitlin was running out of ways to politely respond to this wacky conversation. "Well, thank you, it was very nice to meet you…um, what did you say your name was?"

"Oh, I didn't say, dear," the woman corrected her with a chilling smile. "You have no reason to know me but we have every reason to know you."

Goose bumps rioted up Caitlin's arms. "And why is that?"

"Because you're the only woman smart enough to stand in our way," the woman answered, dropping her smile as she approached Caitlin. "But we can't let that happen. We're doing God's work."

Zak!

Caitlin opened her mouth to scream but the woman was faster than she looked. Something sharp plunged in her neck and everything went black before she could get a sound out of her mouth.

After that, there was nothing.

* * *

Zak's brain was humming. Regina Burke. They should've known something was up with that weird-ass cult in spite of their protests. They should've hauled them in and interrogated them Red Wolf–style.

Maybe broken a few bones.

He exited the elevator to the restricted wing where Caitlin was supposed to be in the lab but found it empty. The way he'd left things with Caitlin flashed in his mind and worry set in. He'd given her strict instructions to let him know if she left the lab at any time. Caitlin wasn't the kind of woman to do things out of spite. He checked his cell but found no messages.

A sick feeling lodged in his gut but he didn't want to jump to conclusions, especially when his nerves were strung taut.

He called Scarlett. "Caitlin isn't in the lab. I'm heading to the cafeteria. Keep a look out for either Caitlin or Rebecca."

"Copy that."

He clicked off and detoured for the cafeteria, scanning every hallway, his anxiety rising every moment.

Zak made it to the cafeteria and knew within seconds she wasn't there. He tried her cell again. It went straight to voice mail. *Pick up, Caitlin, please*. But his gut told him she was in danger. And his gut never lied. He had a sixth sense about these things—everyone in Red Wolf had that. They just knew when things were about to go south. That innate ability had kept them alive and he wasn't about to question it now.

Especially when it was Caitlin's life on the line.

"That bitch has Caitlin, I can feel it," he told Scarlett. "We need to find her. Now."

This time they met up in an FBI facility, courtesy of

Xander's connections. They needed resources that the hospital conference room couldn't provide.

"Patch into the hospital surveillance in the lab," Xander directed a man at a computer. "That should give us facial recognition so we can apply it to our cameras on the streets."

"Give me two minutes," the guy said, his fingers flying across the keyboard. "Got it."

The image of a woman and Caitlin popped up. Zak ground his teeth as he saw the aggressive stance of the woman coming at Caitlin. He saw her stick something in her neck. He watched Caitlin drop to the floor.

Then he saw a man come in and scoop an unconscious Caitlin up and cart her off.

"Follow them," Zak said tersely, his fists clenching. "If they hurt her, I swear to God, they won't have to worry about the virus because I will end them first."

Scarlett didn't try to calm him because she knew it would only make it worse. He needed action, not platitudes. Caitlin had been taken right beneath their noses by a psychopath and they hadn't seen it coming. She'd waltzed right up, bold as you please, and jabbed a needle in his woman's neck and carted her off like a Christmas turkey like no one's business.

And that couldn't stand.

He wanted to put his hands around that woman's neck and squeeze until her eyes popped from their sockets.

Xander knew the look, felt the murderous rage radiating from him. "We'll find her," he promised.

Zak nodded. "We better."

Or there would be hell to pay.

Caitlin's eyes opened one at a time with a groan as her head felt ready to explode. Her mouth tasted like a toad had crapped in it and her neck was sore. *What the hell? What happened?* Did she fall down the stairs and black out? She struggled to sit up but found her hands were tied behind her. *Oh, God, that wasn't right.*

"Look, who's finally awake," a voice said, chipper and full of sunshine and totally incongruous with the fact that she was tied up like a hostage. "Are you hungry? Do you need to use the restroom?"

"Who are you? What are you doing?" Caitlin asked fearfully, staring at the woman who'd jabbed a needle in her neck. "I don't understand. What is happening?"

"So many questions. I suppose that's fair, but really, we should do this over breakfast. Low blood sugar is nothing to mess with."

Caitlin struggled to sit up and found herself on a bed in a loft. Several people, who seemed to find nothing unusual with a kidnapped woman tied up in the room, were milling around.

The woman who'd drugged her helped her to her feet, though Caitlin was a bit wary of letting her get too close. She led Caitlin to a small table where an assortment of breakfast pastries awaited. The woman poured her coffee and prepared a scone as if they were having a delightful tea, instead of a hostage situation.

"You're insane," Caitlin realized with dawning horror. "That's it, isn't it? You're freaking insane and this is your insane posse of followers. That's the only thing that possibly makes sense because otherwise I can't make head or tail of what is happening right now."

"Hush now, you probably have a touch of low blood sugar. Here, enjoy a fresh scone, dear."

"Screw your scone, you psychopath, let me go," she hissed, which probably wasn't the smartest thing to do but Caitlin was running on pure adrenaline and fear.

"We should work on your manners," the woman warned. "Robert warned me that you were a bit prickly."

Robert? Caitlin craned her neck to see one of her team members, Robert Vepp, walk up and join them with an eager, if not hesitant, smile. "Hi, Caitlin," he said, taking a seat. "It's good to see you again."

"Robert!" Her eyes bugged and her jaw dropped as horror and rage warred with one another. "It was you who broke into the lab?"

"Guilty," he admitted, raising his hand as if it were something to be proud of. "Almost got caught, too. But the Lord will always look out for the Faithful."

"Oh, my God," Caitlin groaned. "I vouched for you. How could you do this, Robert? You were one of my team. I believed in you."

"And I believe in you, which is why you're here and not out there," he insisted. "I convinced Mother Regina that you were worthy of conversion. You are worthy of becoming a repentant. When the Purge comes, the Faithful will remain and inherit the earth. We will start anew. The earth will need people like us to shape the world in a better way, a smarter way."

"You're crazy," Caitlin realized, shaking her head. How had she missed this? For crap's sake, she should've listened to Zak when he'd insisted the original theft had been an inside job. Her ego had refused to believe that anyone on her team had been capable of such a betrayal. Not only was this embarrassing, it was devastating. "Robert, please, you can't truly believe this crap. You're a man of science."

Robert's expression hardened. "You'll learn that science is of the Lord but the application of it must glorify His plan. We've gotten away from the beauty of His original vision but we can restore the balance. Wipe away greed and avarice, return to basic core values."

"By killing off most of the human race?" she asked with open incredulity. "Have you not watched any movie or read any book ever? Humans are flawed by their very nature. There's no such thing as utopia and your vision will fail. All you will succeed in doing is wiping out a bunch of innocent people. Not to mention, you can't control a virus like this. It will wipe out the 'Faithful' just as quickly as it will wipe out the rest. What are you going to do about that?"

"That's where you come in, my dear," the woman said, smiling. "You've hit upon how to protect those who've earned protection."

Caitlin barked a hysterical laugh. *Oh, the irony.* "You jumped the gun. I don't know if my theory is correct. I was just getting to the point where I was testing my preliminary findings. I have no idea if I'm wrong or on the right track. All you did was take me away from important work and I can't do my work from a kitchen table."

"Of course not, we are prepared to provide a facility for you to complete your testing," she said with that same smile that was beginning to give Caitlin hives. The woman pushed a scone toward Caitlin. "But first, please eat. We can't have you fainting from hunger. You're much too important, dear."

"Lady, screw your scone, and screw you. I'm not helping you do shit."

The woman pursed her lips as if disappointed. "I was hoping to do this the civilized way but I understand you need persuasion." She flicked her wrist, and two men dragged Rebecca, roughly throwing her to the floor. Without her prosthetic leg, she lost her balance and fell hard.

Caitlin gasped, horrified. "Rebecca!"

"I'm okay," Rebecca assured Caitlin in a weak voice but Caitlin could tell she was hurting. "Whatever you do, don't listen to them. They're nothing but a bunch of cock-sucking cult lovers."

"Shut your foul mouth, unrepentant," one of the men shouted, kicking Rebecca hard in the stomach.

Caitlin jumped and sucked back a scream, too afraid for Rebecca to say anything else, but Rebecca just rolled to her back and gave the man a shaky middle finger. "That all you got?" she moaned, and Caitlin wanted to laugh and cry at the same time.

The man went to kick her again but the woman held up her hand, her lip curling as she turned to Caitlin. "You will do as you are told."

"What makes you think I would do anything for you?"

"Because the Lord always finds ways for the Faithful to open doors."

She nodded and the men jerked Rebecca to her feet, dragging her away. "Where are you taking her?" Caitlin demanded, fear for her friend coloring her voice. "Stop! Where are you taking her?"

The woman met her angry gaze and said, "To the facility, dear. Don't worry. She'll be waiting for you—and the cure."

Chapter 26

CJ cursed loudly and explosively as he paced the room. "Goddamn it, this crazy bitch was in our hands and we let her go? Unbelievable. I'm never going to live this down. I knew I should've just thrown them both in the trunk and brought them in for questioning."

Scarlett tried to calm CJ but Zak understood CJ's rage because he felt it, too. He wasn't feeling very merciful at the moment. "Look, you couldn't have known that Regina was the ringleader. Your focus was on Carl. Your sexism got the better of you. How many times have I told you that women can be the bad guys, too?"

CJ hung his head. "Yeah, I need to get that through my head. Damn it. I should've known. That bun was a dead giveaway. Women in buns are up to no good."

Scarlett returned to the quivering man in their custody. "Now that we've got that sorted out, time to spill the beans, Mr. Browne. We know that Regina Burke is behind the kidnapping of Dr. Caitlin Willows and we can assume she's also behind the theft of a deadly viral weapon stolen from a lab in Vermont. What we don't know is where Regina is holed up right now. That's where you come in. Start talking."

Carl looked bewildered. "I already told you, I don't know anything about this terrible apocalypse you keep talking about. You came into my house, terrorized me and now you drag me into this crazy story about this end-of-the-world nonsense. I'm done with this intimidation. I'm calling my lawyer."

Scarlett leaned in, invading his personal space. "Cut the crap. Regina Burke is already in deep. Just tell us where she is and we'll cut you a deal with the DA, and maybe you won't spend the rest of your life rotting in a federal prison with a bunkmate named Bubba. If you keep holding to your story, I can't promise you shit."

Carl stammered. "I don't know what you're talking about."

CJ scoffed, irritated with the pace of the interrogation. "Tell me something. I don't understand the cult mentality. What could make doing something so idiotic work for you? And where the hell did you get all of the cash for this operation? How do I start my own cult, 'cuz you make this look like a pretty good gig."

Carl seemed offended. "You can mock our faith all you like but we are protected by law to worship as we please."

Scarlett rose, shaking her head with irritation. "Yes, you may worship as you please but you don't have the right to kill innocent people. We've been over this. Come on, now, let's not insult each other's intelligence. You seem like a smart enough guy to know that it's not okay to wipe out the whole western hemisphere!"

But Carl held to his original statement, insisting, "I

don't know what you're talking about! How many times do I have to tell you that?"

They were getting nowhere fast. Zak snapped. "I'm done with this bullshit," he muttered, grabbing Carl by the lapels and yanking him to his feet to snarl in his face. "Your crazy-ass Faithful cult member has my girl. And if you don't tell me where she is right now, I'm going to rip out your tongue and shove it so far up your ass you'll be able to feel it tickling your tonsils. Do you understand me? Am I making myself perfectly clear?"

Scarlett backed him up. "I was willing to do this the nice way but we're running out of time. There are innocent people dying and I'm not about to lose the doc over your stupid beliefs. Just tell the man what he needs to know and maybe he won't rip your arms off and beat you with them."

"You can't do that. There are rules—"

"There are rules for *cops*. And as we told you before we're not cops," CJ interjected with a gleeful grin, all too happy to start busting skulls for the fun of it. "Rules don't apply to people like us. We break rules for a living." He rubbed his hands together, cracking his knuckles and bouncing up and down, ready. "C'mon, let me have a crack at him. I owe him a few licks for wasting my time the first go 'round and making me look like an idiot."

Zak grinned. "You hear that? My friend owes you a few licks. You don't want him to get a hold of you. He's a little crazy."

"Damn straight," CJ agreed as if Zak had just paid him a compliment.

Scarlett tried again. "Do yourself a favor—just tell us what we need to know and we'll go easy on you. You don't have what it takes to go a round with either of these guys. You're soft, like an uncooked biscuit. Save yourself the indignity of pissing yourself and just give up Regina. What do you owe her anyway?"

Carl lifted his chin, the picture of a martyr bravely going to battle, and Zak wanted to punch his face off. "I am of the Faithful. I am of the Chosen. I go into the light with the strength of the Lord powering my fight. You can do what you will. I will never break."

"Yeah, challenge accepted." Zak heaved Carl across the room, slamming the man against a bookshelf, sending books and knickknacks flying. "I don't have time for this goddamn bullshit!" He hauled Carl back to his feet, staring into his blubbering face. "Here's how this is gonna go. I'm going to go to the kitchen and find myself a nice pair of nutcrackers and then I'm going to proceed to break every single one of your knuckles one by one until you tell me what I need to know. Understand? Good." He shoved Carl into CJ's hands. "Keep our friend company while I find what I need to make him talk."

Carl's lip quivered as a trickle of blood slid out of the corner of his mouth. He looked to Scarlett for help. "Are you really going to let him brutalize me like this? I'm going to see every single one of you in court. I'm going to make your life a living hell."

Scarlett shrugged. "Hell, as far as you're concerned we're all dead people anyway, so what does it matter? If we're all going down with this ship we might as well have some fun while we do it. Have you heard a knuckle crack? It sounds terrible but we like to place bets on which knuckle makes you piss yourself."

Zak returned with a walnut cracker, clacking the metal instrument with a cold smile. He wasn't bluffing. He wouldn't hesitate to torture this soft, weak-assed idiot if it meant saving Caitlin.

He would tear the city apart, break any bone, break any rule, do anything necessary to bring her home safe.

"Let's get this party started, shall we?"

Caitlin was shaking all over. Rebecca was gone. She had no idea where they'd taken her but Regina had provided a closed-circuit camera for the room where Rebecca was imprisoned.

Where Rebecca would die a horrible death if Caitlin didn't perfect the serum.

"I don't know if it works," she said, trying to appeal to some sort of logic in a crazy woman, but Regina was humming to herself as if all was right in the world and it was time for a mani-pedi. "Rebecca is a brilliant scientist. You've just condemned her to die!"

"You should spend less time talking and more time working," Regina suggested, gesturing to the rudimentary lab setup. There was a computer without an internet connection and a functioning BSL-4 lab at the most basic level but it wasn't safe by any means.

She cast an accusatory look toward Robert. "I'm assuming you're the one who set up this lab? You know this isn't sufficient for the kind of virology that we're dealing with. You're putting us all at risk with this setup."

"Don't try to scare me. We're fine. We have negative pressure suits for the work done in the class 2 biosafety cabinets and every window is pressure sealed. It might not be as pretty as Tessara's labs but it will get the job done," Robert assured her with a smug expression that made her want to wipe the cement floor with his face. "Now, a true repentant woman does her work quietly for the glory of the Lord."

"Screw you," Caitlin muttered in disgust, wondering how she'd ever been fooled by this idiot. "You've completely ruined my sense that I can judge a person's character, because, clearly, I was blinded by your bullshit."

She didn't see the slap coming. His hand connected with her cheek so fast her head whipped back and she stumbled, sucking back a sharp breath as tears stung her eyes.

"Robert," Regina warned with irritation. "Please mind your temper."

"Of course," he said, instantly remorseful. To Caitlin, he said, "I must give you time to learn how to embrace your new role in the new world. Forgive me."

In spite of the sting in her cheek, she leaned forward and hissed, "Screw. You." She didn't care if he beat her. The idea of Robert thinking that she would ever be in league with his crazy cult made her physically ill. She'd rather die.

"You might not die but your friend certainly will," Regina reminded her, rising from her perch and adjusting her tight bun. "Ticktock, my dear. Come, Robert, let us leave Dr. Willows to her work. We will attend to midmorning sermon and luncheon."

"Yes, of course."

Robert hurried after Regina, leaving Caitlin alone in the lab. Only then did Caitlin break down and cry. What was happening? She didn't dare look at the closed-circuit camera feed. She couldn't bear to see Rebecca writhing in pain as the virus did its part to destroy her from within. She searched the lab for some way to get through to the outside. She had no way of knowing where she was. The lab was sealed; there were no windows. She was surrounded by slabs of concrete, which not only dampened sound but messed with cell signals. Not that she had her cell phone. Or her Apple Watch. There wasn't a phone in the room, either.

All she had was her wit and determination to get the hell out of here.

What did she know about Robert? Aside from the fact that he was obviously crazy like all the rest of the Faithful, he must've been into her, or else he wouldn't have picked her to "save" for the new world. Maybe she could play that to her advantage? *Ugh.* That made her want to vomit but what options did she have? She needed more information and right now she was scraping the bottom of the barrel.

Swallowing the bile in her throat, she knew what she had to do. Play to his ego. Get answers—but whatever she did, she had to avoid Regina. That woman was nuts but sharp.

That was the plan. In the meantime, she risked a glance at the circuit feed, perfect the serum for Rebecca.

Ticktock, indeed.

"Hold on, Rebecca. I got you."

Chapter 27

Zak washed his hands of the blood, ready to punch something and scream at the moon. Carl had given them nothing.

Except a mess on the floor.

"Joshua will handle the processing," Scarlett told Zak, not that Zak cared what happened to that pissant Carl after he left their sight. "Gotta say, I didn't see that coming. I figured after the first knuckle he'd cave."

"Never underestimate the power of religious conviction," Zak muttered with a glower. "I'm going out of my mind, Scar. I have to find her. What if they've already killed her? What if we're already too late? They tried to kill her twice before. Why would they hesitate now that they have her? I'm going insane. I feel so helpless and useless." He flexed his knuckles, ready to punch something, but he held himself in check by the thinnest of margins. His voice broke as he uttered a heartsick "Goddamn it."

"We'll find her. I swear to you, we'll find her."

"They're winning," Zak said with disbelief, dropping into a chair. "I can't believe we're being bested by a crazy bunch of crackpots who believe a super blue moon eclipse is going to bring about the apocalypse. I mean, c'mon, what the hell is happening right now? We've beaten better with worse odds and yet, this is what cooks our goose? I can't believe this. Honestly, that's not even what's upsetting me. I couldn't care less about the world. All I care about is her. It's the ugly truth and I hate myself for it but it's true. God help me, Scar, but I'm so scared."

Zak embarrassed himself by breaking into ugly sobs and Scarlett let him cry it out. Thankfully, CJ and Xander had left to transport the mess that'd become Carl Browne to Red Wolf for Joshua to deal with, leaving Scarlett with Zak.

"What a time to fall in love, right?" Scarlett said with a rueful but gentle laugh as she rubbed his back in support. "I understand. These things happen when we least expect it. We can't control when our heart decides to kick in. Do you think I would've chosen to fall in love with Xander when I did? God, what bad timing was that? He was on the run and being framed for blowing up a senator. Talk about your poor choices. But it happened and I had to just deal with it. So that's what you're going to do. You love her. You deal with it."

"But what if—"

"Don't even go there," Scarlett interrupted sternly, shaking her head. "You're giving yourself too much room to think. You need to act. Put your feet in motion. Your head is going to mess you up. You're a soldier, so act like it."

"I'm trying! We're in a stalemate. We've got no orders, nowhere to march. What am I supposed to do?"

"We go back to our training. We sure as hell don't sit here weeping like a bitch. Look, I'm not trying to say don't feel your feelings. This is 2018—we're allowed to have emotions, according to our shrinks, but we can't wallow in that shit. We don't have that luxury. You've had your cry. Now wipe the snot from your nose and let's get to work."

Zak looked up, Scarlett's advice sinking in. She was right. Nothing was getting done while he sat here crying about the situation. He had to be in motion. Get back to his training. Caitlin was out there and he would find her. He wasn't about to let the first love of his life die at the hands of a bunch of crackpots.

Wiping at his nose, he rose and nodded, his head on straight. "Thanks, TL. I needed that."

Scarlett rose with him. "That's what I'm here for. A verbal ass-kicking."

"You're good at it," he admitted, grinning. "Must be why you and Xander are such a good fit."

Scarlett chuckled. "That and other things."

"Ugh, now I have to wash my brain out with bleach. Thank you for that."

"You're welcome." Scarlett wasn't even sorry. Zak thought she might've even done that on purpose just to be a dick but she was already switching tracks. "I was thinking we should check the electrical grid. Something tells me that the timing of Dr. Willows's kidnapping is important. What if the doc was close enough to a breakthrough that they took her to another lab to finish the details?"

"Why?"

"Well, because what I know about human nature is that no matter what, self-preservation always trumps faith. Regina Burke is going to want her own fail-safe from the virus and she's going to need the doc for that."

"And a BSL-4 lab is going to pull a significant amount of power," Zak finished, snapping his fingers in agreement. "Let's follow that lead. Xander should be able to pull that string, right?" Scarlett nodded but there was something behind her eyes that made Zak pause. "What's wrong? Is there something else?"

"Another patient died last night. I'm hoping my hunch is right for a number of reasons or else we're going to lose all of those patients currently in quarantine and God knows who else is out there."

It was a sobering thought. The fact was, they didn't know who else was contaminated. Even if this had been a test run for the Faithful, it was still a hefty kick in the balls. He muttered an expletive under his breath. He knew a kid was currently fighting for her life. A three-year-old alongside her mom and dad. "Man, this religious cult is a bunch of assholes."

"Most are."

They climbed in the car and met up with Xander. A plan in motion was better than no plan at all, even if the odds were stacked against them.

Zak refused to give up.

The Faithful were going to need God if he caught them because he was going to send them straight to their maker.

Caitlin managed to create the first batch of experimental serum and give it to Regina but she hadn't heard back from the cursed woman before it was time for dinner. The Faithful gathered together to eat in a small group in a place that resembled a mess hall, but Caitlin was always under heavy guard.

However, she was always placed at Robert's table as Robert seemed to hold some kind of high standing with the Faithful, along with Regina. Caitlin hadn't been able to ascertain the hierarchy as of yet, but it didn't matter. She only needed to get under Robert's skin.

Even though he made *her* skin crawl, she pretended to swallow her revulsion and tried to appear humbled through her ordeal, appealing to his ego and his whacked-out faith.

"Regina isn't joining us tonight?" Caitlin noted as she folded her napkin carefully in her lap. "I was hoping to ask her about Rebecca."

"You may ask me about Rebecca," Robert offered with a generous smile, cutting into his braised chicken. "To answer your question, your serum shows promise. We are pleased. But then, I knew you were brilliant. It was just a matter of time before you figured out how to beat the virus."

"Your faith in me is flattering," she said, biting back the urge to spit in his face for being a two-faced, disgusting pig of a man who sold out his own team. "I'm relieved to know Rebecca is doing better."

"She's not out of the woods yet," Robert warned, wagging his fork at her. "So don't get any ideas of trying anything foolish."

"Of course, I wouldn't," Caitlin said, stiffening, her hand curling around her napkin in her lap, wishing it was Robert's throat. "I just want her to be okay. She's an innocent victim in all this."

He shrugged as if Rebecca's pain meant nothing. "She's an unrepentant. The Faithful deserve the earth. Once the earth is wiped clean, you'll see that we will rebuild the earth the way it was supposed to be in the original plan."

"I gotta say, Robert, you really hid this part of yourself pretty well," she said. "I never imagined you were so...*dedicated* to your faith."

"In today's world, you're discriminated against if you have a strong faith," Robert said. "Especially in scientific circles. I never would've been picked for your team if you'd known about my faith."

That was true. If she'd known he was a lunatic she would've had him escorted from the building but that was a different conversation. "So Regina, she's intense," Caitlin said, trying to make conversation and gain information, as well. "Definitely cut from a different cloth than most people."

"She's incredible, isn't she?" Robert agreed, smiling as if in awe. "She's one to take a page from, let me tell you. She truly believes and puts her money where her mouth is. Quite literally."

"What do you mean?"

He gestured to the building they were in, saying, "This whole place is funded by her. She's some mega heiress. This is all her money but she understands that money is inherently evil in the wrong hands. She's going to change all that. Once we rebuild, we're going to eradicate the need for money."

Caitlin snorted. "And what? Pay with coconuts? Use the barter system? There's a reason currency came about. It fulfills a need. Just because you change the system doesn't mean people will stop having needs."

Robert scowled. "Of course not, but Regina has a plan to end the greed that money breeds."

Of course she does—Regina walks on water with the Lord. Caitlin was having a hard time holding on to her dinner. She averted her gaze on the pretense of submission but actually she was searching for Robert's cell phone. She spied the edge of his Samsung hanging precariously out of the corner of his slacks. Her gaze went quickly to the glass of water on the table. She let a few moments pass by, seeming to meekly eat her dinner, until Robert felt comfortable taking his focus away from her.

Just as she went to make her move, a woman joined them, taking her seat beside Caitlin, a look of shining adoration in her young eyes. "You are Dr. Willows?" she asked.

"Yes," she answered, trying hard to hide her sharp disappointment at her chance being thwarted. To this point, Regina had kept everyone away from Caitlin, so she was surprised Robert hadn't shooed her away. "And you are?"

"I'm Teresa. We're so happy to have you part of our new beginning. What an exciting time, don't you agree?"

Teresa was like a puppy, cute and inherently excited about anything. Caitlin wanted to bop her on the nose for being an idiot. However, maybe *God* had just opened a window when previously a door had closed.

"Nice to meet you, Teresa," she murmured with a nice smile. "Yes, very exciting times, indeed."

And just like that Caitlin began making the plan to use sweet Teresa to get the hell out of Crazy Town.

Chapter 28

Thanks to Xander's contacts and clues from power drains on the grid, they were able to narrow down a few possible locations within the city for a BSL-4 lab.

There were three likely places, circled in red on the city map. "CJ, Laird, you take the north. Scarlett, Xander, you take the west, and I'll take the east."

"You shouldn't go alone," Scarlett said. "Xander can send an agent to go with you for backup."

Zak waved off the offer. "I don't want to wait. I want to hit the road now. Every minute counts. I'm aware of the risk. I know how to breach a building undetected. You don't have to worry about me."

"Don't let your emotion cloud your judgment," Scarlett warned, but Zak was already on the move. He had a one-track movie playing in his mind—find Caitlin—and he didn't care.

Zak walked out the door with CJ, of all people, hot

on his heels, calling out, "Wait up, man." When Zak stopped with an impatient frown, CJ, said, "Hey, man, take a breather, you've got a mad-dog look in your eyes and it's not you. You're always the one cooling me down, so I figure it's my turn to return the favor. You're running too hot. You need a cooler head if you want to save your lady."

Zak hadn't told CJ about his feelings for Caitlin. "Scarlett tell you?" Zak asked, narrowing his gaze with suspicion but CJ just shook his head.

"It's pretty damn obvious. You've got the worst poker face. You've been head over heels for the doc since day one. It's cool, man. I envy you, for real. But if you want to save her, you've got to calm down and think straight. You've got that look in your eyes like you want to rush into the place John McClane–style, guns blazing, and that's going to get you killed. Possibly the doc, too. That's not what you want."

Zak didn't want to hear this even if CJ was right, but hell, coming from CJ, the original crazy hothead, it was just weird. Maybe that was why he was able to hear it. It was just weird enough to sink in. He blew out a frustrated breath but nodded, accepted the advice.

CJ grinned, realizing he'd gotten through to Zak. "Damn, maybe I'm good at this. Career change—therapist, maybe?"

Zak shook his head ruefully. "I wouldn't go that far, buddy, but I get it. Thanks. You're right, I was coming in pretty hot."

"Damn right you were. I mean, I respect it. It's how I do things, but we both agree I come at things with a sledgehammer when sometimes a sledgehammer does nothing but break shit."

He chuckled. "True again."

"So you gonna wait for backup?"

"That would be the smart thing."

"But you're not going to, are you?"

Zak cast a shit-eating grin at CJ. "Hell, all I'm doing is a little recon. Don't need backup for that, right?"

"That's what I'm saying."

He laughed, the red cloud lifting for a minute. "Keep your phone handy. I might need backup if my location is the jackpot."

"Ditto."

They bumped fists and parted ways.

Heading for the eastside location, Zak scanned the area looking for anything that seemed to support a BSL-4 lab. GPS put him a half block from the location on the grid and he saw a warehouse looming. It was certainly big enough to support the needs of a BSL-4 lab. Parking far enough away to walk in undetected, he kept to the shadows and crept in the alleys behind the warehouse, watching for potential cameras. If this was the place, they wouldn't take any chances with unwanted visitors. Zak came to the backside of the building and scanned to the top.

Time to do a little snooping around and see what he could see.

Regina came to Caitlin's "bedroom" later that night with a pleased expression. "Your serum is working well. We will move into mass production of your formula starting tomorrow so that we can inoculate the Faithful ahead of the super blue moon eclipse. You've exceeded expectation. Very good. Robert's faith in you was not misplaced."

Caitlin didn't trust herself not to spit something snarky at the woman, so remained silent. She was trying to earn brownie points. "How is Rebecca?" she asked, concerned for her friend. "Is she recovering?"

"Assuming your serum continues to work as expected,

she'll recover. However, she will remain in isolation and under guard until we can determine that you are not going to do anything foolish."

"And by foolish, you mean try to escape because you've kidnapped me," Caitlin supplied with a short smile devoid of humor.

"Your perspective still needs adjusting but I'm willing to overlook your rudeness for this evening," Regina said, patting her bun with a subtle motion.

Then she smiled and said, "As a reward, I've arranged for some company for you tonight. Robert said you and Teresa seemed to have hit it off. She's a kind soul and a good girl. You would benefit from emulating her meek spirit."

Not bloody likely. Caitlin accepted the offer with a subtle nod and Regina seemed satisfied. She opened the door for Teresa to enter and then stepped out. "I will return within the hour. Enjoy your visit."

Teresa had brought ice cream.

"I hope you like vanilla," she said, handing Caitlin a small dessert cup. "I figured that was the safest bet."

Caitlin accepted the ice cream with a smile. "It's great, thank you. Please, sit with me."

Teresa smiled, happy to be there with her. Either Teresa was dumb as a box of rocks or she'd been kept in an underground shelter her entire life and knew nothing about the world in general. One way to find out. "Teresa, do you realize I'm being held here against my will?" Caitlin asked.

Teresa's smile faltered. "What do you mean?"

"I mean, Regina jabbed a needle in my neck, drugged me and forced me to create a serum to protect the Faithful so that when she unleashes a horrific virus on the world, the Faithful don't die bleeding out their assholes."

It was a little on the graphic side but Caitlin didn't have the option of softballing the situation. Teresa looked nervously to the door. "Regina is our leader. God has chosen her to lead us to the new world."

"No, Regina is a crazy loon and she's going to kill a lot of innocent people unless you help me. Teresa, you seem like a good person. Why are you helping a bunch of crazy people hurt innocent people? Do you know what this virus does to the human body?"

"It puts the bad people to sleep," she said, although her voice reeked with uncertainty.

"No, it doesn't do that at all," Caitlin corrected her, trying to remain patient when she wanted to shake some sense into her empty head. "It liquefies your insides and turns you to mush. It's excruciating and it's brutal. One of the first victims was a two-year-old child—practically a baby. Right now, there is a three-year-old in the hospital dying from this virus—" Caitlin stopped, realizing that for all she knew Georgia Burke was already dead, too. Her eyes welled with sudden tears but she sucked them back. "People are already dying horribly from this virus and it's all Regina's fault. Please. Listen to me, Teresa. You can save millions if you listen to me right now."

"What do you mean?"

"I don't know what Regina has told you about how the virus works but I can assure you that the infected don't simply go to sleep peacefully. She's lying to you. Help me. Regina is dangerous and she's crazy."

The wheels were turning enough to give Caitlin hope that maybe Teresa wasn't as dumb as she appeared, until she suddenly shook her head resolutely. "No, she's chosen. You don't understand. All prophets face trials and must endure sacrifice."

"Regina isn't sacrificing anything," Caitlin said, trying again to get through to Teresa. "She's pushing her own agenda and it has nothing to do with anything I've ever seen in any Bible! Show me where in scripture does it say you must unleash a supervirus on some lunar event in order to cleanse the earth? I must've missed that day in Sunday school because I don't remember that lesson."

Teresa insisted, her expression becoming beatific. "No, you don't understand, she's sacrificed her own flesh and blood, much like Abraham!"

Caitlin drew back. "What?"

Teresa bobbed a vigorous nod. "Yes. God knew that Regina couldn't ask of the Faithful the ultimate sacrifice if she wasn't willing to do the same, so she offered her own flesh and blood."

"What are you talking about?" Caitlin repeated, confused. "What sacrifice?"

"Her daughter, Ellis."

Suddenly, Caitlin's throat constricted and three names flashed in her memory.

Wes, Ellis and Georgia *Burke*—the family in quarantine.

Why hadn't she put it together?

"Regina infected her own daughter?" Caitlin asked, horrified.

Teresa said sadly, "She was an unrepentant."

Tears blinded her. "Oh, my God, if I ever hear that stupid word one more time I'll jab a pen in my own ear," she said, wiping at her eyes. "They're innocent people, not unrepentant. Regina might've killed her own damn family."

Caitlin thought of the little girl, Georgia, and felt fresh rage. If Zak didn't find Regina first, Caitlin had a pretty good idea how she'd like Regina to meet her maker, and it was going to end up messy.

Caitlin shocked Teresa, reaching out to grab Teresa's hands, holding them tight. "Do you feel this? Human hands. Warm blood courses through my veins, same as you, same as the people Regina is condemning to a gruesome death over some misguided sense of faith. How can you in good conscience support the murder of millions? The murder of children, whose only crime is being born to parents who don't subscribe to the same faith as yours? Is that really so bad? People can still be good even if they don't believe in the same religion. History is built upon the bones of people killed in the name of religion. Please don't add to the list of misguided people believing theirs is the only way. Please, Teresa. I'm begging you."

Teresa blinked back something that looked like tears, as possibly even doubt crossed her expression, but she pulled her hands from Caitlin's tight grasp and rose to knock rapidly on the door. "Regina, we're done with our ice cream," she said, avoiding Caitlin's crushed gaze. And Caitlin knew Teresa wasn't going to help her.

Whatever Kool-Aid Regina was passing out, Teresa was guzzling it down just like everyone else in this crazy place.

Caitlin closed her eyes and prayed Zak was having better luck in finding her than she was having in busting out.

Chapter 29

Luck was on Zak's side. There was something definitely not right about this warehouse. For one, the windows were facades, and every door had an airtight seal and electronic keypads.

Pretty fancy controls for a warehouse previously used to store medical equipment.

His gut told him this was the place. He was going to make the call. He texted Scarlett the location.

Moving along the brick wall, he searched for a possible weak point, but whoever had retrofitted the building had done their homework. Hunkering down, he watched the points of entry. The side entrance in the alley seemed to be reserved for delivery traffic. He dropped down, first to the dumpster, then to the ground, hiding until he saw a delivery truck rumbling through the alley and come to a stop.

He didn't have time to wait for Scarlett and the team to get there before he made his move. Sliding in behind the delivery guy left in the truck, he cracked him in the head, dragged him behind the dumpster, stripped him quickly of his uniform and then zipped himself in the uniform just in time to pull the hat down low on his head and follow the rest into the building undetected.

Zak, carrying a crate of fresh vegetables, was directed to the kitchen, where he dropped off his load. Then, when no one was paying attention, he dipped into the shadows.

Dumping the delivery guy costume, he exited the kitchen and melded into the small crowd, looking for anyone who might be useful, without drawing too much attention to himself.

The warehouse seemed to be built like a church in certain ways, as there were rows of pews on the first floor and a dais for the sermon. But there was also a large conference room that doubled as a cafeteria with an attached kitchen. He was guessing that the lab was on the upper floor, which was where Caitlin was likely being held.

He slipped out of the first floor and into the stairwell, taking the stairs two at a time as he climbed the floors. It was his guess that the lab would be on the top floor for ventilation purposes, away from the general population for other reasons, as well. Zak went to the door and found a keypad. Using the butt of his gun, he smashed the keypad, sending a shower of sparks into the air and an alarm pealing through the building.

So much for the sneak attack.

Zak kicked in the door and found a woman in a severe dress suit and a bun, her hands crossed in front of her as if she were waiting for him.

Well, this isn't a good sign. He lifted his gun. "Where's Caitlin?" he asked, getting straight to the point.

"You're trespassing."

"Seeing as you're trying to wipe out humanity, I think

I get a pass on the trespassing charge, lady. Now, I'm only going to ask you one more time before I start to get real pissed off," he said, moving slowly closer. "Where's Caitlin?" he repeated in a hard tone.

"What I try to remember is that everything happens according to His plan, even when I am vexed by inconveniences such as these," she said as if Zak didn't have a gun trained at her brain. "I will not miss dealing with such brutish cavemen such as you. I will rejoice in watching your kind die."

He smiled. "And here I thought it was going to be hard to shoot an old lady in the head." His finger was seconds away from pulling the trigger when he heard Caitlin's tremulous voice behind him and he whirled to find Robert Vepp clutching Caitlin, a needle to her neck.

"What are you doing?"

"Making a hard choice," the woman answered with a sigh. "At my word, Robert will plunge a full syringe of the virus into Caitlin's body. You might succeed in killing either of us but she'll be dead within forty-eight hours and highly contagious, which in turn would kill you, too."

"Don't do it," Zak warned with a growl, seeing red. "I swear to God, I'll do more than just kill you. I'll rip you apart."

"My death is nothing. Heaven awaits me. What awaits you in death?"

Zak saw the fear in Caitlin's eyes and it did crazy things to his insides. He knew he couldn't get to her in time before Robert could stick her with that needle but he also knew it was unlikely either was getting out alive at this point.

Maybe if he stalled long enough for Scarlett and the team to get here they'd have a chance but if not, they were screwed.

He was used to shitty odds, but Caitlin wasn't. He'd do anything to save her, anything to increase the odds of her survival.

"You couldn't have gone into philanthropy of some kind with your mega millions?" he asked with a mocking smile. When her eyes flashed with surprise that he knew who she was, he said, "Yeah, did a little digging around. Regina Burke, sole heiress of the Burke Paper Mill Estate, couldn't seem to make friends on her own, so she decided to make a cult instead. Seems a little extreme but each to his own, right? Except, hell, woman, did you have to try and kill the world while you were at it, too?"

Regina's face turned florid and he knew he'd hit a nerve. Maybe he'd keep hitting that spot and see what happened. Pissed-off people made mistakes. But her ire cooled as she replied with squared shoulders, "The Lord chooses His warriors, not the other way around."

"Oh, so you think you were chosen for some holy war? So explain to me, where does North Korea come into play in your holy war? Because you stole the sample from Tessara, who had acquired the sample from North Korea, right? I mean, did you just happen to stumble across the intel from your weekly tea with the Almighty that North Korea was dabbling with some nasty new bioweapon that might fit in nicely with the mumbo jumbo you were cooking up in your head for your village idiots? Please help me understand how this works."

A small smile curved Caitlin's mouth at his scathing sarcasm in spite of the danger she was in and he wanted to kiss her sassy mouth.

Robert looked to Regina, offended on behalf of his leader. "Don't listen to him. He's an unrepentant. Nothing he says matters. Don't let him get under your skin."

Regina held up her hand to silence Robert, her gaze

narrowing. "You think you know something because you can google a person's name? You know nothing."

"I know you're a sad, pathetic excuse for a person who can't function in the real world and so has to change the world to fit her vision of how the world should be. You're weak. I've seen plenty of people just like you out there in the world. You're no different than any other fascist dictator running their regime, forcing people to dance to their tune. All you're doing is packaging your particular rule in a facade made of religion but at the end of the day it's all bullshit and ego."

Caitlin's eyes glowed and her smile slowly widened as she looked straight to Zak and said, "I love you," as if they were the only two people in the room.

He said right back to her, "I love you, too, baby." And suddenly, when their gazes met, everything made sense, as did what had to happen next.

In a blink, Caitlin swung her elbow and jabbed it into Robert's nose, catching him off guard long enough to send the needle flying. Then Zak pumped a bullet into Regina's chest, dropping her to the floor with a thud as glass shattered behind her.

Caitlin shouted for Zak to watch out for the needle as Robert scrambled to get away, holding his broken nose, but Zak was on him before he could get far. He wanted to break Robert into a million pieces for daring to hold that needle to his woman's neck. "I'll make you wish you were never born," he promised, dragging Robert to his feet, getting right into his face. "I swear to God, you'll wish you never set eyes on me, asshole. You want to meet God? I can arrange that right now."

Zak buried his fist in Robert's gut a few times, making mincemeat out of his pancreas before he threw him back down on the concrete floor.

"Zak! Stop!" Caitlin cried out and he stopped midkick, breathing hard, question in his eyes. "We have to find Rebecca! She's somewhere in this building and they infected her so I would work harder to perfect the serum. I have to find out if she's okay. I don't even know if the serum worked."

Zak grabbed Robert and shook him like a rag doll. "Hey, asshole, where's Rebecca?" he asked but Robert was unconscious and wasn't up to doing anything but oozing bloody drool from his slack mouth. Zak dropped the man with disgust but promised Caitlin, "Don't worry, we'll find her," just as Scarlett and the team bust through the doors, taking in the scene and reading the situation.

"Seems you didn't wait for backup," Scarlett said, walking over to peer down at Regina's body. "So much for using a cool head."

"Situation called for immediate action," Zak answered, apologizing for nothing. He looked to Caitlin, who was already moving toward the door. "Rebecca is in this building somewhere. We need to find her."

"You go, we'll deal with this. Watch your six."

"Copy that."

Caitlin had never been so happy to see another human being than when Zak had burst through that door like an avenging angel, gun drawn and ready to kill.

She'd also realized that she'd fallen in love with him long before that moment but that particular moment had sealed the deal forever.

Yeah, if they survived she was pretty much going to marry him.

"If they survived" being the operative clause, because having that needle at her neck had felt like a huge deterrent to surviving.

Her hatred for Regina was eclipsed by her hatred for Robert by the thinnest margin, so smashing her elbow into his nose had been the most gratifying experience of her life.

She'd never been a violent person but that had been more satisfying than popping Bubble Wrap.

"Pretty damn impressive, babe," Zak said as they made their way down the hallway, checking doors as they went. "Seriously, though. You're not only smart but badass."

Caitlin smiled. "Yeah, I am, aren't I?" she agreed. "You have no idea how badly I wanted to do that. Robert deserved that. I only wish I could've kicked him in the nuts, too. He thought he was going to, like, be my husband or something in the new world order. Gross. Like we were going to repopulate the earth with some supersmart babies or something. He had me snowed. This whole time I thought he was gay. Turns out he was just a douchebag."

"Now *I* want to kick him in the nuts. The only babies you'll be having will be mine."

Caitlin skidded to a stop, her gaze swiveling to Zak's. "Excuse me?"

"I mean, if you want kids, that is. I can't promise they'd be supersmart or anything because I'm just a normal guy but I can promise they'd be really cute because between me and you…that's a cute kid."

Oh, God, her ovaries just put on their Sunday best. "You're so damn sexy," she said, pulling Zak straight to her mouth and kissing him hard and deep. Yes, she would have his babies and they would be the cutest, smartest, most adorable babies in the history of babies. They would like science and sports and art and math. In short, they would be a perfect blend of both of them.

Zak smiled against her mouth. "Is that a yes?"

"Is that a proposal?" she countered.

"Well, let me put it to you this way. I'm not letting you be with anyone else, so you might as well marry me."

"Persuasive argument."

He grinned. "I've been told I have a way with words."

"You definitely have a way with that tongue."

Zak's smile turned feral. "And you have a way with that mouth."

She would enjoy spending a lifetime with this man.

They reached the last door in the hall and saw Rebecca lying in a bed, cordoned off with plastic sheeting. Caitlin stopped Zak from going any closer.

"Regina said the serum worked but I don't know that for sure. Stay here," she said but Zak didn't want her going any closer, either.

"Hold up, if it's not safe for me, it's not safe for you."

"Zak, I have to check her vitals."

He wouldn't budge. "We'll get a doc up here or we'll have her transported to the hospital. I'm not about to have you infected if the serum didn't work."

Caitlin wanted to believe in her serum but there was a niggling doubt. It had been created under duress and she hadn't had a chance to do the proper checks, so how could she be sure? In the end, she knew Zak was right but she wanted to let Rebecca know she wasn't alone anymore. Even if it was just to hold her hand.

Zak understood. "We'll get her to the hospital with the right care, and she'll know you were there for her. How pissed would she be if she knew you put yourself in harm's way for her unnecessarily?"

"Pretty pissed," Caitlin agreed.

"Okay, then. Let's get her out of here."

Caitlin nodded. "What's going to happen to all the Faithful?"

"Depending on their involvement, they'll be charged as accessories to attempted murder. Maybe even an act of terrorism. But my guess is not everyone knew what Regina had in store for the big shebang."

"Maybe not in detail but some knew." Caitlin thought of Teresa and frowned. "They should all be put away for accessory."

"No argument there." He grabbed his cell and texted Scarlett, letting her know they'd found Rebecca and they'd need a medical transport.

The door opened, and thinking it was Scarlett, she started to joke that she was Superwoman-fast, but realized too late that it was, in fact, Teresa. Caitlin heard *"Unrepentant!"* screamed at her and something ripped through her skin, sizzling and burning as it went in one side and out through bone.

Her last coherent thought before sinking into complete darkness was "So this is what being shot feels like."

Chapter 30

The thing about getting shot is it really puts things into perspective.

While Caitlin didn't recommend taking a bullet to the chest, unlike Regina, Caitlin actually survived hers because Teresa wasn't as good a shot as Zak.

Thank God for that.

"How's the patient?" Zak asked, coming into the hospital room with contraband, aka chocolate bars smuggled from the gift shop. "I swear if the nurse finds me sneaking these in she's going to castrate me."

"It's fine," Caitlin promised, reaching for the goodies. "I need the endorphin rush. Besides, I'm ready to get out of here already. I don't know why the doc hasn't sprung me yet. I'm fine."

"Well, generally speaking, a bullet wound to the chest is a big deal. That bullet missed your heart by inches, babe. When I said you were badass, I didn't expect you to take it so literally. I never want to see that again."

He joked and made light of it but Caitlin knew how her almost dying had affected Zak. Scarlett had told her while Zak had gone on a burrito run during her recovery—cafeteria food left much to be desired—that she'd never seen him lose his mind with grief like that. It'd been like watching a beast mourn its soul mate. Something poetic and awe-inspiring.

He'd also beat the ever-loving snot out of Teresa to get the gun away from her.

Caitlin couldn't work up an ounce of pity for her because that stupid woman hadn't felt an ounce of empathy for the people who she'd known were going to die of the virus. The Faith of the Chosen were all a bunch of crazies as far as Caitlin was concerned.

Most had been rounded up that day in the warehouse with the exception of a few who'd managed to get away. The FBI handled the arrests, which looked really good on Xander's résumé, but the fact that Caitlin got kidnapped didn't look so great for Red Wolf, though they were redeemed by saving the world. So there was that.

They even got a hefty bonus from Tessara for recovering the sample and all the proprietary materials that were stolen.

Rebecca was expected to make a full recovery, thank God, but just like Caitlin, she was changed from her ordeal.

Speaking of the devil, Caitlin thought, as Rebecca walked into her room, leaning on her cane. "Hey there, they're springing me today," she said, smiling, still a little pale from her horrific experience.

Zak smiled. "You look good," he said, bending to kiss Caitlin on the forehead. I'll leave you ladies to visit while I check and see what horror the cafeteria has in store for us today."

Caitlin waited for Zak to leave and then asked, "How are you feeling?"

"Good. A little sore, but otherwise pretty much back on track."

"I'm glad."

"Hey, I wanted to talk to you before I head back to Vermont. Do you have a few minutes?"

"All I have are a few minutes. I have gobs of minutes, actually," Caitlin joked. "What's up?"

Rebecca smiled briefly, in a subdued manner. Not that Caitlin expected her to be her usual peppy self, but something was different. Rebecca drew a deep breath as she said, "I wanted to tell you personally that I'm not going back to Tessara."

Caitlin's smile faded. "You're not?"

She shook her head. "No. I've been thinking a lot about everything and I just don't think Tessara is the right fit for me anymore. I used to think I wanted adventure, until I got a little bit more adventure than I bargained for. Danger isn't as exciting as it's cracked up to be. Dangerous situations are just that—dangerous. I nearly died. You nearly died. Dead is dead. I have lots of living to do. So yeah, I think I'm ready for something a bit more in the range of normal, you know what I mean?"

The thing was, she did understand. She hadn't said anything to anyone, not even Zak, but she'd had the same private thoughts. Maybe she hadn't wanted to say anything until she'd had time to examine her reasons, or maybe she'd been afraid of admitting her parents might've been right, but the fact was Tessara was perhaps too rich for her blood after all.

She didn't want to worry about being shot at.

Or her future kids being threatened.

She enjoyed being on the cutting edge of science but there had to be boundaries, too.

Caitlin had a hole in her chest from where a bullet had pierced her sternum, six inches from her heart.

Six inches.

That wasn't a lot.

She'd also been giving a lot of thought to her mother's suggestion that she'd rejected, which, as of recently, didn't sound so terrible. She knew all she had to do was make a call and the job was as good as hers. With her credentials, she could create her own team, name her salary and hours. It would be as exciting or glamorous as working for Tessara, but no one would be shooting at her head—or chest—either.

But then, she no longer needed excitement in her job. Zak was exciting enough.

Caitlin cocked her head and said, "How do you feel about organic skin care?"

Rebecca smiled quizzically. "I…like it?"

"Me, too."

"Are you going to expand on that or leave me hanging?"

She smiled. "I need to make a few calls but when I have my ducks in a row, I'll give you a call. I think you're right, though. Tessara isn't the right fit for me, either. Time to move on."

Rebecca's smile widened as she understood. "All right, then. I'll see you back in Vermont. My flight leaves in two hours and I still have to get through security with this sucker," she tapped her prosthetic leg.

Caitlin chuckled and watched as Rebecca walked away just as Zak returned.

"Aw, I missed Rebecca?"

"Yeah, she's heading back home."

"Does she need a ride to the airport?"

"No, I think she's got it but you're sweet to offer."

"That's me, sweet as a pickle."

Caitlin laughed. "Pickles aren't sweet."

"Sure they are. Those little party pickles."

"Hey, so Rebecca isn't going back to Tessara."

Zak's brow rose. "No?"

"Nope—and I've decided I'm not, either."

He released a pent-up breath and the tension dropped from his shoulders like boulders tumbling to the ground. "Thank God. I know the right answer is to say I'll support whatever choice you make, but babe, I never want to lose you. If you're working for the evil empire, well, this kind of thing could happen again and that scares the ever-loving shit out of me."

She smiled, understanding. "Good answer. Because I'm quitting Tessara to possibly work for an organic skin care company in Virginia. It also means I'd have to sell my house and move in with you."

"Well, that works for me because I wasn't sure how 'Netflix and chill' was going to work when you lived in Vermont and I lived in Virginia. Logistically, it was going to be a problem."

She started to laugh but then stopped because it hurt too much. She settled for a big smile. "I love you, Zak Ramsey."

His smile gentled as he leaned in for a sweet kiss. "I love you, Caitlin Grace Willows-soon-to-be-Ramsey."

Somehow, amidst bullets, a deadly virus and a crazy bunch of fanatics, love had found them and they weren't going to let go.

No matter what life continued to throw at them.

* * * * *

COMING NEXT MONTH FROM

HARLEQUIN®

ROMANTIC suspense

Available June 4, 2019

#2043 COLTON'S COVERT BABY

The Coltons of Roaring Springs

by Lara Lacombe

A casual, convenient fling turns serious for Molly Guillford after she finds out she's pregnant. When she and Max, the baby's father, get trapped in a mountain gondola during an avalanche, more than Molly's secret is in danger—and the fight for their lives has only just begun!

#2044 SPECIAL FORCES: THE SPY

Mission Medusa

by Cindy Dees

To maintain his cover, spy Zane Cosworth kidnaps Medusa member Piper Ford. As these enemies fall in love, can they take down a terrorist cell and escape—alive and together?

#2045 NAVY SEAL BODYGUARD

Aegis Security

by Tawny Weber

If former SEAL Spencer Lloyd nails this bodyguard assignment, he'll open up a whole new career path for himself. But he has to make sure Mia Cade doesn't find out he's protecting her—a task made all the harder as their attraction turns to something more.

#2046 UNDERCOVER REFUGE

Undercover Justice

by Melinda Di Lorenzo

Undercover detective Rush Atkinson has infiltrated the crew of Jesse Garibaldi, the man suspected of killing his father sixteen years earlier. His plans are derailed when Garibaldi's friend Alessandra River shows up, but little do they know they're both trying to take down the same man.

YOU CAN FIND MORE INFORMATION ON UPCOMING HARLEQUIN® TITLES, FREE EXCERPTS AND MORE AT WWW.HARLEQUIN.COM.

HRSCNM0519

If former SEAL Spencer Lloyd nails this bodyguard assignment, he'll open up a whole new career path for himself. But he has to make sure Mia Cade doesn't find out he's protecting her—a task made all the harder as their attraction turns to something more.

Read on for a sneak preview of the first book in New York Times *bestselling author Tawny Weber's brand-new Aegis Security miniseries,* Navy SEAL Bodyguard.

Before she could decide, Spence wrapped his arm around her shoulder, yanking her against his side.

"Mia yelped.

So much tension shot through his body that she could feel it seeping into her own muscles.

"What're you doing?"

"Using you as camouflage," he said, looking away from his prey just long enough to give her a smile.

"The guy ran from me once already. I don't want him getting away again."

"Again? What do you mean, again?" He wasn't going to chase the man through this building, was he?

"He crashed your party last week to confront Alcosta, and now he's at the man's office. If the guy means trouble, what do you think the chances are that he wouldn't show up again at one of your Alcosta fund-raisers?"

Mia frowned.

Well, that burst her sexy little fantasy.

"Are you sure it's the same guy?"

Taking her cue from Spence, instead of twisting around to check the other man out this time, Mia dropped her purse so that when she bent down to pick it up, she could look over without being obvious.

It was the same man, all right.

And he wore the same dark scowl.

"He looks mean," she murmured.

The man was about her height, but almost as broad as Spence. Even in a pricey suit, his muscles rippled in a way that screamed brawler. Cell phone against his ear, he paced in front of the elevator, enough anger in his steps that she was surprised he didn't kick the metal doors to hurry it up.

"I'm going to follow him, see where he goes."

"No," Mia protested. "He could be dangerous."

"So can I."

Oh, God.

Why did that turn her on?

"Maybe you should call security instead of following him," she suggested. She knew the words were futile before they even left her lips, but she'd had to try.

"No point." He wrapped her fingers around her portfolio. "Wait for me in front of the building."

"Hold on." She made a grab for him, but his sport coat slipped through her fingers. "Spence, please."

That stopped him.

He stopped and gave her an impatient look.

"This is what I do." He headed for the elevator without a backward glance, leaving Mia standing there, with worry crawling up and down her spine as she watched him check the elevator the guy had taken before hurrying to the stairwell.

Oh, damn.

HRSEXP0519

HARLEQUIN®
TM